OUT OF THE CRADLE

John Kenrick Ellis

MINERVA PRESS
ATLANTA LONDON SYDNEY

OUT OF THE CRADLE

ISBN 0 75410 797 3

First Published 1999 by
MINERVA PRESS
315–317 Regent Street
London W1R 7YB

Printed in Great Britain for Minerva Press

OUT OF THE CRADLE

For Jeannette

Part One

Please forgive a few textual errors.due to inadequate proof reading. A corrected edition is in prparation.

Chapter One

Blurr and burble and a long way down – such a long way down! I never felt good till the face came down, too, and touched all over. That was nice, a pink round with black holes and a funny soft and good smelling. That was the good time until it went away and the light went out and I cried. The dark I just came out of. I was just barely. It's too easy to go back and not be. No! I want to be, to be and see.

Kinky curled her tickle tail, and I sneezed.

'That cat!' yelled Muv. 'Get her out of the bed.'

But she lay down and purred and Muv laughed and I purred but couldn't. It was light for the longest time now. When I woke up it was still light, and there were sounds. A thing ran on the lawn outside the porch. Fizz-whir it went, and grass flew up in Feddy's face. Muv said he was too little to push it and was hers too and my big brother, but how could he be outside when I couldn't? How could he be before I could? Muv says she was always here, but I don't see why Fed… he says it's because he's older. How old is Muv, then, and Kinky and big Daddy and Mrs. Lawrence? I've got to find out, but it's getting dark again and I don't want to go back. I want to stay and see and find out. Please, Muv, leave a light. Then I'll go to sleep.

I found out. People have been here for thousands of years. Not just here. Thousands of people, thousands of years, over there, beyond the woods and far and on. Fed and I couldn't even walk it in a month. I can count, and a dozen is twelve, but Fed's ten and I'm only five. And Muv and Dad and Mrs. Lawrence! I can't count that far. Fed says a thousand is ten times ten times ten, but he goes to school and says I'll find out what times is.

Yesterday I played with Helen and she's got yellow hair and is a girl. Her mother is Mrs. Lawrence. My mother is Mrs. Levin.

Do some mothers have boys and others girls? Girls have dolls they put to bed. Helen tried to put me to bed but I wouldn't. She thought it was funny when I wanted to hold her baby, but I loved it. It went 'waa' and closed its eyes. We had fun putting it to bed until Helen's mother made me go home to supper. Its name is Tina.

Our house is bigger than Helen's, and my Dad makes more money. But he won't give me more than a nickel a day. Muv says to put them in the pig so I can buy a clock that rings, but I'd rather go to the Five and Dime and buy anything in the store for three nickels. One day I bought a bell that dings when you tap it, but Fed sat on it and now it won't. He's a goop. The new nickel Daddy gave me is a fierce Indian and a buffalo. I didn't put it with the lady nickels.

Last night Dad didn't come home until way late, and it thundered outside my window. Fed said it thundered outside his, too, but I think mine was louder. I woke up when Dad came home. He slammed the front door and stayed downstairs. Muv came in my room and looked at the thunder and cried. I was too sleepy to care.

Pencil boxes are silly, but tablets are all right. Mine is yellow and has a big 'five' on the front. Helen took me to school on the streetcar today. Fed wouldn't. It is very far from home and full of noisy boys, but Miss Zarman was nice and made us sing 'America'. She said we would learn to read and how to brush our teeth. I know that already, but she doesn't know I know. The paper said the war is almost over, and Mutt hit Jeff – POW! 'War' and 'pow' are good words, but 'Katzenjammer' is too hard. Fed says I mustn't ever say that. It's German and bad.

Chapter Two

The train curved through the greening woods, ran along the river, and hooted toward the west. The sun slanted into the coaches on its way down, and the passengers tugged at the stiff window-shades or wiped cinders off their faces in the washrooms and then teetered down the aisles toward the dining car. There was no life outside now except the still life of grass and shrubs and trees.

Mrs. Ora Levin and her two sons, Frederick, aged twelve, and René, aged seven, sat at a bouncing dining-car table, waiting to be served. The dark waiters glided about, balancing against the car as it turned around curves. Steam fled from the metal kitchen, briefly exposed through a swinging door. Frederick sat, stiff and important in his blue serge suit, trying to look like the man of the family, but René squirmed and stared and wrinkled his intense little face as he surveyed every detail of the dining car, the people in it, and as much of the outside as he could see.

One of the black and white waiters swooped down on the Levins and deftly served them, pouring ice water into their glasses from a silver metal pitcher. The surging, bouncing movement of the train transformed itself into ripples on the surface of the liquid. Soon the waiter returned, balancing a tray full of dishes on one upturned palm.

'Now, Ren, look at those delicious baked beans, your favorite dish. Do try to eat all of them.'

His mother smiled at him.

'I'll try, Mother, but there are so many.'

'I do wish you'd get hungry again, Renny. You must eat to put muscles on those bones.'

'I know, Mother, but there's so much to see and think about. It goes by so fast.'

'There's always more to see. Now eat.'

After dessert, the efficient waiter placed a small glass bowl of water in front of each of the Levins. Ripples also moved through this liquid, like little waves.

René frowned. 'Mother, we already have water in our glasses.'

'Yes, Ren, these are finger bowls. Dip the ends of your fingers into the water and wipe them dry on your napkin.'

'Oh.'

Frederick Levin listened to this conversation from his Olympian height.

Those two, he thought, how they chatter, and about every little thing too. People shouldn't pay so much attention to little details. That was something new about the finger bowls, though. Good thing I didn't start to drink from mine. When I am president of a company a few years from now I will know all about such things and will have servants to wait on me all the time. But René, he'll never get to be president of anything. He'll always be too busy asking questions.'

'Isn't it strange to be back in our seats after eating supper in another room? It's just like home.'

'Would you rather eat in the coach, René?'

'No, Mother, but it seems strange to be doing things the same as at home when we're really in a string of boxes going sixty miles an hour.'

'Probably only you would think of it that way. Now sit down and read your book while I go wash.'

'Later on I'm going to walk all the way back to the parlor car.'

'All right, but not now. Wait until I get back.'

They call this a berth. It's not the same as birth – Kinky and her kittens. This is a bed in a train. Mother's asleep down here and Feddie's asleep overhead all by himself, and he hasn't got a window, and if it weren't for those green curtains that the porter put up, everybody could see us, even that man with the fat cigar; and I would fight him if he looked at Mother like that again. We are going to California at sixty miles an hour, day and night, Why? Where is Dad? Why did Mother cry at the thunder, and why did Dad go away and not come back? Is Kinky really in the baggage car, and why couldn't Helen come along with me? I would have married her and the dolls, too. What made that hiss when the conductor pulled the cord and the train slowed down? How did the engineer know to whistle at the road? Why doesn't he get sleepy like me and run the train off the track in the middle of the night? Why doesn't Fed and everyone look out the window all the time like me? How can he bear to miss seeing the country? Each tree is different and the river turns and the cows eat and that little boy chases a dog and the windmill whirls. How can I remember all these things and all the other things and all the things I'll see and hear and smell and feel from now on? I will have to write them down. I will start tomorrow. Like Gulliver. I will tell what I see, big and little. Clickety bang, clickety thump, roll and bounce – what a nice feeling – but it is so dark. I couldn't possibly go back now, but the dark is still there – here. No, I want to be. I will be.

Chapter Three

'Fed, we've been going sixty miles an hour for nearly two days. Why aren't we in California?'

'Because it's too far away. Why don't you figure out how far we've come and then how far we have to go?'

'How, Fed?'

'You know how. Like I told you. See. Twenty-four hours in a day and night. Two of those times sixty miles an hour. That isn't right. We don't always go sixty miles an hour. But anyway, forty-eight times sixty.'

'You do it, Fed.'

'All right. That's – let's see – two thousand eight hundred and eighty miles.'

'And—'

'And we have to go about three thousand five hundred miles – so.'

'It's awfully far. It makes me feel sad. Mother, I feel sad.'

'Why René?'

'I will never see Tina again.'

'Who in the world is Tina.'

'Mother You know. Helen's baby.'

'Oh. Well, never mind. You might see Helen again some time, all grown up.'

'Helen's baby!' hooted Fed. 'Oh my, oh me, you poor, poor thing.'

'Make him stop, Mother. He makes fun of everything I say.'

'Enough from both of you now. Look out the window at those big, gray mountains. Don't your ears pop? We're up high.'

Older than the world, the folded peaks flung themselves across the land. The puny train crawled between and through and under them like a furtive snake, puffing and twisting in the canyons, squirming up the slopes and slithering through the tunnels. This was the divide. The world on the other side could not be like the one on this. Something definite and permanent separates the lands cleft by mountains, just as it estranges the lands separated by oceans. The foliage, the trees, the birds, and the rocks change to kinds not seen before by the inhabitants of the plains or eastern river sides.

René held his breath and widened his eyes. To see these masses, to see into them, to understand what they meant, to know them, he must do this. The very shapes of the crags, the sudden turns of the peaks and cliffs, the angles of the slopes, all seemed to contain some fundamentally significant meaning. If only he could penetrate it. The wrinkles in his forehead and the intensity of his quizzical eyes indicated some of the effort – and some of the power – he was employing in the attempt.

During the time between the end of the evening meal and the making up of the berths, the Levins sat in their seats and read, as they usually would have done at home. Fed lolled across the whole of the backward-moving seat and pawed through a John Martin's Book, Mrs. Levin read *Ladies' Home Journal*. René, put his *Gulliver's Travels* aside, and, unnoticed by his mother, he picked up and soon immersed himself in a book that had lain on the seat beside her.

René usually read books with care, starting at the frontispiece and skipping nothing. This picture, a sepia oval, showed a benevolent, wise old man with a full beard. The photograph, as though especially precious, was covered by a page of semi-transparent paper, embossed to look like a spider web. The title on the next page was indeed a puzzle, 'Leaves of Grass'. Abandoning his usual orderliness, René turned to the center of the fat volume.

> Once Paumanok
> When the lilac-scent was in the air and Fifth-
>   month grass was growing,
> Up this seashore in some briers,
> Two feather'd guests from Alabama, two together,
> And their nest, and four light-green eggs
>   spotted with brown,
> And every day the he-bird to and fro near at hand,
> And every day the she-bird crouched on her nest,
>   silent, with bright eyes,
> And every day I, a curious boy, never too close,
>   never disturbing them,
> Cautiously peering, absorbing, translating.

He read on, entranced, half-understanding and greedy. Suddenly, he burst into sobs. His mother looked up from her magazine startled.

'What's the matter, Ren? Are you trying to read that book? There's not much in there that little boys could understand, much less that should make them cry.'

'It's so sad, but it's wonderful, Muv. I didn't know there was anything like this in the world. That brave little bird! But it's the words. Are there many people who use words like this? Can I ever? Oh, I must.'

'No, not a poet in this family, absolutely not,' put in Fed.

'Hush, brother; we could stand one. Yes, René, there are others. You will learn to read them. Perhaps you can write, too. Don't ever be afraid to try. If you can, you will.'

'I must. Oh, I wish I could grow up fast so I would know all you have to know!'

'Don't say that. You'll need a long time to learn all that. Be happy while you are young. Stay young and happy as long as you can.'

'All right, Mother. Now I must throw away all I wrote today. I didn't know how to say it. I must try all over.'

The porter came to make their beds, and the Levins prepared to spend their last night in this wheeling world with the stars outside.

All to do over again. I said the mountain was a mile high and solid rock. I said it couldn't fall down on the train because it was heavier at the bottom, but it didn't look that way. It is hard to tell how things really look. Those mountains mean something, but I don't know what. Those sharp trees mean something different. That man with the board probably knows. That is the way: 'Paumanok'. I would like to hear that said right. 'Fifth-month'. That sounds good. 'Silent, with bright eyes.' That is the way to say it. Tina Wina, Helen called her baby doll. She spanked it and it went 'waa'. Kinky with her crooked tail. How could I say that? Crooky with her kinky tail. Words go backwards sometimes. Like Fed—def—deaf. That man with the cigar. He wouldn't know what 'Paumanok' means, but he looked at Mother again. It's a good thing the curtains are there – even if it is dark. Tomorrow I will try to write like Gulliver and the little bird, too. It is hard.

Part Two

Chapter One

René woke up gradually as the sun gathered its strength and pounced on the little house, breaking through the bougainvillea vine that smothered the eastern wall. A few eucalyptus buttons dropped on the porch roof as the morning breeze swayed the trees.

Soon it would be time to get up and go to school. After breakfast, he and Fed would take the short cut through the canyon and climb up the other side to a road that led directly into the dusty school yard. There more eucalyptus and palm trees outlined the playing field.

He remembered the first day he went to this school. Many of the faces were brown, and much of the hair was black.

'*Buenos dias*,' said the teacher. 'Good morning.'

'Good morning. *Buenos dias*,' replied the children, standing at attention by their desks.

This teacher was not like Miss Zarman. She hoped they could read and brush their teeth, but she liked to play the piano and have them sing out of the gray song books where the words were in English and in Spanish with upside down question marks. The notes ran up and down in patterns.

Sometimes Miss Gomez told René to go across the hall and sit with the brown and white students in the first grade for an hour. He was the top pupil in the second grade, and it was hoped that his presence would inspire the strugglers who were just beginning to unravel the mysteries of the

English language. The brown-eyed, black-haired strugglers were polite and friendly, but few of them were willing to be inspired. The teachers did their best and refused to be discouraged by their pupils' slow or doubtful progress.

Recess was different at this school, too. The students nearly always went outside to play because the weather was so mild. But the school ground was divided by an invisible line. On one side, the boys ran, yelling in their various degrees of toughness and swagger. On the boys' side, tops were thrown, marbles were clicked, and balls were tossed as hard as their small arms could fling them. On the other side played the girls, busy playing ring-around-the-rosy, hopping over ropes and bouncing balls for jacks.

It was on the girls' side that René met Marilyn. The girls invited him to play hopscotch. Recklessly he joined them. This was much more fun than wrestling with bullies or swinging a bat at a ball that was thrown too fast.

'What's your name?' asked a slender girl in a pale yellow dress, with bobbed hair to match.

'I'm René. Can I really play with you? Will they punish us?'

'Oh come on,' piped up a dark little girl in a wine-red dress. 'Probably nobody'll notice, Here, take this green stone. That'll be your marker.'

'Thank you. But you'll have to show me how.'

René's remark was addressed not to the helpful girl but to the one in a yellow dress.

'I'm Marilyn,' she announced, 'and this is Cicely, and that's Bonita and that's Marjorie.'

They giggled and hopped around in circles while Marilyn explained the game to him.

'You can be first,' she said.

'Oh, no. Let me be last. I'll watch to see how you experts do it.'

More giggles. The throwing of colored bits of glass and stone were followed by solemn, serious hopping through the squares. They were all showing off. René was too busy watching Marilyn to pay much attention to the way of the game. The girls noticed this. When his turn came, though, he went through the squares without a mistake. It was beginner's luck. Soon after that, the bell rang and the pupils straggled back to their classrooms.

Marilyn – what does that name mean? What does she mean? She gave me a note:

'Walk home with me after school. I have something for you.'

She is so pretty and there is something in her eyes – green eyes? I wonder if she will let me hold her hand. Why is it good to hold a girl's hand? Why is Marilyn prettier than Cicely? She's better than Helen, even.

After school, Marilyn waited, a little bashful at her boldness, until René, also a little bashful, ran over to the playground corner. He took her books and walked beside her as she danced down the sidewalk, her hair bouncing with every step.

'I don't know where you live, Marilyn.'

'I'll show you. It's on Mission Street. René, what does your father do? Mine's a minister.'

'He is? My father doesn't live with us any more. He's a politician back East. But never mind fathers. You're here and I'm here. That's what matters.'

He took her hand. She stopped skipping and walked with a proud and dignified step.

'Marilyn, Marilyn, what does your name mean?'

She turned to him wide-eyed.

'It means me, just me. And you, René. That's a pretty name, Who gave it to you?'

'Mother, I suppose. Her family is partly French. They lived on the Mississippi River in Louisiana. That's French, you know.'

'Oh,' replied the little girl, who didn't know.

'Marilyn, whispered the boy, squeezing her hand, 'will you be my girl?'

Dropping her sea-green eyes a moment she took her hand out of his, then looked up it him and whispered, 'Yes.'

They stood still and gazed into each other's eyes.

'If you're going to be my boy, René, you're supposed to do something now.'

She held her little flower face close to his.

'Oh, what, Marilyn? I've never had a girl before. What should I do?'

'Silly, don't you remember? I said I had something for you. Here it is.'

Not waiting for the eager, puzzled boy to catch her meaning, she put her little arms around him and kissed him fair on the mouth.

René reddened with pleasure, but before he could recover and kiss back, she untwined herself, ran into the nearby house, and closed the door.

'Marilyn,' he cried, 'come back.'

The door opened a crack and a small voice piped, 'René tomorrow.'

That was all.

Chapter Two

From then on, it was known and agreed that Marilyn was René's girl. These boy and girl pairings were part of the accepted pattern of life in the town. 'Puppy love,' people said and either smiled a little enviously or frowned and shook their heads. In the society of the playground the relationship was taken for granted. Marilyn was René's girl. It probably wouldn't last. A boy usually had several girls by the time he left for high school. But a few of the couples remained faithful if their families or the ridicule didn't break there apart.

Next morning, when René reached the playground he was met by a delegation of toughs.

'Here he is, the little girl-boy who plays hopscotch.'

René tried to brush past them without answering, but they blocked his way.

'Missy, prissy, sissy,' taunted the head bully. 'What makes you think you can go over on the girls' side? Are you a girl?'

'What do you care where I play? Why don't you go tell on me? That would just about be your style.'

'Let's show this sissy how to fight,' yelled the bully, grabbing René's arm and twisting it behind his back.

René lunged out with a kick that caught one of them on the shin. He knew that he couldn't defend himself against the whole gang. Students ran up from all corners of the yard to watch the fight. Among them was Takeo Fujita, who had been friendly to René before, showing him how to peg a top and giving him some fish line to wind it with.

'Hey, Tak,' yelled one of the bullies. 'Help us teach this sissy not to play on the girls' side.'

'No.'

'Whaddya mean, no? All right, we'll do it ourselves.'

'No,' said Takeo again, putting himself in front of René.

'Ah, Tak, whaddya mean? Do you like sissies?'

'No.'

'Then let us at him.'

'No.'

The Japanese boy was larger than most of the pupils at the school because he was older. He was in a lower class because he had entered late, not because he was dull. His age and size made the aggressors hesitate. They milled around uncertainly while he stood impassively, juggling three marbles in the air.

'All right for you, missy sissy, we'll get you after school when your giant isn't here.'

'No you won't. Scatter,' ordered the juggler.

They scattered reluctantly, yelling jibes and treats.

'Thanks, Takeo. They just about had me. You're a real friend.'

'That kind are always cowards. They're always in a bunch. Better hang around with me until they find somebody else to pick on.'

'Good, Tak, but I must tell you. I did go on the girls' side and play hopscotch yesterday.'

'I wouldn't have done that, Ren. Was she pretty?'

He grinned like a pumpkin jack-o'-lantern.

René flushed. He rested his hand on the other boy's arm.

'Just wait till you see her.'

From then on the rule-breaker had to endure epithets of 'sissy', 'girlie', 'hoppy', and 'lover', from the tough element whenever he encountered them on the playground. Most of the time he scowled and managed to ignore them. In defiance he joined the girls at hopscotch a few more times and found that he was a hero among them at least. Marilyn took his hand to show the other girls that he belonged to her. He was too happy to mind this sign of ownership, although he saw Cicely's glance of amusement.

Chapter Three

'Now you must walk home with me,' said René to Marilyn a few days later.

'I don't want to. Your mother might not like me.'

'Yes, she will. I've told her all about you.'

'Oh, that makes it worse.'

'Come on, now, Marilyn. I walked home with you. Now it's your turn.'

'Well. How old is your brother?'

'Fed's five years older than me.'

'Well, how old are you then?'

'Oh, I'm seven, but I'll soon be eight.'

'René when we grow up, let's get married.'

'Yes we will.'

They ran and skipped through the dusty, small-town streets, stopping now and then to look at each other.

'There, we're almost home.'

'I'm afraid, Renny. Maybe Fed will think we're silly.'

'Oh, who cares about Fed? He's probably out running around, anyway.'

This proved to be correct. But more disappointing to René was the fact that Muv was also away. He remembered with chagrin that she would be visiting a friend until almost supper time that day.

'Come in, anyway, Marilyn, and look at our house.'

They sat on a low sofa in the living room.

'Oh, Renny, so many books! Who can ever read all those?'

'Well, we all try. But you have lots of them, at home, too, don't you?'

'Not like this. Your shelves go clear to the ceiling, and a little piano. Who plays that?'

'Muv – that is, Mother.'

'I think your family must be very nice. This room feels good. I think your father was horrid to run away.'

'He didn't run away exactly. I'll tell you about it some day.'

A knock on the door startled the little girl. René looked out and saw that it was the two sisters from next door coming over to play.

'Come in, Leila and Lizzie. Meet my friend Marilyn.'

The two girls, a little younger than René and apparently twins, with long, dark hair in braids, sidled in bashfully.

'Hello, Leila and Lizzie,' greeted Marilyn politely.

They tittered and then each gravely took turns to shake hands with the new girl.

'Marilyn and I are going to get married,' announced the boy.

'Oh, Ren, for heaven's sake,' she said, blushing.

'Well, we are; and I'm proud of it.'

'When?' asked the bolder twin, Lizzie.

'I don't know. Soon, I hope.'

'Why not now?' proposed the twin. 'Let's have a wedding right now. That would be fun.'

'Yes, let's do,' piped up Leila. 'Won't you, Marilyn?'

'Well, all right. It might be fun.'

Marilyn's blue-green eyes danced with anticipation. Her gay and puckish nature rose to the possibilities of this kind of play.

'Who'll be the minister?'

'I will,' replied Leila. 'I know just what to say,'

Lizzie took charge. 'Now everybody get dressed up. We'll use this curtain for the bride's train. And René go brush down your hair and put on a coat. Here, we'll use this bookstand for the altar.'

They dashed about, giggling, under Lizzie's directions. Marilyn went into Mrs. Levin's bedroom, arranged the curtain as a sweeping train, squirted herself with perfume, and stepped into a pair of black, high-heeled pumps.

'Everybody ready?' yelled Lizzie. 'I'll play the wedding march. Now walk slowly across the room to the altar. Marilyn, you first, then René.'

This play ceremony affected the boy strongly. Marilyn managed to look misty-eyed and expectant. And she smelled alluring. Leila made an imposing minister, solemnly mouthing what she could remember of the ceremony in a man's voice.

At the conclusion she said, 'René, you may kiss your wife.'

He did this shyly but joyfully. The new Mrs. Levin reddened, but didn't resist.

After Lizzie played some of Mendelssohn's magic music from *A Midsummer Night's Dream* on the piano they all sat around in the living room solemnly, not knowing what to do next. Then a call came from next door. Leila and Lizzie quickly took off their make-up.

'We have to go now,' said Lizzie, 'We hope you live happily ever after and have many children.'

They flew out the front door in a flurry of giggles. The newly-weds gazed at each other bashfully. Marilyn moved closer to René.

'That was a nice kiss, Mr. Levin.'

'And you are a beautiful bride, Mrs. Levin. Where shall we spend our honeymoon?'

'Oh René, I'll bet you don't know what people do on their honeymoon.'

'Well, I know they sleep in the same bed, if that's what you mean.'

'That isn't all they do, René Levin. But it's late and I have to go home.'

'All right. We'll have our honeymoon later.'

'You're a bad boy. Oh, there comes your brother. Let me out the back door. I don't want to meet him now.'

Chapter Four

The he-bird and the she-bird. That's really not very good, is it? It's the whole poem that's good. You can't really take it apart. I must find out how to say these things myself. To think of all the other poems… so many. I must go to the library. Why do they call me a sissy? Fed says that's a pantywaist who's afraid to fight and likes girls. What in the world is a pantywaist? I don't like to fight, but I'm not afraid. Why do boys want to be tough and noisy and hit each other all the time? Girls are nicer. Marilyn smelled good. And the way she looked, so proud and important. 'That isn't all they do, René Levin,' she had said. What then? Helen and Tina and Marilyn. I came out of Muv, she says. Kinky had six kittens, one at a time. Why does Takeo like me? Good thing, though. He wants me to go home with him and meet his parents. They have a big field full of vegetables. They bend over all day picking, even his little sister. And they are happy. I should go see him.
Let's see, it could go

> *Nowythen the guavas, glary-eyed,*
> *Bend and kiss the fuzzy dew.*
> *And all the sheep in all the areywide*
> *Lie down and lick the favored few.*

Fed would say that is crazy. Maybe it is, but pretty-crazy. It tells a story, too.

> *The poor Girl laid me on her Bosom, and fell a-weeping with Shame and Grief. She apprehended some Mischief*

> *would happen to me from rude vulgar Folks, who might squeeze me to Death, or break one of any Limbs by taking me in their Hands.*

They called Takeo my giant. Would he like to read Gulliver's description of Brobdingnag? That was a different time, with different words, so straight and true. Tak could squeeze that bully to death. Rude vulgar folk. Muv and love and Muv and love and love… Muv… Mari… lyn… Nowythen…

Part Three

Chapter One

'Oh, look, René,' gasped Lizzie, running after him down the path into the canyon.

She wore a Hallowe'en mask she had made in school. It was crudely outlined in black and white crayon, and consisted of a piece of heavy paper with holes for eyes, nose, and mouth. It was in the shape of a skull, and had cutouts at each end to fit over the ears. She looked like a lively young body with a long-dead head.

'Didn't you bring yours?' she asked.

They were on their way home from the third-grade class.

Although it was only a little after three o'clock, dark clouds were scudding in from the ocean. The wind bent the palms, rattling and scattering their fronds, and flung the eucalyptus trees into the frenzied attitude of tall ladies wringing their hands.

Lizzie's mask flew off and sailed away as they emerged from the far side of the canyon. She started to cry, but the boy stopped her.

'Never mind, Lizzie, you can have mine. Here, it's in my pocket. Don't put it on until you get inside.'

'Oh, thank you. I wanted so to show it to Mother.'

She touched his arm gracefully and flew on into her house.

He started calling Kinky, as was his habit upon returning home. There was no answer. He looked around disconsolately and then stopped, suddenly seeing something. He was afraid to look at it more closely. It was Kinky but she lay halfway under a guava bush, quiet on this windy day. A gust caught at the fur on her back, ruffling her gray fur, but she didn't move.

The boy approached slowly, as in a bad dream. The cat still didn't move. He reached out and touched her with a trembling hand. She was stiff and cold.

Oh, no, not yet. Kinky can't die yet! She came with us all the way on the train. She had kittens at home, one at a time. She was our cat, part of the family. Dad might go away but Kinky can't. Perhaps this is different. She didn't have any choice. It came and got her, all of a sudden. So it can do this? All of a sudden. You don't have to be real old. You don't know it is there behind you. Out of the dark. Pounce. Now I see. It will get me and Muv and Fred and – Marilyn. No. No. No. No. No. But it will. Why are we here and then not here? Why are we not here and then here and then not here? That isn't fair. It isn't right. It just is, and we can't do anything about it. Absolutely nothing about it. We can do so much, but not about that. I will write about Kinky now so that we will never forget her. That is all I can do.

He ran wailing into the house. Mrs. Levin was not at home. She found him later, scribbling furiously, tears falling on the disordered tablet. She had a difficult time persuading him to put down his pencil, wash his face, and come to supper. He went to bed early. Then she and Fed got out the shovel, dug a deep hole, and buried the cat under a guava bush.

Chapter Two

On his way home from Marilyn's white house on Mission Street, René sometimes passed through a district of smaller, plainer houses in various stages of disrepair. 'Shacks,' sniffed the better citizens. They wanted to tear them down, although they were happy enough to have the help of their inhabitants during the harvest season. There was a charm to these houses, nevertheless. Bright red geraniums swarmed over them in profusion, mingling with purple bougainvillea blossoms and passion flowers. Black-haired children swarmed half-naked in the disorderly yards, Smells of chili peppers and the sound of tortillas being made floated out of the open windows.

One day, walking through this neighborhood René was suddenly confronted by a rather skinny boy, brown-skinned, of about his own age and size.

'I'm Juan Mendoza, sissy, and now I'm going to beat you up.'

René then remembered him as one of the bullies who had tormented him for playing on the girls' side.

'All right, Juan, if you must, go ahead.'

'Aren't you going to fight back, sissy?'

'No. You're a good fighter. You like to do it. I've never done it. I wouldn't know how.'

'Too bad for you, then.'

He tripped René, turned him over on the ground, and sat on him. Several little boys and girls gathered around this triumphal scene and giggled and pointed, jabbering in Spanish.

'Now I'm going to black your eye, *gringo*.'

He placed his fist in the other's eye, experimentally.

'Will that be fun?' asked the fallen boy mildly.

'Jesus, no, not if you don't get mad and fight.'

'I'm not mad at you, Juan. Why should I be?'

This seemed to put a new light on the matter. Why was he mad, really?

'Well, since you're such a sissy, maybe I'll let you up if you say you give up.'

'Oh, I gave up before you got me down, Juan. Remember?'

'A real, honest-to-God, pantywaist sissy,' said Juan, almost incredulous.

'Yes. I guess so, Juan. But what is a sissy?'

'Everybody knows that.'

'I guess everybody but me.'

He got up on his feet and smiled at his tormentor.

'Well, I bet nobody ever called you one, anyway, eh, Juan?'

'You're damn right. I'd punch his *cabeza*.'

'Look, I suppose you wouldn't want to help a sissy, but I'd like to know a lot more about Spanish and things like that. Perhaps you could help me?'

The dark boy spat in a final attempt to express his disgust.

'Hell, *gringo*, I must be *loco*, but, well, let's be friends.'

'Oh, Juan, that's great. Do you live here? Are these your sisters and brothers?'

'Come here and I'll show you something.'

He led René to the rear of the house and started to dig in the ground. Soon he had unearthed a number of what looked like large seeds.

'Ground nuts,' he said. 'Eat some. They're good, *muy buenos*.'

The white boy looked at him dubiously but then popped one in his mouth and started crunching away.

'They are good,' he agreed. 'Will you show me how to dig them?'

'Nothing to it. You just have to know where to look. I'll show you some good places.'

From then on René learned from Juan. He found out that Juan's people were charming but also volatile. They were poor but had dignity, and were violent but also forgiving. He loved the sound of their language.

He sat in the kitchen watching Senora Mendoza slap tortillas between her hands and fry them on top of the hot old iron range. He tried to learn the name for everything in Spanish. Juan's little sisters and brothers got used to him and finally came to sit on his lap, looking up at him through their liquid brown eyes. Then they would run across the room and get under Mrs. Mendoza's feet. She chased them all outside including René.

Strings of dried red chili peppers hung in festoons across the back porch. Juan would grab one occasionally when Mrs. Mendoza wasn't looking. He would break off a small piece for René, who would manfully chew and swallow it with tears streaming down his face. The Mexican boy enjoyed this tremendously, and punching René on the upper arm, would yell, 'Hot, eh, *gringo*, *muy bravo*, *muy bravo* make a man out of you yet.'

Then he would laugh and dance while he nibbled on the rest of the hot pepper.

The language that René learned from Juan was not the most polished Spanish. He would probably have been surprised to know how much slang he was picking up. But at least he could talk to the Mexican boys now; he no longer sounded like an American sissy. Instead he sounded just like tough Juan Mendoza.

Mrs. Levin worried a little about her son's new vocabulary and occasional tough swagger. She didn't really know how vulgar the language was, and decided not to protest. It was perhaps a desirable facet of a young man's education. She knew that he would drift away from it and into something else given time.

Chapter Three

June had come and school was finished. The brown and black and red and white pupils scattered like leaves in a winter wind. Umbrellas bloomed on the beach. Hot-dog and ice-cream stands popped up over night like mushrooms.

Mrs. Levin now worked in the newspaper office in the mornings as a typist and occasional secretary to the publisher. Fed had expanded his paper route and was well on his way to becoming a supervisor. He had several grubby little boys under his charge, each with a bicycle and a canvas bag labeled *News-Post.* They hurled tightly folded copies of the paper at numerous front doors every afternoon. René could not refuse when Fed pointed out to him that this was his chance to help earn his keep. So late each afternoon, he folded a set of the ink-smelling journals, carried them to a north-side residential area, and threw them, one by one, at the waiting houses.

The rest of the day was his. He could read, write, or wander as he wished. He shunned the noisy, crowded, competitive life of the beach. Instead, he hiked farther and farther back into the canyons, as far as the foothills, and inland along the small, sluggish river. His only problem was remembering to get home in time to deliver the papers. He was often late, which led to sarcasm from Fed and complaints from the customers.

One day, near the head of one of the canyons, he came across the body of a small animal, which was partly decomposed and swarming with ants. He never went back there again and tried hard not to think of Kinky. He could not believe that Kinky was that way, decaying, ant-ridden. No, she must be somewhere else, surrounded by mewing, sucking kittens. He could not face death, that enemy again.

The canyons and river valley were carelessly, generously strewn with wild flowers; yellow violets, blue lupine, red Indian paint brush. No one came to look at them. They were all his. He found secret places to hide, and places to lie flat and look up at the sky. If you lay long enough and looked hard enough at that high dome you could feel the earth turning beneath it. It was like looking at the wind. If you held a leaf or a blade of grass at right angles to the wind and put your eye close to the edge, you could barely see the wind pouring over, like looking at a waterfall.

There were places where you could dig up ground nuts. Juan had shown him how to find them. After brushing the soil off, they tasted better than anything bought at the store.

Then there were the caves. He didn't tell Mother about them because she would have worried. They were carved into a cliff where the river joined the ocean. In one of them you could hear the waves at the bottom of a deep hole and you could smell sea air and kelp. They were hard to get to, but once inside them all was safe. One of them was called 'Indian cave' and had white Indian writing and pictures painted on its smooth, brown walls.

One Sunday René decided to explore Indian cave further, since he didn't have to hurry back to throw papers that day. He told Muv he was going up the river, and set out early. Fog had left the cliff sides slippery, but he managed to wriggled into the cave mouth and look at the paintings.

These mean something. They are trying to tell me. They wouldn't spell Paumanok. That was far back East. But if we could know.

I'm going to sit down here and look and think. The tide must be up. The waves are pounding – all the way from China.

> *Way worn and moon pulled,*
> *Rolling through the spumy air,*
> *Wind tossed in storm,*
> *And sun sucked in fair,*
> *You have arrived, are here*
> *As messengers. Plenish now my ear.*

It's strange that I don't mind the dark in here. Of course, it's not very dark. But even so I've come so far out now I don't believe I can go back. Is that growing up? Is dying going back? It must be. But there is something left behind, especially when you write. The Indians said something with these marks. I will tell something more with mine. That makes us alike. Muv said something once about a great chain of being. Maybe that chain is made of writing, those old Egyptians and these old Indians and me – a chain without an end, a circle.

There was nothing more in the cave. Whatever had meaning in there had been said. René scrambled up the side of the cliff into the sunshine. Since several hours remained before he would have to return home, he wandered up the river valley. Mocking-birds swooped and yelled at him as he entered a eucalyptus grove. He picked up a handful of droppings where they had fallen. The clean, pungent odor of the oil rose to his nostrils when he crushed t hem.

How could this be? Did the One who made the eucalyptus trees in the beginning, under the world in Australia, decide to make it oily and to make that oil pleasant and healing to human beings? There must be a connection or a pattern that ties things together. Not just living things, either. What about the minerals in the earth? There is so much to be learned and understood. Even old men disagree and dispute angrily the real nature of the earth and man's place in it. What I want to do is not to try to find out and tell why but to see and tell what, the what and the meanings of the whats, how the whats are connected together. I think I can see this. Perhaps I can make other people see. That is what I want to do. To see everything and to make everything see. Well, perhaps not quite everything, not that thing in the canyon and the ants, not yet anyway, I don't think that is a 'low and delicious' thing. No.

As he walked out of the grove and up the river the day grew warmer. He decided to take off his shoes and stockings and wade. He knew this might be dangerous. There could be pot-holes and quicksand. But he would be careful, and the cool water felt so good. It was just a little California river, not like that muddy monster back home.

Suddenly he stopped. In a deeper pool on the other side, a shadow moved. A black water snake came up from the bottom, coiled and whipped and writhed. It waited, suspended near the surface for a moment, and then moved out towards him. He stood frozen in fascination and fear. As the snake swam forwards, René jumped up in an ecstasy of fright and ran toward the nearest bank. The snake, startled, pulled back and writhed quickly away towards the pool. But the boy did not see this. He stumbled up the pebbly shore and ran toward the town, forgetting shoes, stockings, and sunshine. Some time passed before he stopped, trembling, and began to feel that he was no longer being pursued.

That night he awoke several times. It would be difficult and frightening, he thought again, to see and make see everything. Perhaps it would be better to write only about what is beautiful. He decided to try to do that.

Chapter Four

Returning home from a ramble later in the summer, René called for Kinky, forgetting she was dead. Only the guava bush moved in the ocean breeze. Then he saw a new automobile parked in front of the house through the grape arbor. He ran into the kitchen; Muv wasn't there. He could hear her in the living room, talking to a man.

'Hello, René,' she greeted him as he slipped into the book-lined room. 'This is Mr. Hornbeck.'

Then, to the neatly dressed man with the gold watch chain, she said, 'This is my youngest.'

'Pleased to meet you, young man. You bear a strong resemblance to your mother.'

René looked towards her questioningly.

'Mr. Hornbeck is a businessman, Ren. He has been kind enough to take an interest in our affairs and has advised me how to handle some of them.'

'Thank you, Mr. Hornbeck. Do you have a family?'

'He gets straight to the point, doesn't he?' said the insurance man, laughing comfortably.

His gold watch chain bounced and glittered.

'Mr. Hornbeck is a bachelor, René. He lives alone and spends much time on his business.'

'Like Fed,' said the boy.

Mr. Hornbeck laughed again, this time a little uncertainty.

'Fed, Frederick, is our oldest,' Muv explained. 'He has a head for business and is a distributor for *The News-Post.*

This keeps him hopping outside of school, and his activity impresses René and me. We are inclined to spend too much time reading and doing other unprofitable things.'

'You do have a lot of books, don't you?' asked the insurance man, eyeing the loaded shelves dubiously. 'But where is Fred... Fed? I would like to meet the businessman of the family.'

'Oh, he's out with his boys and their papers. He may return in a little while, though.'

'Well, René, what do you do to keep busy?' asked Mr. Hornbeck in an obvious attempt to make up to the boy.

'Not much, really,' René replied, putting on his owl-like scowl in an attempt to appear serious. 'I read and write and hike. Mostly I write.'

'That's interesting; what do you write? Cowboy-Indian shoot-em-ups?'

René looked at Muv hopelessly.

'No, poetry.'

'Oh,' said Mr. Hornbeck in shocked disbelief.

'He has quite an imagination and a gift for language,' put in Mrs. Levin, unable to keep the pride out of her voice. 'Now, René, you can run along if you want to. Mr. Hornbeck may come see us again, and I wanted you to meet him.'

The boy rose with relief.

'Glad to know you, Mr. Hornbeck. Please do come again.'

He ran through the kitchen to the back bedroom, pulled out his tablet and began to write a description of a small-town businessman who wore a shiny gold watch chain and a rather fatuous smile.

Later Mrs. Levin asked René how he liked Mr. Hornbeck. She seemed to want him to care for the man. The boy, always anxious to please his mother, tried to discover something he could admire, but without success.

'Does he like you, Mother? Is that why he came to our house?'

'Yes, he does, René. Will that bother you?'

'No, well, except that he doesn't seem to be our type at all, Muv.'

'He isn't. But we must be careful not to limit ourselves to "our type" son. For one thing, there aren't very many of "our type" here and we might become narrow and ingrown. Also, some people who are different from us can be very agreeable once we get to know them. We might be able to use our way of life to help other people, even people who perhaps don't know they need to broaden their horizons. Mr. Hornbeck might like to know some people like us despite his small-town businessman ways. He might be lonely and dissatisfied with his narrow little life and not know why. He lives all by himself, you know.'

'Poor Mr. Hornbeck. It must be dull. But, Muv, he *likes* insurance, and he doesn't like poetry.'

'Yes, but it might be possible to learn to like both. Shall we give him a chance? We might even learn something from him. Remember, we have an up-and-coming businessman in our family now.'

'All right, Muv. I'll try. But don't *you* ever go into insurance. You are the only one who can read what I write.'

She gave René a hug. Just then Fed came stomping in through the back door, asking where the peanut butter was.

Chapter Five

In the fall, when school took up again, René reluctantly gave up his summer rambles, his explorations of sea caves, and his dreamy mingling with nature. He came back to the world of people. It was not a very satisfactory world. Fed was exceedingly busy with his newspaper distribution. He became more down-to-earth and businesslike than ever. His evenings were spent totting up accounts, making lists of possible customers, planning sales speeches. Of course he prospered. He treated René as the useless appendage of the family, who ought to give up the contemplative life and pitch in to help fill the family purse.

Mother still received Mr. Hornbeck on occasional evenings. He beamed approvingly at Feddie's business activities but looked puzzled and askance at René's dreamy book reading and interminable writing. Mr. Hornbeck was, of course, far too polite a man to express any disapproval. From time to time he stated, in his unimaginative commercial speech, his pleasure at being with such obviously cultured people. He vaguely felt the lack of any such interest in his own uncluttered, straight-forward mind. But he could always reassure himself with the success and the thrill of running the insurance agency. There, things that mattered took place. His heart swelled with pride to think of it. Mrs. Levin, Ora, was bound to see the virtues, of becoming the wife of such a successful businessman. Besides, he wanted to possess her French good looks. He thought her quite an asset, any way he looked at it.

One morning Miss Paddle, the fourth-grade teacher, a large hearty woman, announced to the class that a new kind of test was to be taken that day by every pupil in the school. She warned that no one was to get excited or worried that it was not a test that could be failed. Rather, it was a way of finding out how well the school was doing by comparison with other boys and girls in other schools.

She said, 'Now the papers are to be passed out. The instructions are printed at the top of the first page. Read them first and then a bell will ring for you to start. Do the answers as fast as you can, but don't get scared. Remember, no grades.'

As usual, the teacher and her monitors kept a sharp eye out for cheating and shenanigans. René rushed headlong through the test and then sat quietly. Soon Miss Paddle motioned to him to step out into the hall.

'What's the matter, René? Aren't you going to cooperate with us? Go back now and finish the test.'

'But I did finish it. It wasn't very hard, as you said. Do these problems really mean anything?'

'René Levin, this is a scientific test made up by experts back East. Do you mean to say you think you are smarter than they are? Go get your answer sheet and bring it to me.'

This was done and the boy was sent to the library for an hour.

Early the following week, Miss Paddle told René to come to her desk after class. Her expression was a mixture of disbelief and awe.

'Here is an important note to your mother, René. Be sure to take it straight home to her. It's from the principal. You're not in any trouble. He just wants to talk to her. Now, don't lose it.'

'No, Miss Paddle. Thank you. I'll give it to her.'

As a matter of fact, the boy almost did forget the note in his shirt pocket. In going down through the canyon on the way home, he discovered a lizard sunning itself. He took a long time to look at this creature from every angle. He observed its bright, heavily-lidded eyes and long tail, and its prescient immobility as it froze to protect itself from harm. It moved only slightly in breathing, like a small leather bellows. The boy and the reptile stared at each other for long, pregnant minutes. Finally, the lizard, seeing no harm, scuttled off, and the boy straggled home.

'What's that in your shirt pocket, René?' asked Mrs. Levin as he dashed into the kitchen to give her a kiss.

'Oh, I almost forgot. It's a note for you from the principal. Here.'

She read it hastily and smiled.

'He just wants to talk to me about some test you took. Nothing wrong, you scamp.'

'No, Mother. I haven't made anybody angry in a long time.'

'Good. I'll go see him tomorrow.'

Chapter Six

The principal ushered Mrs. Levin to a chair beside his large golden-oak desk. He seemed a little uncertain how to begin. He looked at her with curiosity and peered at her face.

'Mrs. Levin, perhaps René told you that we administered an unusual test to all the students last week.'

'No, he didn't, as a matter of fact.'

'Well, you know that educational people and psychologists have devised tests to determine the level of natural intelligence that each of us possesses. You've heard of "IQ"?'

'Only rather vaguely, I'm afraid.'

'"IQ" means "intelligence quotient". These tests are supposed to produce a figure to indicate a person's mental age. If he is above the normal mental level for his age group, his IQ figure will be above 100, supposedly about the average. The average has been determined by testing large numbers of people of every age. It has been found that feeble-minded or retarded youngsters score below 100, while brighter children score over 100. A score above a certain level is taken to indicate actual genius. Mr. Levin, we were pleased and astounded to learn that your son, René, has made the highest score on this new test that I have ever heard of: 200. Mrs. Levin, if this score is valid and if these tests are to be relied upon, your son is a genius!'

'This is rather overwhelming, isn't it? Do you believe, personally, that the test is reliable?'

'I don't see how we can doubt it. This particular test is supposed to be the latest and best and apparently has been thoroughly authenticated. I have sent René's answer sheet to the people who publish the examination, and we will see if they think we should give him some more tests. But in the meantime, Mrs. Levin, take a deep breath and tell me how it feels to be the mother of a genius!'

'It is quite extraordinary, of course. I have always known that René was unusual in many ways. I suppose that we who are close to him have become used to his insatiable curiosity, his surprising flashes of insight and his unusual vocabulary.'

'May I say without embarrassment that it is obvious where some, nay much, of his superiority comes from, Mrs. Levin.'

'Well, you flatter me. As far as I know, neither his father's nor my family have ever produced a genius.'

'Seriously, though, you must be very proud. I can't think of anything on earth that could give me as much joy and satisfaction as being responsible for the production of a genius.'

It was obvious that the principal was sincere and deeply moved. René's mother couldn't help feeling a sense of exultant joy well up in her throat.

'But, now, what a responsibility,' she said, half aloud.

'Yes, I have thought of that, too,' the principal sighed. 'Unfortunately, this is not the kind of community that can support a first rate public school. We do our best, but—'

'Now I begin to regret the fact that we are almost poor. He should, I suppose, be sent to a special school.'

'That would be the logical thing. But don't despair. We will figure out ways to enrich his school work. Although my position as a principal should prevent me from saying this, a boy like René is going to go so much further on his own, that I don't think lack of expert schooling is going to matter too much now. Later, his performance will undoubtedly provide him with ways to study at the best schools, perhaps even abroad. We will help you all we can. In the meantime, you have the job of keeping him well, out of trouble and as happy as possible.

'I do congratulate you, Mrs. Levin. Yours is the greatest honor I can think of. Now, do you agree that we should keep this quiet? I won't tell anyone here, none of teachers, and of course not René or any of the students.'

'That is for the best. Thank you.'

'I think it is best to keep him in the same grade as other students his age, rather than to skip him far ahead. Do you agree?'

'Yes, indeed. He needs time to learn all about life.'

'Precisely. Then this will be between the two of us for the time being, at least. And let me say again how much I admire and envy you, Mrs. Levin. Be proud and happy at this opportunity.'

'You are very kind, sir. I *am* proud. I cannot deny it. Thank you for your understanding.'

'Goodbye, Mrs. Levin. I will keep in touch with you.'

Chapter Seven

'Hurry, René, and get up. You'll be late for school.'

The boy opened his eyes and the room turned slowly around as though mounted on an axle. He tried to get up but fell back. His mouth was dry and his face hot.

'Sorry, Muv, I can't. I must have caught something.'

'Your head is hot,' she said after feeling it. 'Stay in bed and I'll get the thermometer.'

'One hundred and two. You'll stay in bed all right, and we'll ask Dr. Horace to come by and see you.'

René thought this would be taking things a little too seriously, but Mother insisted and he was too weak to protest. She arranged to stay home from work for that day at least.

'Well, I'm not sure yet just what he has got. There are a lot of illnesses running around school,' said the doctor later. 'Give him these tablets every three hours. Keep him quiet in bed, of course, I'll stop around again tomorrow.'

He dropped his stethoscope into his black bag, patted the invalid on the head and left as quickly as he had come.

'And don't worry,' he added to Mrs. Levin as he whisked out the front door.

'Here's our little bell, René. I'll be in the kitchen or living room. Now lie quiet and try not to fret.'

'All right. I think those pills are making me sleepy.'

Did Kinky have a fever? Maybe I've got what she had. Wouldn't that be sad; 'René Levin, promising young writer, dead at the age of nine.' He might have gone far. Oh. I didn't see you, Mr. Grahame. Say, was that really Toad's last song: 'When the Toad-came-home... Shout – Hooray!'? You should have let him sing that at the banquet, poor Toad. But I suppose he had to be restrained – for his own good. That man with the cigar is looking at Muv again. But now he's put on a shiny gold watch chain. He's laughing and its bouncing on his stomach. No insurance today, Mr. Hornbloom. Close the green curtains. Clickety-clickety Paumanok. Lyndall is a pretty name. I will name my daughter Lyndall and my son Waldo, and they will herd ostriches. Mrs. Marilyn Levin, will you come to bed with your husband? That isn't all they do, pretty-smelly Marilyn. Let's go out on the karoo and sit on a kopje and eat mealies... or is it chilies? Por favor, Juanito, show me where to dig the groundnuts, and then if you don't vamos pronto I'll bash in your cabeza. Ratty, you and Mole come over here and look into the eyes of the Friend and Helper. I, too, have heard the glad piping and seen the baby otter, Fizz-whir. Fed, you're too young to push that thing, but how can you be older than me? When you were four where was I? Not to be and then to be, and then – no! Ants are not nice and neither was Miss Paddle. Paddle-waddle-woddle. The lizard breathed and covered his eyes and ran. Did he hear the pipes? The wind blew Lizzie's skull away and then shook Kinky's fur because she was dead... dead... dead. The black snake came and got her. There were giants in those days and Takeo pulled the fleet of Blefuscu all the way over to Lilliput. Quinbus flestrin fujita. Wind tossed in fair, and sun sucked in storm. That isn't right. All the sheep bend and kiss the fuzzy dew while nowythen the messengers plenish my ear. It used to go better, Off in the distance... see a canyon under the ocean... look closer... in it float people with sea weed for hair and green faces... they are dead... I know them...! that's... oh no...! Muv, come quick... oh Mother!... Mother!

Part Four

Chapter One

The public library, surrounded by palms and oaks, sat in a small park on a side street in the oldest part of town. The building was old, wooden and much used. Many feet had worn hollows in the wooden steps leading up to the heavy oak front doors.

Mrs. Levin often went to this house of books. Both she and her sons were insatiable readers, and thus could hardly escape the attention of the gray-haired man who usually sat behind the desk and stamped out the books. She gradually became aware that this collection was unusual, even remarkable, for a small town public library. Mr. Phineas the librarian noted that this family, especially the younger boy, withdrew unusual books. Volumes that had lain untouched on the shelves for months and even years began to go out in this boy's hands: Macaulay's histories, Scott's and Dickens' less popular novels, Keats and Melville and Hawthorne, Audubon and Darwin.

One day Mr. Phineas, seeing Mrs. Levin alone, asked if he could speak to her in his office. Surprised but compliant, she agreed.

'Please forgive me for being so bold,' he began, 'but I have noticed with pleasure your use of our library. It is obvious that you are people of taste and knowledge. We are pleased to have you here and would be happy to order any books that you might want; within the limits of our budget, of course.'

'Thank you, Mr.—?'

'Phineas. Excuse me for being so thoughtless. And you are?'

'Mrs. Levin. My boys are Frederick and René.'

'Is René the younger one?'

'Yes, Mr. Phineas.'

'If I may continue to be bold, since you are so pleasant and courteous, I am very much taken with your younger son. I have noticed his unusual reading and his intelligent face. I hope you will understand that I mean no disinterest in you and Frederick. In a small place such as this, one cannot help noticing people like you; I am gratified for your presence. But you will probably agree that your René is a remarkable boy.'

'Yes. We have known that for a long time.'

'I have expressed myself crudely. Of course you have. Mrs. Levin, you may well believe that I am a busybody or an eccentric or something even worse, in making the following proposition, but I will do so nevertheless. I am very much interested in helping people like René. I haven't had the opportunity to do it often in this backwater. I don't think I'm a "nut", but I have a strong conviction that we must do whatever can be done (and much can be) to further the development of superior people in our society. Our world depends largely upon the wisdom and genius of a few gifted people. Who knows? Your René may turn out to be one of them.

'Mrs. Levin, you must know the problems and limitations of our public school. The town does its best, but—'

'I know, Mr. Phineas. I wish I could afford to send him to the best private school.'

'Well, not many people can afford to do that. But I propose something else. Would you let René spend an hour with me every afternoon after school? I have had some experience in helping intelligent young people. You might say that it is a hobby of mine.'

'This is most generous of you, but I don't know. Are you sure that you want to?'

'I am anxious to, Mrs. Levin. Now you may have some doubt.

'Perhaps you will feel that I am not qualified to do this or that I have some ulterior motive – to indoctrinate or worse. It would be right of you to want to know more about me. Just talk to Mr. Meadows, the school principal, and Dr. Horace, the physician. They will vouch for me.'

'Oh, I don't feel that is necessary, Mr. Phineas, René will tell me all about you soon enough if I decide to let him come.'

'Bravo. I'm sure he will. Now do send him over. We'll plan a reading program that is agreeable to you. But mostly we'll just talk.'

'Thank you so much for your kind offer. It *is* a problem to know how to keep his restless mind occupied. He reads and writes so much, but indiscriminately, I'm afraid.'

'I had a feeling he might be a writer. Now, do you think he will want to come? Do you think he will like me?'

'If you can answer even half of his questions, Mr. Phineas! But really, he likes nearly everyone – and especially people of ideas and enthusiasms. I just hope he won't wear you out.'

'Not at all, Mrs. Levin, I am looking forward to this.'

Chapter Two

René had been wandering along the sea shore. This summer he discovered that after walking nearly a mile south of town, past the dunes, he could reach a part of the beach that was usually deserted, even in warm weather. A marshy inlet, locally called 'the slough', made the sand here so shallow and so overgrown with swordlike grass that few cared to frequent the area. The only human being he saw was an occasional surf fisherman. But it was a gathering place for birds. Sea gulls, petrels, pelicans and sand hoppers all found a refuge here. Finally they seemed to get used to the boy. When he first walked into their domain. they flew up in large groups, fluttering and complaining. But now he could pass through without ruffling more than a few timid wings.

He had found a place where he could sit and watch and meditate. Surrounded by reeds, it was a perfect hideaway, except at high tide when the water backed up enough to dampen the sand. When that happened he would walk out to the wet edge of the beach where the waves flowed in and then out. Juan had taught him to look for little short-lived holes that appeared in the wet sand as each wave retreated. He would quickly dig his fingers under one of the holes until he felt a small creature wiggle in his palm. It was a camaron, a tiny white shrimp. He would wash the sand gently out of his palm and peer at the creature as it writhed in his hand. 'It wants to live, just as much as I do,' he would marvel. Then he would put it down on the wet sand, where it would immediately burrow out of sight.

Today he hurried home from this sanctuary, late as usual. As soon as he entered the yard he dropped down on the ground near a pile of papers and began to fold them tightly, banging each one on his knee in authentic delivery-boy style.

Leila and Lizzie, no longer in pigtails, but still tomboys, were clinging in a large pepper tree at the rear of their yard next door. They hooted at René when they saw him and started to flip pepper berries at him. He pretended to ignore them. They hit him seldom and not hard enough to hurt.

'Leila, I've used all of mine up,' shouted Lizzie. 'I'll have to climb up higher to get some more.'

'You be careful,' warned the more cautious twin. 'It's too high.'

'Lizzie stuck her tongue out at Leila and stood up in the crotch where she had been hanging. By lifting one leg up high enough and grasping the main trunk with both arms she should be able to pull herself up to the next higher branch. She started, blushing a little as René grinned at her exposed panties.

'Bad boy. Turn your head till I get up there.'

'All right. But I bet I'll have to come up there to get you down,' he teased.

'No. I don't need any help from *boys*.'

With a mighty pull she gained the higher branch. It was a little scary up there, but she would never admit that with René looking on. She started to inch slowly out on the smaller limb to reach the berries.

'Lizzie, you come back,' yelled Leila. 'That's not safe.'

She slid farther out, in defiance. Suddenly the limb gave way under her weight. She plummeted to the ground unable to hold onto any branch to break her fall. Her little body hit with a sodden thump, bounced once, and then lay deathly still.

Leila screamed and sobbed. René vaulted over the hedge and reached Lizzie's side. She lay crookedly, like a rag doll, and her face was dead white.

'Now shut up Leila and stay here while I run in your house and have your mother call Dr. Horace. Lizzie'll be all right. She's just knocked out.'

'Mother's not at home,' wailed the twin.

'*I'll* call him then. You stay here.'

'No.'

'Quick. Yes. You must.'

He ran into the house, jiggled the telephone hook, and told the operator to get the doctor. She got the address from him and told him to wait by the phone, It rang in a short time with the news that the doctor was on the way. He ran back to Lizzie. She hadn't moved. He touched her wrist and felt a faint pulse. There was nothing more he could do.

'Oh, she's dead, René. She doesn't move. She's dead,' wailed Leila.

'No. She's got a pulse. Besides, here comes Dr. Horace.'

The familiar Ford chugged up and out hopped the doctor with his bag.

'Dear me,' he said. 'This is no way to find my little twin.' He felt her pulse and then all over her body for broken bones. Then he felt her head and neck, turning it gently.

'Now, don't fret, Leila. She's tough. I think she'll be all right. But we will have to get her to the hospital. René you stay with her. Leila, you show me the phone.'

The ambulance carried the unconscious girl to the hospital, with her distracted mother, who had since come home, inside.

René suddenly collapsed. The customers would just have to do without papers tonight.

She might die. She is too young. What is it, who is it that decides who and when? Why wasn't it Leila? Why was it Kinky? When will it be me? The she-bird went and the he-bird stayed.

> *O darkness O in vain!*
> *O I am very sick and sorrowful.*

But it was not Lizzie's turn. She had a fractured skull and several broken ribs. She came close to dying but youth and providence saved her. The decision was that she would live, René wrote a poem of thanksgiving and gave it to her when she came home from the hospital.

Chapter Three

One afternoon after school the boy presented himself to the librarian.

'Excuse me, Mr. Phineas, Mother said you would like to talk to me, I'm René Levin.'

'Of course, René. Let's go back to the office.'

He led him to a room at the back of the old building, formerly used as a place to prepare books for circulation, repair damaged volumes, and carry out other mechanical duties necessary to a small public library. It had been converted into an office of sorts for the librarian. However, a faint odor of glue, paste, ink, and paper still floated in the air. Large windows on two sides of the room admitted sunlight filtering through the leaves of large, ancient oak trees standing just outside. An old rolltop desk stood against one inside wall. Drawings and photographs of authors covered another wall. Two old upholstered chairs and a large oblong wooden table completed the furnishings.

'Sit down. Make yourself comfortable. I suppose you think I'm at least mildly crazy. What did your mother tell you?'

'She said you were very kind and wanted to help me learn more than I could at school here. She said you noticed that I took out books of poetry and other… unusual things.'

'Well, what do you think of the idea? Do you think this will be a bore? Mostly we'll just talk about things that probably interest you… and me, but which you probably can't talk about elsewhere.'

'It sounds great, Mr. Phineas, assuming that you like me after you get to know me and that you aren't disappointed.'

'Well, well, that could work the other way, too, but hopefully not. I'm looking forward to this. Now then, tell me something about yourself. Or perhaps I should be the one to begin.'

'Yes, please.'

'Yes. Why in the world am I stuck away in a small town library like this? Well, let's see, I was born in England. I went to a grammar school there. Then my parents moved to this country. We came to *New* England, Boston. I was lucky. My father did well enough. He was able to send me to Harvard. I loved it. I taught there for a few years. Later I got a scholarship to Cambridge in England. Then bad luck: my father died, my health went bad. I needed a warmer climate. I found this little town and my health improved here. They needed a librarian, and that tells the whole story. Now, how about you?'

Mr. Phineas' gray-blue eyes beamed intensely as he sat back in his old chair and leveled his eyes at the boy.

'I was born in a middle-sized town in the Middle West, on a river. I can still remember the river. I can remember a lot about our house and the woods outside. When I was quite young, just in first grade, my father left us. Mother and my brother and I came out here on the train. It took more than three days. I had never seen mountains or the ocean. Mother said her friend told her about this town. It was a good climate and a cheap place to live and she could probably get a job. She types. Fed and I started to school. He has a paper route.'

'Now we know all about each other, don't we? Isn't it funny about these things, about where we were born and used to live and so forth? They don't really mean a thing, do they? But we'll get really acquainted in time. Do you think, though, that two people ever can really, completely get to know each other? Have you ever thought about that?'

'Yes, that is, no. I don't think anyone can ever be completely understood by anyone else. Not even Mother. Sometimes she says the darndest things.'

'I agree. My mother did, too. I suppose we get to know them, or more likely they get to know us, better than just about any other human beings, though. Now, René, let's be friends. But don't ever think that I'm trying to pry into your private life, that I'm a curious old goat who has to live on other people's lives. Don't ever tell me anything you don't want to. Keep some secrets. Remember I'm an Englishman, and we Englishmen respect another man's privacy. But nevertheless, let's explore the world together. It's an enormous world. Neither one of us can ever discover it all. But you can tell me some of your discoveries, and I can share some of mine. Mainly, though, we'll discover things by taking advantage of those marvelous people who see and tell better than any others – the artists.'

'You mean poets, writers and historians, don't you, Mr. Phineas?'

'Right, but also musicians, painters and photographers. Everyone who can teach us to hear, see, feel, smell, taste and think better than ordinary people.'

'How shall we go about it?'

'Well, let's work out some ways together. You like to read. You can read poetry and good literature. Maybe I can tell you about some things you haven't seen. Better yet, if you don't mind, we could make up a sort of program so that you could progress logically from one thing to another. You can't understand some things very well until you've learned the background material. For example, we can't read a poem in French until we've learned that language. By the way, do you know any foreign language?'

'No. Mother talks a little French but hasn't taught it to us.'

'All right. Let's get started on French. You don't have to wait for high school where you can take courses. I'll give you a book and we'll start speaking it together. Now, next perhaps it would be a good idea for you to make a list of all the books and poems you have read that you can remember. Will you do that?'

'Oh, yes. I will start tonight.'

'Good. Now in that list you might underline or star your favorite ones.'

'Yes. I will.'

'It will take a while to make such a list, but bring what you have of it tomorrow. Later we'll make lists of music, pictures, and other things you know and like. Do you sing or play any music?'

'No. I wish I could.'

'We'll find out if you have the knack. It's best to start young. I'll ask you to go to a music teacher friend of mine. She'll try you out on various kinds of things. You will be a busier boy now. Will you mind?'

'No. Just so I don't have to drudge at anything I don't like and am no good at.'

'Well said. However, when you find something you do like, you'll work at that, eh?'

'I don't suppose I've ever really worked hard at anything. But I think I will when I find just what I want.'

'Next to having a good brain and a good soul, that is the most important requirement. Some lucky people get so absorbed in what they're doing they never realize they *are* working hard.'

'I do hope I will feel that way about writing. I already do about reading.'

'Well, now, we've made the whole business sound pretty grim. It's not like that at all. It's a great adventure, better than climbing mountains or discovering a pole. You'll see.'

'Mr. Phineas, what does that mean?' asked the boy, pointing to a printed card thumbtacked above the old desk.

'Oh, you mean *En archei en hob logos*? Have you read the Bible?'

'Not much. No.'

'Ah, there's a book we'll begin soon. It's one of our very greatest. There's the real foundation stone of most of what's been written in our world. Those words mean "In the beginning was the word."'

René's eyes shone. In the beginning was the *word*. The power was and is in the word. No wonder Mr. Phineas, a word man, likes that statement. It will be mine, too, forever from now on if I can make it so. In the beginning and in the end.

'Now of course we writers might get a big head if we forgot the rest of it. "In the beginning was the word, and the word was with God, and the word was God." Nevertheless, whether we are Jews, Christians, or unbelievers, you can't avoid the fact that the first thing, the thing that started it all and is still starting things, was a word. It's good for our writers' egos, isn't it? The word is our tool. Look how mighty a tool it can be.'

'It is very good of you to talk to me this way, Mr. Phineas. You act as though I were a writer already. I do so hope I can be one.'

'I also do so hope, but in addition, I do so believe, René Levin.'

Mrs. Levin took note of the books her youngest son brought home from his first session with Mr. Phineas.

'May I see them, Ren? How do you like him?'

'Here's a literary Bible, he calls it. It's easy to read because it's printed like a regular book. Then this is a beginning French book. Will you talk French with me, Muv, when I learn a little? And I'm to go see Mrs. Briscecov who's a music teacher to find out if I have any talent.'

'It sounds like he's given you an awful lot to do, son. I hope you won't turn against him for working you too hard.'

'No. He's wonderful. And he talks to me just like a grown-up. He acts as though I know as much as he does.'

'That's good. I'll help you with the French as much as I can after supper.'

'And I must start a list of all the books I've read and can remember.'

'Well, you're off with a bang I must say. Just don't overdo everything and then turn against it.'

'No. I'll try not to.'

Chapter Four

René heard a piano as he neared the small, green house on Olive Street. The series of *bravura arpeggios* followed by ascending and descending octaves almost frightened him away, but he resolutely stomped up the wooden steps and twisted the old-fashioned door bell. The music stopped in mid flight, and a little, dark-haired, dark-eyed lady opened the door.

'Mrs. Briscecov? I'm René Levin. Mr. Phineas said you would see me?'

'Oh, of course, Mr. Levin. Come in. I am pleased to meet you.'

The eleven-year-old boy was not used to being addressed so formally but he thought the twinkle in the lady's black eyes showed that she was not really formidable.

'Sit down. Have you ever played a musical instrument? Do you sing? Can you read music?'

'Only the little bit of singing and reading we do at school. Practically nothing.'

'That's a shame. Better to have started when you were four. Do you like to listen to music? Have you heard much?'

'Not much. My mother plays the piano some.'

'Do you go to concerts, symphonies?'

'No.'

The lady clucked her tongue.

'Well, never mind. We will fix all that. Do you know what note this is?'

She pressed a key in the middle of the piano sharply.

'I think that's "C", isn't it?'

'Well, that's a beginning. Can you sing this little song?'

She handed the boy a book.

'Here, I'll help you.'

She played a soft accompaniment, nodded her head for him to start and sang along with him for a while. Then she stopped singing and nodded to him to continue. Then she stopped playing and nodded vigorously at him to keep on singing. When he finished, she looked a little more pleased.

'Phineas says you have a piano at home. You said your mother plays. What are your favorite pieces?'

'Oh, some Chopin mazurkas, and the Erl King, for instance, and Kammenoi Ostrow.'

'Wagner?'

'Not much.'

'Mozart?'

'Yes, all that Mother plays of him. Oh, yes.'

'Good.'

She turned toward a cabinet in the back of the room and took out a small wooden case. She opened it and took out two rounded, polished tubes of wood with holes in their sides and a mouthpiece She fitted them together quickly and handed the instrument to René?

'I'll bet you've never seen one of these before, eh?'

He handled it delicately, curiously.

'No. Is it a flute? But flutes are not like this.'

'Not now they aren't. But this is what the flute used to be a long tine ago. Have you read Hamlet? Do you remember the line, "Come, the recorders"?'

'No. I've forgotten.'

'Well, this is a recorder, the English flute of Shakespeare's time. Phineas has one, a large one called the treble. He plays it very well. Hamlet said it would "discourse most eloquent music." It disappeared for a long time when the more modern flute came along. The modern one is louder, but this one is sweeter. It is seeing a revival as are all the old instruments. They sound much better for the music that was written for them. Bach never played or wrote for the piano, you know; that's the way we hear it, but he meant it for the harpsichord. Someday you will hear Madame Landowska and they you will *know*. You have a great deal to learn, but I think you can do it. The recorder is easy to learn but hard to play well. Would you like to try?'

'Oh yes, please.'

'You say that, but you have never heard it. I will play a little piece for you. It's a shame you can't accompany me on the piano, but never mind. Listen.'

In high mellow bird notes the recorder sang, flying the scale. It warbled and trilled and then settled to an affable *arioso*. Finally it flew up again and finished with a ravishing trill and cadence.

'Oh, that is beautiful. It sounds like a different world. But could I ever make it sound like that?'

'That remains to be seen. But why not? You can try with one of my instruments. I will let you take it home if you will read this little book on how to take care of it. Instruments are delicate, like children. They need loving care. If you take to it, we will order one to be made for you by Mr. Dolmetsch in England. It will take some time.'

'Will it be too expensive?'

'We won't worry about that. If you can play it well, you can pay for it. Now then, would you like to start learning?'

'Oh, yes, but again, what must I pay you for lessons?'

'Phineas and I have an agreement. Ask your mother if she can afford a dollar a week. If not, fifty cents. If nothing, come anyway. He and I have our ulterior motive. I will be honest with you. We need another player so that we can play trios together; at the moment we can only play duets.

But that's not the real reason. You must develop the music that is within you. I will give you piano lessons and you will try the strings and the other instruments. Perhaps you will like them better than the flute, but this will make a good start. Here.'

She handed him another recorder that she had put together while talking. She showed him how to hold it and how to blow, softly but steadily. She showed him where to put his fingers to make 'C'. He tried, and it sounded dreadful, like a peanut whistle. She was not disturbed. She quoted Hippolyta:

'At first you will be "Like a child on a recorder – a sound, but not in government." But the government will come.'

She gave him a tutor book and told him to do the first lesson at home and come back next week.

The world is very big, René thought on his way home. There is so very much I didn't know. Now I will get to learn more. How good of Mr. Phineas. How can I ever repay him? But I will, I will.

Chapter Five

Frederick Levin at sixteen was tall for his age, but thin. He had an air of seriousness about him which helped him to keep the boisterous paper boys in order. They respected and liked him because he was always absolutely fair with them, never mean or petty. He patiently put up with their continual bookkeeping troubles. They did not collect payment from their customers; he did that. But they were required to account for the number of papers they delivered and to keep a currently accurate list of regular, new, and dropping subscribers.

Fred's excellence at his work did not escape the notice of the newspaper's circulation manager. When this man became incapacitated by a heart attack early in September, Mr. Brannigan, the publisher, asked him to suggest a successor. He was surprised to hear him recommend young Levin. Although he seemed too young, (he had a year or two more to go in high school), Mr. Brannigan decided to offer him the job. Since Mrs. Levin had been working for him in the mornings for two years, he spoke to her the morning after his decision. In the small town way he addressed her by her first name.

'Ora, that boy of yours has done very well by us. He is our best dealer. What would you say if I offered him the job of circulation manager?'

'Poor Mr. Stainbock. Is he really that ill?'

'Yes, Doc tells him he must quit work and retire now. I know he'll hate it, too. But guess who he recommended to take his place?'

'Frederick?'

'Right, and I think he can do it. But what do you think?'

'I suppose he could do it if Mr. Stainbock and you agree, but you know he's still in school.'

'Yes. However, it can usually be arranged to take a lighter schedule of classes, say in the morning only, if a young man wants to work.'

'In a way I'd hate to do that. But he has always done very well in school. If his grades don't suffer... he does like the newspaper work. It is really very good of you.'

'Not really. We'll all profit if he does well.'

'Let me think it over and talk it over with him. I imagine we'll say "yes".'

'Fine. Let us know tomorrow, please, Ora, and don't *you* get sick on me. We rather lean on you Levins. How's the younger son doing?'

René is spending his boyhood in one long preparation. His tutor is sure he'll be a great writer. His music teacher is certain he'll be a noted musician. With all that faith, and mine too, he should amount to something one day.'

'I hear good things about him, too, every now and then. You are a lucky family in spite of being without a man. Well, let us know about Fred soon.'

'I will Mr. Brannigan. Goodbye.'

She left the office and walked slowly up the business street.

I'm afraid I don't really know my son Fed as well as I should, she thought. I must constantly try not to spend all my affection and thought on René. I'll have a real talk with Fed tonight, if he just will. He mustn't get into business too deep too early unless he really wants to. I know he pretends to be displeased or at least different with me and René when we go off on our wild speculations or artistic discussions. But he's a good boy not to be jealous. I hope I do right by him.

At home she embarked upon a flurry of housekeeping to settle her mind and calm her conscience. Of course her elder son talked her into the feasibility, the desirability, of his taking the managerial job, and of course she was proud of him for doing so.

Chapter Six

The library was warm and quiet when René visited the little office a few days later.

'Come in, René. I have been looking over your list of books. Quite a *mélange*, eh? But that is all right. We must absorb the good and the bad. Everything is grist to our mill. Now, however, since life is short (you probably won't agree, but it is), we should begin to discriminate and select. I have made out a list which includes some of those on yours and many more. Will you be willing to stick to it, at least for a while?'

'Of course, Mr. Phineas. I have just read around at random. Some books and poems stick in my mind, and I wouldn't give them up. But it will be great to have a list to go by.'

'If possible I would like you to slow down a little, too. I will suggest that you read these in order. Some will be re-readings. If you feel like plunging ahead, please don't. Instead, read some of those earlier on the list again. This way we can dive in deeper instead of trying to swim a race.'

'All right. I'm getting pretty busy with the music and the French, anyway.'

'Too busy?'

'No. These are things I like to do. I just hope I can learn to play the recorder.'

'You are impatient, of course. Practice every day and it will come. You do like it, though, *n'est-ce pas*?'

'Yes, rather better than the piano. I hope Mrs. Briscecov; doesn't mind.'

'She won't. She will understand. She knows, though, that you need some piano as a sort of musical foundation. It is like a one-man orchestra. You are the treble and bass all at the same time.'

'Yes, I see. But I do like the sound of the recorder. It sings when she plays it.'

'Yes, doesn't it? Well, now, let's look at literature again. You seem to like some of Walt Whitman's poetry. That is interesting.'

'I started to read some of it when I was pretty young. Mother had *Leaves of Grass*. I didn't understand it very well, of course. I still don't altogether. But I like it very much.'

'Some people don't think it is really very good poetry, you know. they say it sprawls and needs more form and discipline.'

'Well, all poetry can't be alike. Do they want him to be like Keats?'

'Perhaps. To be more formal and controlled, at least in language.'

'I don't know. I do see he is different. You can't take his poems apart very well. He is doing things another way. They affect me and I don't want to take them apart, but I think some day I can figure out how they work. The words sort of pile up and keep piling up. I suppose it would be easy to make fun of them; do people make fun of them?'

'Oh, yes people do, even people who know poetry. But other people write "perfect" poetry. It doesn't sprawl, it isn't repetitious or grandiose. Perfectly turned little gems, they hope. But one reads them because the words are dead. Walt was alive, big bellowing. He had something to say. A lot of it may turn out finally to be nonsense, but what writer can avoid admitting the same of much of his work?

Is it better to be careful, precise and polished all the time or to say what you have to say, in a big, bold way if necessary?'

'It demands on what's right for you, doesn't it, Mr. Phineas? I suppose the greatest writers who ever lived can do both these and other things, too, all at the same time.'

'*Ipse dixit*. You are describing Shakespeare. Wait until you are a little older.'

'I hate to wait.'

'I suppose so. Well, you can get what you can get, even now. Let's put down *A Midsummer Night's Dream* next on the list. There is a world of magic and delight.'

'Oh, thank you.'

'Now then, Genesis.'

'Overwhelming.'

'Remember how it starts, "And God *said*, Let there be light… And God called the light Day, and the darkness he called Night… And God called the firmament Heaven…" and so forth.'

'Yes God said and God named. *En archei en hoc logos*,' recalled the boy excitedly.

'The names of things are fundamental. Thus there is

much in a name after all. And writers are callers of names, too. Are we little gods? Are we creators? The Greek name for poet is "maker". Am I blasphemous?'

'No, Mr. Phineas.'

'Most church members would certainly say so, René, and I suppose we ought to talk about this before we go any further. You know that only a comparatively short time ago in history people were burned at the stake for deviating from the accepted pattern of religious beliefs. One of the reasons for this, of course, was that up until very recently some of our most avid concerns were our relationship to God, how to please and worship Him, and how to prepare our immortal souls to join Him in eternity. This is much wider than Western Christianity, of course. Man everywhere has this concern in his various ways. Now I am the kind of man who feels that it is absolutely none of my business what people believe, in a religious or philosophical sense. This shows you right away that I am not a Christian nor a Muslim either. This means, too, that it is absolutely none of my business whether *you* are a Christian or Muslim. But obviously, this is ridiculous too. You and I can't go exploring together if I am going to be stepping on your toes in terms of religious belief or if you are going to be boxing me into some highly formal narrow view of life that stems from an orthodox creed.'

'I think I see what you mean, Mr. Phineas. You mean that a man's religion is none of your business as far as liking him or trying to help him is concerned, but that you can't really know him if you don't know his religion.'

'You, have put it better than me.'

'Well, I guess I'm not a Christian. That is I, we don't go to church. We never have.'

'I did until I grew up, but I can not call myself a Christian, either. Still, René, we here are all Christians of a sort, aren't we? Our whole civilization grew up on Christianity as understood and practiced by the church and state and people. Our whole heritage and literature is soaked in that religion, so if we're going to know them we're going to have to know much about Christianity; actually Judaeo–Christianity. So you won't think I'm trying to convert you when we read and talk about this so much, will you?'

'No.'

'Good. But it isn't that simple, either. Things never are. We say we aren't Christians, but we certainly have a code of morals and ethics, of what's right and wrong, and we have ideas on matters that used to be the concern of religion such as: why are we here? what is life and the universe all about, if anything? They will always be the concern of man;

so, above all, they are the concern of literature. Therefore, we'll grapple with these concerns constantly. Hope you don't mind?'

'No. I should think about these things more than I do. It is good of you to bring them up.'

'The Bible and Shakespeare and Walt Whitman are bringing them up, so you and I will, too.'

'I hope you won't dislike me, Mr. Phineas, though, if you find out that I am not very religious or philosophical. I'm afraid that other things I can't talk about too well are more interesting to me.'

'No. I don't dislike you. In time you can probably tell me more about these other things.'

'I hope so. In poetry, maybe. But I can't write it well enough for you, yet.'

Mr. Phineas looked a little disappointed.

'Well, I'm not really such an ogre, you know.'

'Oh, it's not that, but for you it has to be good. You know too much.'

The librarian sighed, remembering his unpublished manuscripts.

'Goodbye, René. See you tomorrow. The next part of Genesis, you know.'

'Yes, and *Midsummer Night's Dream*. Thank you, Mr. Phineas.' He walked out of the old office quickly.

Chapter Seven

'*One*, two, three, four,' droned Mrs. Briscecov. 'Now, now, don't forget to put your little finger down on that low "F". Couldn't you hear it sharp?'

'Yes, now that you mention it. But I was so busy changing notes there. That is a hard one.'

'Yes it is. But we must always hear the right note in our head before we play it. Then we play that note we have in our head, like singing.'

'I will try. Do you think I am getting better?'

'Of course you are. Remember the peanut whistle? Now it sounds like music part of the time.'

'Yes, part of the time.'

'Finally it will be all of the time. You are reading well, too, which is good. Soon you will join us in a trio. But now let us rest. Has Phineas told you what we are doing soon?'

'No,' René said, his eyes lighting up expectantly. 'What?'

'Ah, the Merof ensemble is coming to the city: Baroque and Renaissance, viols, recorders and harpsichord. We hardly ever have the chance to hear these inside Europe, let alone outside. You and I and Phineas are going.'

'Oh, how marvelous! But how can I pay?'

'It is all arranged. We will go up on the train Friday night and stay with a musical friend in Pasadena. The concert is on Saturday. We can look around the city, see some pictures, perhaps buy some music. Let's hope it doesn't rain.'

'That is so good of you. I can hardly wait!'

'Yes you can; you can practice. Now to the piano. The Bach. *One*, two, three. *One,* two, three.'

They made a holiday of it. Mrs. Levin saw to it that René wore his best suit and a white shirt, which made him look surprisingly older. Late that afternoon, she walked with him to the station where Mr. Phineas and Mrs. Briscecov were waiting, who were also dressed up and expectant. The lights of the train soon appeared around the south bend. Mrs. Levin waved as they smiled at her through the window, and the train pulled out toward the north.

'I must be on my best behavior now,' said René gaily as they sat back in their seats.

'Yes, we have our eyes on you, young man,' twitted Mr. Phineas. 'But let's look at the ocean now while the sun is going down. See, for once it is clear. There is the island; that sharp peak is over a mile high.'

The island. To be surrounded by the ocean. Half-way to China. Oh no, not half-way. Just barely started in fact. And you could stand on the top of the peak and see half-way. No, still not that far, but far. Do the waves on that side come from the east, I mean the west? Of course they do. How silly. For us the far east is the far west. But the waves, they are messengers. Plenish now my ear. When will I have something good enough to show Mr. Phineas? It must be soon. He showed me one of his. It wasn't very good, really, and such a fine man.

In the city a pleasant young lady met them at the station and drove them all the way to Pasadena. René had never seen such a large house.

'It belonged to a millionaire once,' she explained. 'He willed it to my mother. Of course it is too large. But it is comfortable and a good place for music.'

An enormous grand piano reposed in the formal music room. A violin case sat on a side table. Old prints of composers' heads hung on the walls and a bust of Beethoven scowled from a pedestal near the front window.

René had a huge bedroom all to himself. It was luxurious but he felt a little lost. He read for a few minutes after going to bed but soon fell asleep, the light still burning. He dreamed of an island that moved in the ocean like a ship, carrying people to China.

Back in the city the clang of street cars, the roar of truck motors and the angry surging of people in the streets made René want to shrink and stop his ears. Yet it was exciting, because all the purposeful activity, (although engaged in by hard-faced, selfish-looking people) implied that something important was being accomplished, implied that here one could influence men, move the world.

They visited an enormous music store, filled with instruments, phonograph records, and printed music. Yet even in this huge place there was very little music for the kind of instruments they played. It would have to be ordered from Germany, England or France. Nonetheless, Mrs. Briscecov found a wealth of literature for the piano beyond even her desire. She bought what she could afford and a little more.

There was much else to see and do. They visited several private art galleries and a museum. This was too much for René's unselective perceptions; the pictures, forms and colors ran together in a dizzying blur. Occasionally one did stand apart and speak in an insistent language that would not be denied. One of these was a canvas of a lady in a bonnet and frilly dress, bending over to examine something in a formal garden. It was in the brightly lit French impressionist style, and the light was everywhere, painting the picture. But the light was controlled artfully and didn't dazzle or become over dramatic. One was left with the impression of the artist as a man who saw and told but didn't shout. 'Look at me. Aren't I clever? Isn't this beautiful?'

The other exhibit which stood out for René was one of salon photographs. Mr. Phineas refrained from talking and explaining during these gallery visits. He waited for questions and answered them only briefly. At first René was worried by the photographs. Was it wrong for a man to hang them and exhibit them as though they were equal in importance to painting or sculpture?

'Just hold this matter in abeyance,' said Mr. Phineas. 'See if these speak to you for themselves. Don't try to relate them to paintings.'

By the time he was half-way through the exhibit the photographs were speaking for themselves. The artist had selected, and had chosen the right objects and the right views of those objects; this artist was honest. There were no soft-focus evasions or 'arty' angles. It became clear to René that in the medium of photography, honesty is all. The form was short, the printing brilliant. The objects were not 'arty' in themselves. They were chosen for their form and line, not for their content. The photographer was another man who saw selectively, and told honestly.

The concert was given in a rather small auditorium. It appeared to René that the audience had been selected, reminding him of the photographs he had just seen. They were not the same people who had been rushing through the streets, noisy, hard-faced, impatient. It was the first concert he had ever attended.

Mrs. Briscecov and Mr. Phineas had already spoken of the music to be played. Mrs. Briscecov went on to tell him about the history and character of the harpsichord and viol da gamba. It seemed to René that his two friends were almost as excited as he was.

The first piece was very old, from the French Burgundian court. It sounded ancient and quaint, but nevertheless suave and sure. The old instrument blended perfectly with one another and with the spirit of the music.

However, the Baroque, played later in the program, fired René's sensibilities more. Here was verve, realized concord, variety and harmony. The driving rhythm complemented the inventive melodies. This music was satisfying, not subtle but honest. It was from a time when man had not started to doubt or niggle and the music expressed this clarity; it saw clearly, said things clearly.

They arose early the next morning to be driven to the station by the musical lady. It would take several days for René to get used to small-town reality again. He lived on the promise that this was to be the first of a series of musical and artistic adventures. Operas, symphonies, ballets and exhibitions lay ahead of him like a chain of islands leading to Cathay.

Chapter Eight

Something had gone awry between René and Marilyn. Every day she seemed to become more of a small-town lady and less of a lovely, teasing little yellow-haired girl. She had grown taller than the boy now and gave the appearance of being considerably older. Less and less often did he walk home with her, carry her books, or stop to scratch her name in the dusty road. Now, he usually went straight home and then on to the library or to the house on Olive Street where Mrs. Briscecov set him to his musical tasks.

They were growing away from each other; Marilyn to become a proper young lady, and René to immerse himself in words, music and worlds far distant from the little town.

This afternoon, though, he was free. He caught Marilyn's arm as she came tripping out of the school ground.

'*Bonjour Marilyn, comment vas-tu? M'aimes-tu toujours*?'

'All right, smarty. Now say it in English.'

'I just asked how are you and if you still love me.'

'I don't think you care, but the answers are "well" and "no".'

'Young lady, that's no way to talk to the man you married.'

'Oh, René, let's grow up now and not always talk like we're married.'

'All right, so we're not married. And we never even had a honeymoon.'

'Of course not. How would kids know how?'

'I think you know how.'

She flushed a little and turned away.

'René, I feel like I'm growing up now. I'll soon be fourteen. There are things you don't understand about growing up – with girls anyway.'

'That's probably true. The only things I know about girls are what you have told me.'

'You're so young and have so much to learn.'

'You never used to mind, Marilyn.'

'Oh, I don't *mind*. It's just the way things are.'

'Let's stop here in the park a minute. You don't have to rush home so.'

They sat down on the fresh green grass under a camphor tree. Marilyn self-consciously bent her knees and stretched her short skirt down as far as it would go. Then she pulled her sweater tight across her chest. René looked at her intently. She was beginning to look more like a young woman.

'Are you mad at me? Have I done anything mean?' he asked.

'No, René, but things change. I'll soon be in high school. Would you take me to a prom? Do you know how to dance? Oh, it'll be exciting to go to the football games. Will you?'

The boy sighed.

'No. I don't like things like that. I just want to sit and look at you and write about you.'

'The girl softened a little.

'You are nice, René. I'm not really good enough for you at all. I can't speak French or Spanish or play music or write poetry. Mother says she heard you are a genius.'

'None of these things matter, though, when I love you.'

'You can't really love, René; you're not old enough. I like you very much, but let's not go together for a while now.'

'All right, Marilyn. There are some things you don't know about boys, too, though. But let me carry your books home for you and then I'll not bother you any more.'

They got up and walked toward the white house on Mission Street, both feeling miserable and mean. Each had tears in their eyes when they turned away at the screen door. It closed with unaccustomed softness as the girl disappeared into the house.

Chapter Nine

'René, you and Fed come in here now and let's talk.'

Mrs. Levin thus summoned her sons to a family conference, an old custom of theirs. The boys sat on the living-room sofa and looked at her expectantly.

'How do you like Mr. Hornbeck by now? Do you like him?'

'I do,' said Fed promptly. 'He's got good sense. He knows his business. They like him around town.'

René's heart flopped.

He's asked her to marry him, he thought.

'Do you like him very much, Mother?' he asked.

'I asked you first, Ren.'

He sighed.

'I haven't changed my mind, Mother. I'm really, truly sorry.'

'Well, he wants to marry me, which of course would make him your stepfather. Don't you feel that you need a father? It isn't good for boys to grow up without one.'

'But Mother, what about love? Surely you don't really love him?' asked the younger boy.

'He says he loves me, and you, very much.'

'If you like him, why not?' put in the practical Fed. 'You sure could live a lot better and you wouldn't have to work.'

'Mother?' asked René again.

She seemed to find it hard to face him directly.

'Well, René, love is a very complicated thing. I don't feel about Mr. Hornbeck the way I felt about your father. You will understand better about these matters some day. But he is kind and would be a good father to you. Wouldn't that be good?'

'No,' wailed René. 'He doesn't begin to understand people like us. Remember what we've always said about these people: "Be among them but not of them".'

'But are we becoming intellectual snobs? Is it right to cut ourselves off so?'

'No, it isn't,' spoke Fed. 'You have a right to live, Mother. After all, this is our town and we are part of it. We can't live in some kind of ivory castle. What are we saving ourselves up for? Heaven?'

'Yes!' said René with passion. 'Exactly, Fed, Heaven. No compromise, Fed, not me. You know we're not like Mr. Hornbeck. You know he's probably never read a real poem in his life.'

'Well, that's no calamity. Neither did Henry Ford or – Woolworth.'

'Now boys,' Mrs. Levin intervened, 'let's not go down that track. It's true that Titus Hornbeck will never be an art lover. The question is: would he make a good second father for you boys?'

'No, that's not the question, Mother,' cried René. 'The question is; first, do you love him, and, second, is he our kind of person?'

He looked hard at her and she dropped her eyes. He got up, took her hand for an instant and then walked out of the room.

'Of course he'd have to make something dramatic out of it,' snorted Fed. 'Mother, you do whatever you want to about Mr. Hornbeck. He's all right with me… but we don't need another father, if that's all you're thinking about.'

'Very well, Fed. I think maybe you do, but I don't know where I could ever find him.'

'Nonsense, Mother, we'll get along fine. Why don't you

quit work now?'

'Oh, I rather like the work, Frederick. No, you save what you can. I want you to go into business for yourself some day.'

His eyes lit up.

'Oh, fine, Mother. I will some day, and get rich. You'll see. Then you can marry a *big* businessman.'

She smiled at him but then moved toward the closed door of René's room. He was lying on the bed crying.

'All right, René, you're growing up now. Don't take things so hard. I'm not going to marry Titus Hornbeck.'

He jumped up and hugged her with a bear's grip.

'Oh, Mother, you couldn't. I'm so glad… but am I selfish? Do you want a husband? After all, I had Marilyn. Does Fed want him for a father?'

'Fed said we could get along very well without another man in this household.'

'Are you lonely, Muv?'

'No, no, not now. We will get along by ourselves. I do think you boys should have a father, but Mr. Hornbeck is probably not the man. Maybe I will meet someone later. After all, you boys won't be around here a whole lot longer.'

'I will. I won't leave.'

'Of course you will. You must. But what do you mean, you *had* Marilyn?'

'She grew up all of a sudden and doesn't want me any more.'

'Did some other boy take her away?'

'No, but she thinks she's almost in high school. You know, football and proms. She things I'm such an infant.'

'Poor boy, we just don't seem to be ready for partners yet, do we?'

'No, Mother, not yet, not yet.'

Part Five

Chapter One

The night of 21st June, 1925 was unusually warm in the sea-coast town. René awoke with a start and looked at the moonlight filtering through the bougainvillea blossoms. The house was quiet; everyone else was asleep. The thirteen-year-old boy felt a strange, light excitement, an excess of gaiety. Something pleasant had been vaporizing at the bottom of his soul, and was now about to come forth. He turned on his light, seized tablet and pencil, sat back on the bed, and happily began to write.

Pillows of laughter,
Hollows of sad,
Bounce in the maybe
And fell on the had.

He tossed up a merry,
She caught a delight.
They fumbled the mustn't
And stepped on a might.

If then was forbidden,
Often was worse,
Never would always,
And sometimes came first.

Her now is the future.
His will be is past.
There wasn't was isn't,
and beginning came last.

Having produced this, he calmed down and fell into a reverie. The air was warm and the usually well-loved room seemed confining. It was a night when only the starry universe is big enough to hold a single soul.

He turned out the light and padded quietly out of the kitchen door and into the garden. Not until he was outside did he remember that he was naked. He ran to the large pepper tree at the rear of the yard. It was here that he and Fed had built the tree-house. It was gone now, but he remembered how the pepper gum had oozed out of each nail-hole. It was as though this kind of tree were more alive than others. It had seemed like wounding a friend.

He scrambled up the finely channeled bark of the main trunk and along a large side branch. The moonlight made lacy patterns on the ground of the symmetrical fern-like leaves. The shadows danced in the light puffs of the inland breeze. He found the site of the former tree-house and stretched out on his back along the curving limb. He lay there long enough to watch the moon move through the stars and the stars move round the earth.

A strain of music drifted through his head, the air from 'Giselle'. He imagined her dancing madly with the Wilis in the forest, dancing her lover to death. He sprang up, leapt down from the tree, and started to dance on the leaf-carpeted ground, lightly, silently and gracefully.

I need a partner, he thought, and there she was. Was it Cicely or Leila or someone else, a little dark girl with flashing black eyes and white skin, naked. They joined hands and leapt through the forest. They bounded and floated in sweeping arcs. The Wilis would not let them stop. Higher and faster they flew. Suddenly a cock crew. A faint wind bathed René's bare skin. A wisp of fog drifted past and the girl was gone. He ran quickly into the house, plunged into bed, and instantly fell asleep.

When she made the beds the next day, Mrs. Levin wondered where the sprig of pepper tree leaves had come from that she found tangled in her son's pillow.

Chapter Two

As always, René was the top student in his class. In eighth-grade Latin the next student was Kyoko Kitagawa, a bright-eyed little girl with dark bangs, almond eyes, and a wistful, appealing face. When the class was divided into teams to compete in conjugation games or a spelling match, René usually headed one team and Kyoko the other.

One day at lunch time René found the small Japanese girl sitting in his favorite spot.

'Hello, Kyoko, let's eat lunch together,' he proffered gallantly.

She smiled shyly and said, 'Yes.'

They ate in silence until he noticed that she was eating some curious objects out of a little sack.

'What are those? They look like shells.'

Kyoko flushed in embarrassment and put the sack behind her.

'*Konoha senbei*, ginger shells,' she said. 'Have you ever eaten them?'

'I would if you would give me some.'

She fished out a few of the hard, crisp, folded cookies and dropped them in his hand.

'You probably won't like them,' she suggested tentatively in her little, musical voice.

'Oh yes I do,' he protested, crunching them heartily. 'They're good.'

The girl looked both grateful and pleased.

'René,' she began hesitantly, 'would you like… I would like… would you…'

'I would like to do anything you would, Kyoko.'

She smiled a smile that illuminated their corner of the school yard.

'Then come with me to the *nihon-go gakuen* after school. They will fix the tea, you know, Japanese style. You will like the ceremony. You will understand. It is pretty. Come!'

'Oh, I will. It is good of you to invite me. I like you, Kyoko, very much.'

This was almost too much for the girl. She ran out of the corner in a fluster, then ran back and said, 'After school, here,' and flitted away again like a happy butterfly.

Visiting the Japanese culture school with bright-eyed Kyoko opened up another corner of the world for René. He remembered Takeo now and regretted not getting to know him so that he could go home with him to meet these delightful people. Although this world was new to him, he could see that it was really a very old world. These ceremonies, customs, dresses, and objects, (the mats, the bowls and the whisks), and above all, the stylized and courteous bowings, were beautiful in a way he had not known before, but which he now determined to explore.

They watched *cha-do*, the 'way of the tea', with reverence. He turned to Kyoko and started to say something, but when she put a finger to her lips, he realized that one should not talk during such a ritual. Soon, however she hesitantly put her hand in his and, though he doubted that even this was decorous under the circumstances, he felt happy and flattered.

I wonder if she would let me kiss her, he thought, but then remembered that he had heard somewhere that Japanese felt kissing to be vulgar.

I want to, anyway, he thought, and I will when we are alone.

Kyoko did not think it vulgar, but she did cry a little.

'Oh, René,' she said, 'I love you too much, and probably you don't love me at all.'

'Oh yes I do, very much, but how can you love too much?'

She sighed.

'My people say we must not fall in love with your people. We must stay together and keep up our customs. They say you cannot really like us or understand. They will not think I should love you. They will think I am bold and bad.'

This speech from Kyoko, spoken in her soft, musical voice and with her unusual accent, was so appealing to René that he put his arms around her little body and pulled her to him.

'I never heard such nonsense in all my life. In this country we can love whomever we like. Let's show your people and mine that we do love and understand. I want you to come to our house for dinner. I am proud of Kyoko. Will your family let me come to dinner some day?'

'I hope so. I will try. If they don't I will run away.'

'Don't be silly. We'll win them over somehow. Tell me how to act with them and what to say.'

Thus began René's initiation into Japanese manners and customs. He learned to take off his shoes before entering the rooms whose floors were covered with mats, *tatami*. He learned to bow and to suck in his breath when talking to older people. He did go to dinner at the Kitagawas and ate raw fish dipped in soy sauce and learned to slurp his soup politely. He watched Kyoko arrange flowers in the sparse, elegant Japanese style. He looked on curiously as Mr. Kitagawa tended his bonsai, aged, dwarf trees that were perfect in shape and line.

Kyoko even tried to teach the boy some songs and games.

'René, say after me:

Hotaru koi, hotaru koi,
chichans chochin motte koe.

René repeated the delightful sounds as best he could. She giggled behind her hand and made him say them again.

'That is better,' she said.

'But what does it mean?'

'Come, glow-worm; come, glow-worm; and bring your little lantern.'

'All right, grow worm. I will.'

'René, you are making fun of me. I can't say it the way you do.'

'No, I am not making fun, Kyoko. Really. But you did giggle at my Japanese. Don't you wish we had glow-worms here? Our name is not nearly so pretty, though. We call them lightning bugs.'

'Oh, René!' the little girl exclaimed in disbelief and then covered her face and giggled uncontrollably.

'Now who's making fun?' asked the boy. He pulled her hands away from her face and kissed her pretty eyes.

Another day Kyoko showed him origami. She swiftly folded a colored sheet of paper many times, made a few deft scissor cuts and then shook the paper out. It was now a pattern of symmetrical beauty. He took it home and pinned it to the wall of his room.

'Teach me some more, Kyoko. I can say *Hotaru Koi* now.'

'All right. Guess what this is:
Chi-pa-pa, chi-pa-pa
Suzume no gakko no sensei wa.'

'Is it about crickets?' guessed the boy.

She giggled and then tried to assume a serious face.

'No, silly, it's about the sparrows' school teacher.'

'Let me see you write it, then.'

She rubbed a black ink-stick against a smooth stone in a dish filled with a little water and twirled a brush in her lips to tip it. Then she brushed the characters onto a yellow strip of paper with quick and graceful motions. He took this home and hung it beside the paper cutout.

Kyoko's family came to accept René when they learned that he was interested in their ways and that he really loved beauty. He saw, though, that it would take time to persuade the shy Kyoko to come to his house. She said she was afraid of his mother.

Chapter Three

During the next visit north it was decided that René would go into the city alone since the lady from Pasadena would be engaged and Mr. Phineas would be conferring with friends at the Pasadena library. René planned to visit the downtown music and book stores. He also wanted to explore parts of the city alone, although he did not reveal this desire to his friends.

The ponderous red streetcar clanked through a neighborhood of large houses set back in spacious yards covered with spreading live oak trees. This area, while pleasant, handsome, or even luxurious, seemed to lack a quality of humanity. The large front doors were tightly closed and appeared always to have been so. René could not imagine any of his small-town friends being welcomed or even admitted to these opulent but sterile domains of the wealthy. Later, however, the character of the houses changed. They grew smaller and dirtier and soon gave way to industrial buildings. He descended in the heart of the noisy, swarming, central business district and walked to the second-hand book stores. It would be easy to spend the whole day here, and he browsed for more than an hour, buying two old volumes and a magazine, all for less than one dollar.

Blinking in the bright sunshine outside the dim and cavernous shop, he walked south and east without any particular destination in mind. It was too fine a day to spend inside. He would explore on foot. Here the houses had obviously seen better days. Two- and three-story wooden residences, the former homes of citizens of substance, were now swarming with humanity of various colors, mostly dark. As he walked south, the houses became smaller and dirtier. No bougainvillea vines or bright geraniums graced these squalid shacks.

It gradually occurred to the well-dressed boy that he might be conspicuous in such a neighborhood. Several children eyed him suspiciously as he walked down the next block, and a large, tough-looking man in dungarees and undershirt sitting on a dilapidated porch, followed him with his eyes.

'What you looking for, white boy?' asked a boy about his age, from the sidewalk.

'Nothing,' answered René mildly. 'Just walking.'

'Just walking,' mimicked the dark boy. 'Just snooping you mean, and we don't want to be snooped.'

He turned to the man on the porch for a hurried consultation. René walked on slowly.

'Just a minute, you,' said the youngster. 'Let's talk.'

The white boy kept on walking slowly, but the other one came up and grabbed him by the arm.

'I said to wait. You're so interested in us folks, we're going to show you around. Come on in and visit with some real people, pale face.'

He pulled on his arm and steered him back to the man on the porch.

'What's your name and what you doing here, white boy?' the man snarled.

'I'm just exploring,' René answered, now becoming a little afraid. 'I'm René Levin from Pasadena.'

'Hoity, toity,' jeered the man. ''We'uns don't usual have the honor of visits from quality like you. Come on in and meet a real American Indian family, straight off the reservation. That'll be something to tell your folks back home.'

'All right. I'd like to,' lied René. 'What tribe are you?' At first it seemed as though the man was going to hit him. His eyes narrowed and his nostrils widened. But then he looked at the white boy again and burst out laughing.

'Indian!' he shouted. 'He thinks we are! What tribe? Hell, we're Cherokee-Chickasaw, can't you tell? This is just war paint we got on today. Come on, boy, you're too green to be safe around here.'

They went in through a shabby screen door which was full of ragged holes and had a large bulge at the bottom where it had been kicked repeatedly. A rickety table and two chairs, the stuffing erupting from several tears, made up the furnishings of the front room. The windows were so dirty that the room was dim in spite of the sunshine outside.

A fat but rather pleasant-faced woman with shiny skin rose from one of the dirty chairs.

'Melia,' said the man, 'want you to meet our new frien' Ren Levin. He's an explorer, lost in darkest Indian land.'

She looked at the man rather than at the boy.

'Rafe, you be careful. If you get in trouble one more time you're gonna end up in the jail permanent, and I won't stick around neither.'

He glared at her angrily, but then his voice softened a little.

'You be quiet and behave or there won't be anything lef' to stick around. Now be nice to our guest. He's from Pasadena and he expects manners.'

She glared at the boy. 'What's those books? They worth anything?'

'Not much,' René hastened to inform her. 'I bought the lot at a second-hand store for fifty cents.'

Her face fell and she turned to the man.

'Now what did you bring him in for? He ain't got nothin' and you'll probably get in trouble.'

'I told you, Melia, he wants to see how us Indians live. He don't know. Now be friendly.'

She snorted, got up, and walked into a room at the rear of the house.

'Nemmine her,' he said to René. 'She don't know how to act. But what do you think of our domicile? Ain't it grand?'

'Do you own it, Mr.——?'

'Oh, pardon me. Caber's the name, Rafe Caber. 'Course I don't own it. Nobody like us can own a house. We pays thirty dollars a month for this mansion, includin' the furniture a'course.'

René was genuinely shocked. 'Why for that in our town you can get a… a really very nice house.'

'Not the likes of us can't. Now ain't you glad you're not sooty?'

'I'm really sorry, Mr. Caber, I didn't know.'

''Course you didn't. That's why you went exploring, ain't it? But lemme tell you, white boy, it really ain't safe to traipse around in Indian territory. We're mean, and you could get an arrer in your back. Now you better go back north. Jed here'll go with you. We'se been glad to meet you. Tell your Pasadena friens about us. Some of them could help a little if they would. You tell your millionaire friens what it's like down here.'

'I will, Mr. Caber, I will.'

'No you won't, and it wouldn't do any good if you did. Go 'long now. So long.'

Jed pulled René out of the house and up the street. They walked in silence. When they got to the fringes of the business district he turned back without even looking at the white boy. René almost ran to the streetcar station, but he felt not so much fear as sorrow, or rather guilt. He had been living such a happy, carefree life while thousands of people lived in ugliness and despair. What could be done? What must be done?

Chapter Four

On this windy March day the live oak branches swished dryly against the old library windows. René and Mr. Phineas had just finished another lesson.

'I noticed some references to a story I don't recognize in one of your papers, René. Here it is: "Lyndall, Waldo, and Tant' Sannie hold an upsetting," and so forth.'

The boy squirmed a bit.

'Never mind if it's a private matter, but I was naturally curious since it's there for me to read,' continued the old man.

'Oh, it's nothing, really. Only I'm pretty sure you'll think it's silly. A long time ago I found a little old book one day in Mother's library: *The Story of an African Farm* by Olive Schreiner.'

'I think I remember it. It was popular in the late Victorian era,' Mr. Phineas said, smiling.

'I've never heard anyone say anything about it, but for some reason it appealed to me. I couldn't put it down until I had read it all.'

'It's very emotional, isn't it, and what we would call sentimental, melodramatic these days?'

'I suppose so. Yes, of course. And some of the characters are, ludicrous, like Bonaparte Blenkins. Tant' Sannie's not bad. Lyndall and Waldo will almost do when they're young. I knew you would say it's no good. But I feel I won't let go of it even so.'

'Well, well, don't be so defensive. You know me well enough by now. All of us, I think, have certain pets that we like even though we believe or know we shouldn't. Certainly I have a few that would disgrace me in front of most of my literary friends. I was hoping you wouldn't feel so constrained with me by now.'

'It's only because you set a very high standard, Mr. Phineas. And of course that's good. I owe most of my taste to you. It's just that some times I feel like liking something else. Am I *supposed* to be a little rebellious at this age?'

'Heavens, yes. At thirteen? I'm surprised you don't throw over the whole business and start reading funny papers or join the circus.'

'Now you're making fun. All right. So I got off the track with Lyndall. But I *do* feel sentimental about her in spite of that dreadful allegory about the hunter climbing the mountain of perfection and the one white feather floating down into his dying hands.'

'I have forgotten, but it sounds typical. But keep your Lyndall. It's a beautiful name, isn't it? And I know you, young man; you will find beauty in a name or a word, and why not? The logos.'

'Yes. Thank you.'

'Now, this last poem you gave one. I like it. You said it has one or two bad lines. Perhaps. It's slight. But that's what you meant. It's true to itself. I've always known you have the lyric gift. Let's read it aloud.'

I
Dancing,
The wanton wind
Advancing,
Gestures throw,
Kisses blow,

Movements show,
Glancing.

You
Being
Open eyed,
Seeing,
Take my hand,
Join the band,
Tread the sand,
Gleeing.

They,
Singing,
Their dulcet voices
Ringing,
Citherns play,
Garlands lay,
Till the day
Bringing.

The old librarian read it beautifully.

'That is good, simply good, Mr. Levin. Now, may I ask you a few questions about it?'

'Yes. Although I don't like to talk about a poem after I've done it. But I know I must.'

'Well, we won't talk about it much, but of course I'm interested. Did you find this stanza pattern and rhyme scheme somewhere, or are they yours?'

'The poem just seemed to fall that way. I hardly ever follow a pattern. Each one seems to fit the particular poem.'

'That's remarkable. This one would be difficult because of the two triple rhymes in each stanza, and one set always participles.'

'I suppose so, now that you point it out. I didn't think of these things at the time; it just had to be that way.'

'Let's see; "the wanton wind". That sounds a little familiar.'

'Yes. I didn't know it when I wrote it, but it's Will's. It's in *Midsummer Night's Dream*.'

'Oh, yes. Well, that's no real theft; chances are others have used it too. I like "gleeing". Perhaps it's not really a verb, but it is now. And of course, "citherns" is nice. I suppose you're a little doubtful about "Movements strow"?'

'Yes, that's weak.'

'Well, I don't know. I think it'll do, especially after "Gestures throw". It has the right fancy. Perhaps you could fix it if you continue to feel uneasy.'

'Perhaps. And "Join the band". What band?'

'I think that's made almost all right by the "They" in the next stanza.'

'I hope so. I can't work on it any more now. Maybe some day.'

'You must read Ezra Pound some day, too. You will appreciate his love of Medieval beauty, Now, I know you will be inclined to say "no", but may I send this to a friend of mine at Harvard?'

'Oh, I don't know, Mr. Phineas. At Harvard? Who is he?'

'Now don't shrink up. His name wouldn't mean anything to you I'm sure, but he knows poetry, and especially modern poetry. He's honest but kindly. He won't eat you up or tear it apart.'

'Well, all right, if you really think it's good enough for him.'

'I do. Now one more thing. Have you thought of writing anything in a conventional form, say a sonnet? And perhaps with a philosophic slant?'

'Yes, I'm working on a sonnet right now. I'll bring it as soon as I can make it work.'

'Fine, fine. See you Friday, then, and don't forget to practice the Handel. I'm so glad you got your treble recorder.'

The boy smiled as he walked out of the office. He was glad that Mr. Phineas liked 'I Dancing'.

Chapter Five

'René, come with me to a party. It will be *hana-no-kai.* Tonight we are going to watch a flower bloom,' Kyoko said, looking up at him through her dark almond eyes.

'How wonderful. Do you mean that you give a party just to worship a flower?'

'Yes. But afterwards there will be music. Samisen and koto and shakuhachi. René, you will not mind if we have to be quiet? It is impolite to talk at a flower party.'

'Oh, that is the kind of party I would like, Kyoko. But you will have to tell me what else to do and not to do or I will disgrace you.'

'No, you will not. I will show you.'

They were sitting on the sofa in the Levin living room. René had thought he would never get the shy little girl to come home with him. He knew his mother would return shortly from town, but he knew better than to tell this to the girl. She looked up at the shelves of books and then ran to the piano where she moved her fingers lightly over the keys without depressing them.

René watched her constantly.

It's not possible for her to do anything ugly, he thought. Every movement she makes is graceful. And her voice is like the tinkling of bells. And what a light dancer she would be.

She flitted back to him and put her hand on top of his. She pressed each finger in turn as thought she were playing a musical instrument. Then she pulled him over to the piano.

'Play for me,' she said.

Her words sounded more like 'Pray for me.'

He launched into the Bach toccata and fugue.

'No,' she said, putting her fingers over his to stop them. 'Play something soft and light, a love song.'

She blushed.

He smiled and played the Schubert softly.

'That is beautiful, René. Now I will teach you a song. No, not on the piano. You will have to learn to sing it.'

She sang the foreign words in a small, pure voice.

'Oh, that was lovely Kyoko. What does it say?'

'I will tell you after you learn it. Say the first line after me.'

He did his best to imitate her clear little voice. Then he heard the back door open, and Kyoko started.

'Don't be afraid. It's just Mother. She is pleasant. You will like her.'

When Mrs. Levin came into the living room, he introduced the little girl.

'Mother, this is Kyoko Kitagawa. I have tried so hard to get her to come see us.'

'Hello, Kyoko; René has told me many good things about you. I see he was right.'

'Mrs. Levin, he has exaggerated.'

She had a little trouble with the last word.

'You see I haven't, Mother. Kyoko has invited me to a party. They are going to watch a flower bloom.'

The girl looked anxiously at Mrs. Levin as though fearful she might laugh.

'How very interesting, Kyoko,' she said. 'I know he really will enjoy that.'

The girl beamed. René grinned. Mrs. Levin smiled.

'You were singing something when I came in,' she said. 'Don't stop, I will be working in the kitchen.'

Kyoko's voice was still fainter as she taught René the rest of the little song. It was about a disappointed lover. This time she sang it in English.

'But, Kyoko, that is so sad, not like us. We are happy together, aren't we?'

'Yes, now.'

'Oh, always.'

'Don't say that,' she said, putting her fingers over his lips. 'That is bad luck.'

He took her little fingers and put them in his mouth, biting them playfully. She withdrew them with a little squeal as he repeated, 'always.'

At the *nihon-go gakuen* a group of people sat on *tatami* and gazed at a single, large flower, dramatically arranged in a low, dark-blue vase in the *tokonoma*. The warmth of the room apparently acted upon the petals. They had partially opened out from the center. Everyone looked happy and worshipful and peaceful, but in spite of what Kyoko had said about being quiet, there was a certain amount of conversation murmuring in the room.

Later in the evening the flower had fully opened. Then the musicians appeared and seemed to be responding to requests to play favorite songs. The *kotoist* gracefully plucked several selections from his horizontal harp with its movable bridges. A girl sang in a thin, child's voice, accompanied by the querulous *samisen*. But René was most fascinated by the *shakuhachi*. The impassive player shook his head from side to side to produce a vibrato from the bamboo flute. Kyoko did her best to answer René's eager questions between selections. The flutist even allowed the boy to try to play his instrument, but it would not respond like the recorder; René could see that it would require a very different playing technique.

'Kyoko, you are a flower, and I would like to put you in my *tokonoma* and watch you bloom,' said René after the party.

The little girl turned up her face for him to kiss.

'Thank you, René-san. I love you. Be careful walking home. It is so dark.'

'Do you dislike the dark, too?' he asked.

'Yes, I always have. I am afraid sometime I will not be able to come out of it again.'

'Yes you will. I will carry you out in my arms. Good night, Kyoko.'

'*Sayonara*, René.'

He walked home along the roads and familiar streets under a moonless, starless sky. In the far distance, along the coast, a lighthouse flashed its code: long, short, long. He slipped through the back door and into his room, where his mother had left a light burning and had folded back one corner of the bedclothes.

Chapter Six

René entered the local high school, as a freshman when sessions resumed in September, 1926. Mr. Meadows acted as principal of this school as well as of the grammar school. The high school sat across the street from the other and was mainly distinguished by being built of stone rather than wood. It lacked a bell tower such as graced the lower school, but had a playing field and a small, separate gymnasium.

Marilyn was by now a junior and could hardly be expected to consort with a lowly freshman. He caught the occasional glimpse of her when she passed in the halls. She always walked in the midst of a group of girls. Kyoko, however, was in his section and in many of the same classes, so he saw a great deal of her. She continued to excel in her studies and to worship René as at a Shinto shrine.

The only real problem he encountered in his first year was boredom. Only the Latin class posed enough of a challenge to keep his interest. His other teachers complained to the principal, and the principal decided to call a conference on the subject of René Levin, IQ 200. He sent word to Mrs. Levin, Mr. Phineas, and even Mrs. Briscecov to meet with him one evening in April of the spring semester.

They met in the principal's office in the grade school. He said one office was enough for one man and besides there was less room in the high-school building.

'Let's review the situation to date,' he began. 'Our young man has just turned fourteen and is finishing his freshman year. He is, of course, the leading scholar in Latin and English, but seems to find the other subjects boring. *We* know why, of course, but are continuing to keep his teachers in the dark about his IQ score. You want this to continue, don't you, Mrs. Levin?' he said, smiling at her paternally.

'Yes, if you don't mind.'

'Well, I think it is the best idea. Now, of course, you, Mr. Phineas, and you, Mrs. Briscecov, are working with him more closely than we can and this explains why he is so far advanced. What do you think about his continuing here in the high school, Phineas?'

'Well, I believe that it was very wise of Mrs. Levin not to advance him in grade or send him to a private, advanced school… up to now. Now, however, he is so very far ahead of his classmates that it is beginning to create problems. You all know, I think, that I hope he will go to one of the great English universities. I have been corresponding with a friend at Cambridge and there seems little doubt that he can qualify for a scholarship – for American boys of promise. However, he is not quite ready for that now. The universities are heavy on the classics and languages. He needs more Latin and French. The literature we have been working on for a long time but he needs more philosophy and history and resists these studies. But we'll keep him at it. Now perhaps we should hear from Mrs. Briscecov.'

'Thank. you, Phineas,' she flashed. 'I am sure that René Levin can become a fine musician. He is almost a prodigy now, even if he did start late. Naturally I would like to see him go as far as possible in music. But I know that his first love is literature and poetry. You got him first, Phineas.'

'Not I, Wazlenka. Mrs. Levin and Walt Whitman did it, eh, Ora? You don't mind our way of discussing your son, almost as though you had little to do with the prodigy?'

'Of course not, Mr. Phineas and Mrs. Briscecov. It is thrilling to hear that you think he is so good, but this subject always makes me regret not being wealthy. Think where he might be now if the finest schools... pardon me, Mr. Meadows...'

'Well, I don't think I'm being vain, Ora, when I doubt that René would be much better off if he were a rich man's son in an eastern prep school,' said the librarian.

'I think Phineas is right, you know, Mrs. Levin. I think the boy is actually better off. These over-precocious college students or scientific geniuses... I don't know. They often don't seem to be real people. René is so happy and good, which is worth a lot. Now in regard to musical success,' the principal went on, 'I suppose that's another matter. We know about Mozart and Haydn when they were mere infants.'

'He could be a real success in music,' put in Mrs. Briscecov. 'He has the ear, the timing, the feel, even the discipline. But I am resigned. I don't think he wants to be a musician except for the pleasure of it. I don't doubt that he will make a big name, but it will be in writing, I am glad, though, that he likes music. It will make him a better man, a better artist.'

'Amen to that,' resumed Mr. Phineas. 'But to get back to Mr. Meadow's problems, I do believe that we should skip the boy up to at least the junior year... without missing any Latin, that is. Can this be done?'

'Yes,' said the principal, nodding in agreement, 'and I am so glad you suggested it; it was on my mind too. Would you agree to it now, Mrs. Levin?'

'Oh, of course, gentlemen. He is old enough now that he won't be with classmates who are too mature.'

'Good, then, ladies and gentlemen. In the fall René will be a junior. We can probably get him through high school in three or even two and a half years. Do you think you can arrange to get him into the university by then, Phineas?'

'I feel sure of it. Mrs. Levin and I will discuss the matter and get things rolling. By the way, have you seen any of his poems lately?' the old man asked with pride.

'No, I haven't.'

'Well, they are remarkable, simply remarkable. I think we and the rest of the world will first hear from him in that discipline.'

The committee broke up and went its several ways through the spring night. Mrs. Briscecov shook her head now and then all the way home. After entering the house she shrugged her shoulders and sat down at the keyboard. The music she played that evening sounded rather sad. But she would get used to it. Too late. Too bad.

Part Six

Chapter One

Benny Beadle was a big heavy, friendly member of the junior class. His weight and prowess made him an outstanding football player, which in turn made him a hero to be worshipped by the rest of the student body, especially by the girls, who at this age must worship someone violently. He took this adulation modestly and was actually a rather likeable fellow. For some reason he became fond of René. This was fortunate since they were members of the same gymnasium class, and the more aggressive boys would have delighted in pummeling the 'sissy'.

Though now sixteen, it was obvious that René could not play football because he was too light. Since everyone had to participate in some sport, it was decided that he would become a short-distance runner. So every day while most of his fellows puffed and grunted on the football field or fanned at baseballs, he and a few other light-weights jogged around the track, sprinting occasionally and timing each other with an old stop-watch.

'How you doing, Ren?' barked Benny as he stripped for the shower at the end of class. 'Gonna break that world record, Saturday?'

They were all in training for an athletic exhibition to be held on the school ground at the end of the week. Although it was not now football season and they were not competing with teams from other schools, the coach had arranged a 'tournament' to allow his athletic charges to show off and compete among themselves.

'You know I'm not going to set the world on fire running,' replied René, 'so just how many touchdowns do you plan to make against the scrubs?'

'Now, Ren, I've told you over and over, that's not the way to talk. You got to really believe you're gonna win. Then you will.'

'It works with you, anyway, Benny. Of course your weight and skill have something to do with it, too.'

Benny punched his arm in what was meant as a friendly gesture.

'You get out there and *run*, kid, or I'll sit on you.'

By now they were naked and running for the shower, Benny's body gross, powerful, streaming with sweat, René's delicate and white, like that of a dancer. It was customary to whoop and holler in the showers. It helped relieve the shock of the cold water, and the sounds echoed from the shiny tiled walls in a satisfying way. Steam rose in billows from these animal stalls and the animals pranced and cavorted, throwing soap and good-natured obscenities at each other.

There was something rather good about this crude, primitive rite. René would have to try to capture this in a poem. What would Mr. Phineas think of that?

Afterwards the animals dried themselves with large, coarse towels, and then inevitably, using them as weapons, began snapping at each other's bare bodies. Before this new pandemonium got out of hand, however, a large electric bell clanged and everyone rushed into their clothes to be ready for the next class.

'Actually,' said René to his friend as they walked out of the gymnasium, 'I shouldn't tell you this, but I ran it in ten yesterday. But I doubt that old stop-watch or the fellow who snapped it.'

'Ten seconds. Boy,' exulted Benny. 'I told you you could do it. Now get things fixed up there,' he tapped the other boy's forehead, 'and you'll win yourself a championship.'

'Well, let's not get carried away. But maybe I can win the dash Saturday.'

'No maybe. Hell yes, you're gonna win it, or we'll never talk to ya again!'

Saturday turned out to be a sunny day but cool and windy. Benny worried about the wind much more than René, not because it might blow the football away from a pass receiver, but because it might slow the track runners.

The bleachers soon filled with students and parents. A shortened baseball game led off the program, to be followed by track events and then a short football match. René could not share the excitement of the other athletes as they changed their clothes in the gymnasium. The coach's nervous 'pep talk' failed to arouse a competitive spirit in his heart. Benny's right, he thought. You have to want to win. You have to take the whole business seriously. It means a lot to most of them.

They marched out onto the field self-consciously, to be introduced to the spectators, while the wind whipped around their ankles. René looked up and saw Marilyn in the stands. She was wearing a green 'beanie' hat on top of her pale yellow hair. She was indubitably a young woman now. He thought she smiled at him.

The boys lined up for the one hundred-yard dash. They looked puny compared to the other athletes. The coach gave them last minute instructions and pats on the back. One of the runners made a nervous false start and they had to get set again. The gun sounded and the short race seemed over almost before it had begun. René felt unusually light and ran away from the rest easily, breaking the tape a winner.

'One hundred-yard dash. The winner, Levin; the time... ten seconds... a new record for this school.'

The crowd cheered deliriously. Benny pounded René's back so hard he nearly knocked his breath out. René returned to the gymnasium feeling more sheepish than triumphant. But Marilyn had waved at him unmistakably this time.

A high-school athlete, that's what she wants, he thought ruefully. But he was smiling as he took his shower. Maybe there was something good about being an animal, after all.

He let out a whoop as the cold water tightened his skin.

Chapter Two

It was the last day of school in the spring of 1928. When René walked out of the high-school grounds early, there stood Marilyn, waiting for him.

'I'm sorry, René,' she said. 'I've been a fool. Will you forgive me?'

He tried to make light of it.

'Of course, Marilyn, nothing to forgive. But what is a graduating senior doing talking to a junior who is really just a sophomore? Your friends will never forgive you.'

'All right René. I've gotten over that. Can't we be friends again?'

'No, not friends... lovers.'

'She smiled. 'That is what I meant.'

'Give me your books, senior.'

He took them in one hand and her arm in the other. They walked toward her house. The world seemed to be enveloped in a scintillating yellow cloud. The birds turned somersaults and piped madrigals.

'May I touch your hair, Marin-lyn?'

'Oh, it is good to be called that again. You may not touch it here, but later. René, they say you really are a poet. Can I read something you wrote?'

'Well, I'm afraid you mightn't like it.'

'I still want to read something. I can try to understand, can't I?'

'Of course. I will give you something if you'll promise on your father's Bible not to show it to anyone.'

'Oh, yes… but René… have you ever written anything about… us?'

'There speaks a woman,' he jibed gently. 'No, nothing to satisfy me. Maybe you will now inspire me, Marilyn. Try very hard.'

'I guess that means you've never really loved me,' she said pretending to pout.

'Maybe it means you've never really loved *me*.'

'We'll have to go somewhere and settle that.'

'Yes, it will take a long time, at least all summer. But be careful, Marilyn; I now know what they do.'

'Oh, not with someone else! You didn't find out with someone else?'

'No, no. But I know, so be careful.'

'No, *you* be careful. Here's my house and I'm the minister's daughter, remember?'

'Marilyn, can you go hiking with me tomorrow?'

'I don't know. Mother's getting stricter with me now. But she likes you. Come around about nine and we'll talk her into it. Where will we go?'

'To a secret place I want to show you. You'll see.'

'Goodbye, René. Bring a poem.'

He ran home to write it. He was still struggling with it when his mother made him turn out his light and go to bed.

He brought her instead, the poem he had written after the Japanese party with Kyoko. He couldn't see that there was anything wrong with this. It wasn't a love poem and Kyoko wasn't in it:

The voice rose and fell
Like a wizened baby's,
Seven hundred years old
And querulous.
Meanwhile the wood blocks
Mocked a jumping figure
In the samisen,
Played by a lady
In kimono.

No time. Time was not marked,
And time was not felt.
Time was not.
But sound was.

Bamboo shoot and water ouzel
Were contemplated into eternity
While a shaking shakuhachi
Pulled down the moon,
Dipped it in black water,
And hung it up again.

Strings of a koto
Plinked into blossoms
That floated, petal by petal,
Down from bare branches,
Slowly, lightly,
Into the river.

Later the drums
Called in a samurai,
Fat, fierce, and funny,
But serious, grunting.

Then we bowed,
Sucked in our breaths,
And walked home
Beside the crawling, creaking crickets.

Marilyn concealed her disappointment artfully. If she had not just returned to the boy she might have thrown a tantrum. It would take time to turn his thoughts to her alone.

They sat on the bank of the little sandy river. There was no sign of the water snake, so they took off their shoes and stockings and waded in the clear, cold water. Then they returned to the bank and sat in the sun to dry their feet. In the sunshine the girl's hair shone lighter and finer than ever before. He took it in his hands and kissed it reverently. She put her arms around him and kissed him on the mouth.

'You are beautiful,' he said.

'Would you like... love me if I wasn't?' she asked.

'No.'

'Oh, René, you are cruel. I want you to like me for *me*.'

'Your beauty is you. You can't help that. Why mind? Luxuriate in it. Let me luxuriate in it.'

He ran his fingers again through her silky hair. She jumped up suddenly. 'You're right. We are going to have to be careful.'

She started to put on her stockings.

'We are so much older than we used to be.'

'And you move more gracefully than you did then,' he commented.

He tried to persuade her to go into one of the caves, but she wouldn't. They walked back into the town holding hands but not talking.

'René, I do love you... too much. Someday you will know how it feels. Then you will write a poem for us. Goodbye. See you tomorrow.'

It seemed to him that she was forever running away from him through that screen door, into the white house. But he walked home with the feel of light, silky hair still on his fingers.

Chapter Three

After the Christmas and New Year holiday, Mrs. Briscecov bore down on René and Mr. Phineas in earnest. It had all been arranged; they were to play several trios at the Kramer concert in the city. Mr. Phineas and she would play some duets, and she would solo. There would even be a harpsichord and a young man to play it.

'Now, René, you are rushing that passage. Those are only thirty-second notes, not sixty-fourths. And Phineas, that low "F" is too weak. See if you can strengthen without going sharp.'

Mrs. Briscecov was a merciless master when driving them to perfection. She was sarcastic and cajoling by turns. More than once René felt like throwing down his instrument and stomping out. He did in fact do this one frustrating evening, but soon came back, sheepishly, and resumed where they had left off. Mr. Phineas would try to break the tension now and then with a joke or prank, but the lady was not amused and drove them harder still.

'We are to be the first in the 1929 series. Most of these people have never heard these instruments. Many have never heard this music. We must do right by the recorder, otherwise the people will not like it. We must spread the gospel,' the indomitable lady exhorted.

Mr. Phineas' eyes twinkled.

'You are right, Wazlenka. You are St. Paul, and we the Ephesians. But may we rest a few minutes now? Have you some coffee?'

'Soon, soon Phineas, but now once more through the Telemann allegro. *One*, two, three, four.'

Judging by the applause, the concert was a success. The harpsichord stayed in tune and the young man played it nobly. Mrs. Briscecov's solos from The Bird Fancier's Delight brought down the house. The duets and trios sang sweetly. Afterwards people swarmed up to the stage to look at the strange old instruments and to press a key or two of the harpsichord. Many new people listened to the gospel that evening and a godly number were converted.

Next day the press notices were favorable. Some of the critics were obviously not at home with this sort of music, but they just as obviously enjoyed it. And the whole event was seen as incredibly distinguished, a new height in cultural accomplishment in this, the fastest growing city in the world.

The music lady arranged a reception for the performers after the concert in her Pasadena mansion. René looked forward to this, not because he enjoyed babbling with a crowd of socialites and dilettantes, but because he knew that Mrs. Hilden-Thurber would be there. Known as a crotchety philanthropist, this immensely wealthy old lady could be the one to whom he might deliver his gospel.

When the boy was introduced to the dowager, his heart quailed. Mrs. Hilden-Thurber was a toad; fat, swarthy, with big, blinking eyes and a croaking voice. She sat in a large chair, like a throne and people were brought to her. However, although she seemed repulsive, he could sense that she was shrewd and intelligent. He realized suddenly that she must have been the recipient of innumerable importunities and that she must have acquired a vast contempt for most favor seekers. Nevertheless, he was determined to make a plea.

'How do you do, young man,' the toad croaked and blinked its eyes. 'How did you happen to learn to play that unusual old instrument?'

'Mrs. Briscecov and Mr. Phineas were good enough to show it to me, Mrs. Hilden-Thurber. Mrs. Briscecov actually taught it to me. Mr. Phineas had the first recorder sent to him from England.'

'Humph. You play very well. Do you think I could learn?'

'Oh yes. It is really not too hard to learn.'

'Flatterer. I don't even know one note from another on the piano. But I know good music when I hear it,' she pronounced flatly.

'I'm sure of that, Mrs. Hilden-Thurber. We are so glad you came to the recital.'

'Well, did you know I was there?'

He had noticed the heavy old lady in a front-row seat.

'Oh, I saw you.'

'Perhaps. Perhaps you did. Now, Mr. Levin, tell me something about yourself. What are you most interested in? What do you most want out of life, a young man like you?'

'I am happy that you asked, Mrs. Hilden-Thurber. I do have a special interest to ask you about.'

'Of course; everyone does. I should think yours might be a need to go to a good college. Is that it?'

Her frog eyes probed him and blinked.

'Oh, no. Thank you. I do hope to be able to go to a good college, of course, but Mr. Phineas thinks he can arrange a scholarship for me.'

He looked her straight in the face.

'Mrs. Hilden-Thurber have you ever been in the south-eastern part of our city?'

She seemed to prick up her ears.

'No, what do you mean? What is there?'

'Oh, I wish you could see. Or rather I suppose it is better that you haven't. It is dreadful. The poor people and their nasty houses.'

'Oh, you mean the slum neighborhoods. If you think those are bad, wait until you see St. Louis or London. But how do you know about this?'

I walked down there one day. I didn't know what I was getting involved in. A man made me go into his house. It was horrible but he has to pay thirty dollars a month for it. Isn't that awful?'

'Don't look at me so hard, young man. I do not derive my income from those rents.'

The toad seemed to deflate a little.

'But I must admit I know some who do.'

'Oh. Mrs. Hilden-Thurber, isn't there something we can do for these people?'

'What would you suggest?'

'I don't really know.'

'No, you don't. What do you think would happen if we dropped dollar bills on them from an airplane?'

'It might save some lives.'

'Don't you think most of the money would be spent on foolish things instead of on food and clothes?'

'I don't think so,' the boy said.

'I do. You figure out a really effective way to help these people, Mr. Levin, and I will do what little I can.'

Some other people were being brought before the throne. He strained to hear her last words.

'It was good to talk to you, young man, to talk to someone who wants help for others, not himself. I mean it. Write me a letter when you figure out how to do it.'

'Oh, thank you, Mrs. Hilden-Thurber. I will. I really will.'

She dismissed him with friendly skepticism. He felt that he had failed. He went to bed that night disheartened.

Chapter Four

It was June again and time to graduate from high school. René could not partake of much of the sentimentality of the occasion. His eyes were now focussed on faraway places. He felt distant in spirit from the old stone building and the steaming gymnasium. Marilyn had graduated the year before. Benny was graduating with him, but Takeo and Juan were long gone. Kyoko would be there for another year.

It was inevitable that René should be chosen valedictorian. His intellectual and artistic superiority could no longer be concealed. Somehow the word that he was a 'genius' had spread, though no one really knew what this meant. The rumor that he was also a poet was less widespread. This was simply too embarrassing to be countenanced. Everyone but him was trying hard to bury the 'sissy' charge that had followed him from the earliest days and hence his verse writing was ignored or denied.

At first the boy flatly refused the honor. The idea of speaking to a large audience gave him nightmares. He was gradually won over by Mr. Meadows, Mr. Phineas, and Marilyn. Their pride and faith were too much to resist. His mother, too, was proud, but she didn't push him. Benny Beadle insisted vociferously, of course, with many bruising punches to the arm.

So René resigned himself and composed what he hoped would be a suitable address. Mr. Meadows edited out a few sections which he knew would be over the heads of the audience and suggested additions which the boy tended to reject.

The high-school auditorium was warm and stuffy that June night, filled with parents and relatives of the graduates.

The seniors were seated in rows of folding chairs on the stage. The superintendent of the school district droned through a dull speech, followed by Mr. Meadows, who tried to inject some humor into the ceremony. He introduced the valedictorian as 'a young man we have come to admire and who will very likely make our school loom large in the eyes of the world some day.'

When René rose to speak he saw Mr. Phineas and Marilyn in the third row. The rest of the audience, even in this small auditorium, looked like the proverbial sea of faces or the many-eyed Argus.

'We, the class of 1929, bid farewell to our Alma Mater with fondness and regret,' he began.

There she is with the funny hat: Mrs. Briscecov. Now I see her raising her hand and counting: One, two, three, I wish I hadn't disappointed her. Let's see, it's time for the Latin quotation. 'Let us not forget that, in the words of Horace, "Dimidium facti qui coepit habet; sapere aude; incipe!"' That's for you, Marilyn. Don't you understand? I will convince you. Incipe! How did you like that, good old Mr. Phineas? Well, now I will knock their eyes, or rather their ears, out. 'Friends, those of us who are leaving tonight are determined that we will now conquer the world as an old poet put it.' I would not just put it. I would throw it at them. There is Fed, looking bored. He would probably agree with the old Greek's words. Fight and conquer, that's Feddie. Make the money while it's hot. He'll do it, too. Now I see Mother. Does she think it was really worthwhile bearing us and bringing us up? She probably does, and it must be lonely. Mr. Oscar Levin, State Finance Commissioner; will I ever see him again? Succeeded by Titus Hornbeck, insurance salesman. That just couldn't be. 'We graduates have one question uppermost in our minds as we close our books and walk out into the world. Will we justify the hard work, the love, and the faith that have been expended upon us? I feel that I speak for us all when I assert confidently that we will.' (Applause) I knew that would get them. The real question is how many of us will keep out of trouble and finally become able to support ourselves. Whoever heard of a poet earning a living? Will I ask Fed for a job as clerk in his big, important office? Pardon me, President Levin, I just wanted to remind you, I was a boy genius, you know. Perhaps I could help with the inventory. I could put it in rhyme. I should really worry about the future, but I can't imagine living to be old. It seems to stop early. There is a wall of water... But this is no time for that. 'In conclusion we wish to express our gratitude to the faculty, our principal, and our parents for not only bearing with us but for bearing us up, and out. From all of us then, a heartfelt Ave atque vale. The class of 1929 departs, but hopes not to be forgotten.' (Hearty applause) All our little egos, brought into the world without our desire or volition. But here we are, and once here we want to eat a big slice of the world pie. Too bad about those thousands of Chinamen starving to death. They didn't have a chance, but we mean to get ours.

René bowed and resumed his seat. The principal stood at a pulpit-like desk and handed each graduate a diploma as he filed past and down the stairs to the auditorium, The superintendent shook each eager hand lukewarmly. Another batch through the mill.

Chapter Five

Because it lay on the seacoast the town usually experienced a mild cool, damp, summer climate. In summer the fog, having withdrawn in the morning to a position several miles off the coast, would float over the water like distant sails. Then by four in the afternoon it would start to move in, partly obscuring the sun, but during a few days in August, the wind would blow from inland and the fog would evaporate, the sky sparkle, and the temperature rise. In the evening the air would still be warm and the stars would flicker brightly overhead.

On one such summer evening, René, who had not seen much of Marilyn since school let out, felt impelled to run over to the white house on the corner and knock on the screen door. Marilyn was out but soon returned, clearly happy to see him. They obtained permission to go out, ostensibly to the movie theater, but actually to fly to the beach and walk along the shore.

'I realized suddenly again tonight that I love you, Marilyn. I had to tell you again, to see you again.'

'And yet you haven't talked to me in weeks, René. How can I believe you suddenly don't love me and then, suddenly do?'

'Oh it isn't that way. I have thought of you much. But I have been writing again and Mother has been having trouble and...'

'I don't know, René. I wouldn't want to be married to a man who could stay away from me like that.'

'Oh, no. I wouldn't be that kind of a husband, Marilyn. 'Doesn't that sound like old times: "married", "husband"?'

'It sounds good to me now.'

At the beach she took hold of his hand in the old familiar way and led him along the hard, wet sand. They walked across it, digging their toes into its cool graininess. Then they drew back to a small dune, sat on the top of it, and looked out over the dark water and up into the glistening stars.

'You make me feel so mean, and I really didn't forget you. You don't understand how boys… men are, Marilyn; but they aren't mean. Sometimes they have to go away and think and figure things out. You girls seem more sure of yourselves, somehow. You frighten us by seeming so sure and wise.'

'Really? I hadn't thought of that. I'll tell you a secret, though; you scare us sometimes. You don't know how you make us feel. We go all weak and jelly fishy.'

'That's cute, and you're sweet, Marilyn.'

They sat in silence while the warm land wind blew the sand grains into swirling patterns and seemed to push the breaking waves back into the oncoming swells.

'Marin darling, we were ninnies to come down here without bathing suits. Here it is one of the few nights of the year when it's warm enough to go in.'

'Yes. Well… it's pretty dark… If you'll promise to behave, we could…'

'Oh, let's do. Last one in's a rotten egg.'

They shyly but gaily shed their few summer clothes and ran together into the wine dark sea.

Old mother, here I am, back in your wet womb with your other creatures, the ones who stayed, the fish and the eels and the octopi. And here beside me, glistening like another sea creature, is your daughter, a beautiful daughter with light yellow hair – like wet silk

– and sea-green eyes. And she sees me and I am not ashamed. And I see her, and she is not ashamed. We are proud to be your children as we float in you and touch each other, and it is good. This must be the right way to live: to plunge in unafraid and unashamed. What have we done to run away from this, to lock ourselves up in clothes, houses, cities? Give me your hand, Nereid. We will swim down to the caves of the sea!

'René, come out now. You'll get too cold, and we don't have any towels. Honey, come out now, please.'

He awoke as from a dream, and yet it was still a dream. Marilyn, her silky hair streaming, her wet, white body glistening, pulled him out of the surf. The wind was still blowing, the stars were still glittering, the waves behind them were still susurrating. They lay on the grainy sand while the wind dried their salt-tightened bodies.

They looked at each other in wonder and in ecstasy. Then they twined together in the ancient and purposeful act of love while the million-year-old sea swelled and drew nearer. The tide came in full. The salt water ran up the slope and flowed under them softly as they fulfilled each other in the old ecstatic ritual that is ever mysterious and ever new. Foaming under the girl's body, a wave floated her up to him. He knew her. She was Aphrodite – light haired, white skinned, and beautiful – just born from the womb of the sea.

Part Seven

Chapter One

'You have a great treat in store for you, young man. England, even in the autumn, is beautiful.' Mr. Phineas smiled nostalgically.

'I know it must be from what I… we have read. No one loves his countryside as fervently and as constantly as the Englishman. I suppose I first felt this in *The Wind in the Willows*.'

René was visiting the library office for the last time before leaving for Cambridge.

'Yes, that is a good example. Oh, I suppose most everyone feels that way about his country, really. Russians, Frenchmen. I'm sure we could think of many literary examples.'

'But there still seems to be a special flavor about the English appreciation.'

'Yes, I think that the English countryside is especially suited to inspire poetry. It can be encompassed. It is never really frightening or overwhelming like the Grand Canyon or the Rockies or the Steppes. In it man feels that he belongs and that nature is cognizant of him and feels kindly toward him. Only when the tempest rages, as at Lear, or in the grip of winter, does it scorn him. Or am I being sentimental? Well, you will soon see and can let me know.'

'I can only think of the forest of Arden or Hardy's farms.'

'Yes. Now you will discover whether it is the country or the literature that is magic.'

They sat in silence for a while.

'Now, have we forgotten anything of practical import? You have the letters? Mr. Phillips will meet you in Southampton and get you through London. You must take a day or two to look around. Then it's on to Cambridge.'

'Mr. Phineas…'

'Yes?'

'How in the world am I ever going to thank you or repay you? I have not been at all adequate in expressing my gratitude. I have been selfish. What have I ever done to deserve all this… Mother, Mrs. Briscecov, you? I am spoiled rotten. How can I *earn* all this?'

'I am glad that you asked, not because I believe you are actually ungrateful but because it is right to acknowledge help and good fortune. You remember what happened to Ulysses and his men when they failed to thank and sacrifice to their gods. I think everyone who has helped you has done so because we saw that this help would bear fruit. Your creations will repay us.'

'If faith and help bear fruit, I can't fail.'

'It takes more than that, of course. It takes the magic fire, which we believe you have. But, René, you know that a high IQ does not make a real genius. Whether or not you are the real thing remains to be seen.'

'Sometimes I feel something within me that is much more powerful than I am. I hope I can live up to whatever it is. But I say again that I have not been nearly grateful enough, especially to you.'

'Well, well, you know that geniuses are often not especially grateful. Some of them are dreadful people… selfish, immoral. You can't be like that unless you produce the very greatest art. But, really, writers are usually all right. It's artists and musicians who are sometimes so dreadful.'

'Perhaps someone should have made me a Christian after all,' René said smiling ruefully.

'Perhaps. What could be better than a real Christian, or Buddhist for that matter? But no one can *make* us religious.'

'No. But I will put this in the form of a prayer. Lord, do not let me forget to give thanks to those who have made it possible for me to live such a wonderful life.'

'Amen to that. And don't forget that the best way of all to give thanks is to help others. Pass on the torch.'

'Yes, and that worries me most of all, Mr. Phineas. I am always taking, seldom giving.'

'Remember two things: you are young, and there are many ways to give. You must find your way to do it. Happily it may be in the creation of art, which is not a small way and is as worthy as any other. I am very happy to know that this concerns you, however. You are growing.'

'Do you think so? I have sometimes doubted it.'

'Yes, and you will grow much faster now. You will be a man when you return. I am glad that Cambridge will be your Alma Mater. She is a good one.'

'And you are a good Alma Pater, the best.'

'There, that is thanks enough. See, you have grown.'

Mr. Phineas stood up and reached out his hand. René clasped it fervently and then walked out of the old office quietly.

En archei en hoc logos, and God saw that it was good.

Chapter Two

René and Marilyn sat on their dune and looked at the ocean. A chilly, damp wind blew white wisps of fog over their heads. Their sweaters failed to keep them warm, and they put their arms around each other, partly for comfort.

'I hate to leave you, goldylocks Marin-lyn. How will I ever get along without you?'

'Oh, you'll get along. Just think, England, Cambridge. You'll soon forget about me. The real question is how will *I* get along?'

'I've been thinking about that. Marilyn, you mustn't wait for me. If a nice young man falls in love with you – and many will of course – and if you fall in love with him, you must take him seriously. Who knows what I'll do for a living? You don't want to wait for a starving poet.'

'You've got it all figured out, haven't you?'

She took her arms from around him and turned his head to face hers.

'Just any old nice young man will do for Marilyn while you're off having the time of your life with who knows what sophisticated English girls. I've heard about the college student parties over there.'

'You know me better than that, goldylocks.'

'Well, if you're going to stay pure and single, then why can't I? And why should I believe you won't fall in love with other girls? All they have to do is to be pretty. What about that pretty little Japanese girl?'

'You weren't speaking to me when I knew her, Marilyn.'

'And I won't be speaking to you for the next three years because I can't.'

'Marilyn, I can't pretend about you. I *should* pretend not to love you any more, I should make you angry with me if I were a gentleman. But let's look things squarely in the face.'

He took her chin in his hand and gazed lovingly into her blue-green eyes.

'I don't know if I have any kind of future. I'm not a money-maker like Fed. It may be years before I could ask you to marry me. You must not be tied to me all that time. Besides, you're older and so beautiful. Now promise me you will not wait for will-o'-the-wisp me.'

'I promise you nothing, René Levin.'

Her eyes were wet.

'You still have so much to learn, so much; I promise you nothing of the sort.'

'All right. I have promised you nothing either, remember.'

They stood up and brushed the sand off their clothes. It was too chilly to stay there any longer. The ocean glinted steely gray and the beach lay empty and cold before them as they walked across the wet, dark sand.

When they got back to the white house on Mission Street the girl turned and looked at the solemn-faced boy.

'René, I am not going to the station tomorrow when you leave; your mother will want to be alone with you. And another thing, I am no good at writing letters. I won't write you, so I don't expect you to write me. But, when you come home three years from now I will be here waiting for you. And don't you forget that.'

She kissed him passionately and he kissed her back.

'All right, Marilyn. Goodbye, goodbye.'

Surely, she will get over this, he thought as he walked home. When I come back surely she will have married and have almost forgotten me.

However, his shaking head seemed to imply doubt of this confident hope.

Mother and Fed saw him off on the train. He had made the trip so many times by now that it was hard for him to realize that this time he would not be coming back, that this time he would go on and on, half way around the earth. This fact was not hard for Mrs. Levin to realize, however. She looked solemn, serious, and sad. She clung to her younger son as though reluctant to let him go even for an instant. When the train came in she cried a little and kissed him on the forehead. Fed took his bags and carried them into the coach.

'So long, René, you lucky dog. Knock those Limeys dead, now.'

'All right, Fed. Good luck. I expect to find you president of a corporation when I get back.'

Fed grinned.

'You just might, you know.'

He winked and walked off the train just before it started. René waved at Muv and Fed as the station began dropping behind. He wondered which was hardest, to be left behind or to be leaving home for the first time.

After waiting in the city for an hour, the passengers from the south boarded a longer train that would take them to Chicago. That name always had a harsh sound for René. It sounded like crude men driving heavy machines at reckless speed through a rough, unplowed field. And it was there that for the first time since infancy, he would see and talk to the man who had generated him.

I was hardly out of the dark when he left, he thought. Now, in the full daylight, what will my father be like? He must be at least a little like me. Can we understand each other or will he hate me?

The train wheels seemed to click out the rough word Chi-ca-go, Chi-ca-go, again and again as he fell asleep in the dimly lighted coach.

Chicago was like the big California city only more so: more cars, more noise, more people, more confusion. The sleepy young man stepped into a taxicab and gave the address of the building where his father's office was. The taxi whirled and darted through the teeming streets, skidding to a halt to wait while the road ahead divided and swung up vertically to allow a vessel to pass in the river below. Soon, however, they were moving along a wide, busy boulevard fronting the lake, and shortly afterward they stopped at the entrance to a multi-story building. René took the wrong elevator and had to transfer in order to reach the floor where the finance commissioner's office was located. Finally, he opened the frosted glass door and stood in a large reception room. The lady at the desk looked up sharply when he gave his name and led him to a more private office to wait until his father was free.

These rabbit warrens and the scurrying creatures inside them. No longer human beings… automatons, Imagine spending the best part of your life in one of these cubicles, holding a telephone in one hand, scratching on innumerable papers. 'Get the Saunders file, Miss Johnson. Call Jacobs for me and find out when he can deliver those supplies.' 'Yes, Mr. Wilson, right away, sir.' 'Take a letter. Answer that phone. Post-these accounts.' 'Yes, Mr. Wilson.' And the great world just outside the window, a blue sky, white clouds, birds wheeling over the lake. But not for us, Mr. Wilson, Miss Johnson. We are in jail for life. Business, you know, the life blood of the nation.

The lady motioned to René. He followed her into an enormous room. Ponderous drapes fell to the heavy carpet beside thick-glassed windows. Copies of *The Wall Street Journal* and *The New York Times* littered a large conference table. At the far end of the room stood a huge walnut desk on a slightly raised dais, behind which sat Commissioner Oscar Levin, in all his majesty, murmuring into one of the two telephones that sat on the nearly bare desk.

The king put down the telephone and stood up. He walked down from the dais and held out his right hand.

'Hello, René,' he said quietly. 'Are you glad to see me after all this time or do you hate me?'

'I am glad to see you, Father, of course, and of course I don't hate you.'

'That is good. You are good-looking, better than I was at your age. But you are slight; that is from your mother. How is she, and how is Frederick?'

They sank down into two adjacent luxuriously leather-upholstered chairs, studded with brass nails around the edges.

'They are well, Father. Fed looks more like you than I do. He is taller and a little heavier, and he is a business man.'

Mr. Levin laughed.

'Yes, I understand that you are an artist and a good one, a musician and a poet. We have not had any such in our family until now. But it is a good thing. We mustn't be all business.'

'Well, it is obvious that you are doing all right, Father.'

René ran his eyes around the enormous office.

Mr. Levin waved his arm.

'Mostly window dressing, you know. We must impress the politicians and the businessmen. They expect this sort of thing. It is all part of the game, you know, a big game with high stakes and a lot of bluffing.'

'You must be a good bluffer, then, Father. I'm sure there's more to it than that,' laughed René.

'Well, now, I understand you're going right on to New York. I'm sorry you didn't plan to stay over a day or two, although it's true you would have to be on your own during the daytime. But let's go get something to eat. At least we can break bread together.'

Oscar Levin took a hat and coat from a concealed closet and then guided his youngest son through a back door to a group of elevators. They dropped swiftly to the ground floor where an obsequious doorman whistled up a taxi for them.

'To the Shore Club,' he said to the saluting cab driver.

In a few minutes they glided up to another tall building. They were soon seated at a white-linened table in a room on the top floor, which was glassed in and overlooked the blue-gray lake far below, the miniature waves breaking on the miniature beach.

'What do you prefer, René? Are you very hungry?'

'No, I'm not, Father. Order me something simple, will you?'

'It's a wonder you didn't say baked beans; yes, I remember. Well, let's each have a beef filet, small but good, and coffee right away.'

The waiter bowed and silently disappeared.

'Well now René, you were so young when it happened. I suppose you have always wondered how it could happen. You could hardly avoid blaming me and it looks bad, I know. It was bad. Soon you will be old enough to understand how these things take place and then perhaps you will be a little sympathetic.'

'You don't need to explain or apologize, Father. Of course I don't really understand. I don't know enough to. But I have never felt resentment, only puzzlement.'

'Well, I'm glad it's been no worse. How about Fred?'

'I'm sure he feels just as I do.'

'Good. I want to see him some day soon.'

'I'm sure he would like to talk business with you.'

'Here are our steaks. Now try to eat everything. You might have to miss a meal or two on the ocean.'

Later the elevator sped them back down to the ground. René's father put him in a taxi with directions to the railroad station. They shook hands. The older man looked a bit wistful.

'I wish I were going with you, son,' he said, and waved as the cab shot out into the stream of traffic.

I see now, thought René. He is one of the prisoners, too. His cell is larger, but he can't leave it for long, Too bad.

Chapter Three

'And do you wait a moment you husky-nois'd sea...'

The Atlantic ocean would not wait. Nor would the iron-hulled ship. It butted its way eastward through the leaden waves which endlessly reached and fell under the woolen sky. The ship's stubborn screws pushed it forward through the resisting gray water. When a swell threw up the stern of the vessel, the screws raced in impotent fury and the engineer cursed. Throttled back, they bit again into the dark liquid valleys and in this manner the ship moved eastward. It would apparently finally reach its goal. This sea was not as it now appeared to be, interminable.

René was sick. He lay in his bunk and tried to read. The steward had brought him one of Scott's endless tales, *The Heart of Midlothian*. It was good under the circumstances, a story that went on and on but required no thought. It was better to be in Edinburgh with Jeanie Deans than in this pitching cabin.

Next day the sea moderated. The sun came out, and so did the young man. He sat on deck and nibbled a sandwich of dry, white chicken flesh. Later he walked as far forward as possible and stood at the prow. It plunged inexorably eastward.

So this is the way to Cathay. It is eastward after all. Back there behind the stern, behind the Atlantic beaches and the Appalachians, behind the great river valley and the plains, over and behind the

Rocky mountains that don't tip over because they are heavier on the bottom, behind the desert and the Grand Canyon, behind the Sierra and the coast range, in a narrow little strip of land fronting the Pacific: there is the place from which I come. What time is it there? Much earlier than here. Busie old foole, unruly Sunne, are you shining on them at the same time you are shining on me? I could see the earth turn when I lay on my back near the river. Now, come what may, to the motherland go I. Methinks I see ahead a noble and puissant nation, home of Mr. Phineas, Phineus the sage, who taught Jason his future course. Argo, carry us thither quickly. But am I really a scholar? Do I want that golden fleece? I love the old names and the old places but I do not want to dig up minute facts about unknown writers and present them in dry, careful language. I will be a creator, not a parasite. Everything is grist to our mill, but I will be the mill, although I will not grind exceeding fine. No, I will be an illuminator, a transformer. I will throw new light on old things. That photographer made a thing of beauty out of a kitchen grater or a common garden vegetable. But it took him to discover and reveal their beauty. Not for me the vomit of Zola. It is not truth, but beauty, Mr. Keats, true or not, that matters. We are now afraid of beauty. It has turned into cheesecake and sugar-water in wrong hands. We'll none of it. Ugliness is new, exciting, unhackneyed. Ours is not a matter of encompassing ugliness in a transcendent beauty as old Walt tried to do. No. we will preach that only ugliness is real, that beauty is an effete illusion. We will be original or be damned. Well, they are damned. Only a few are singing in this wilderness. Esse, videre, cantare!

The audience clapped vociferously as the brilliant young poet stepped down from his podium. Homer, Horace, Ovid, Lucan, Vergil, and that upstart Alighieri, each patted him on the back and smiled.

René was seated at a table with three other people in the dining room. Now that he was able to appear for meals he decided that he should make an effort to be sociable. Across from him mooned a young married couple who were not interested in anyone but themselves. Next to him sat a pretty thirtyish little woman with blue, twinkly eyes. She said she was Scottish and was on her way home from a visit to relatives in Canada.

'Have you ever been in my country?' she asked.

'I've never been outside my native land until now,' the young man answered. 'Is it beautiful, Scotland?'

'Wild and beautiful. You must see the lochs and the highlands.'

'A coincidence I have just been reading some Walter Scott. He, too, makes me want to see more. But I am on my way to England.'

'To visit friends?' she asked.

'No, to go to school… Cambridge.'

'Oh, I say. That will be an adventure.'

'Yes, I only hope that I am well enough prepared.'

They had finished dinner and rose to walk out of the teeming room.

'Let's turn around the deck a few times. It is good for the digestion.'

She led him up the stairway.

'All right. By the way, my name is René Levin. What is yours?'

'Oh. I'm Gail McInness.'

'Well, Mrs. McInness, did you find Canada worth the visit?'

'No, not the part I was in anyway, nothing but plains as far as one can see. I want to see some glens and braes. I will be glad to get home. And I am Miss.'

'Oh, excuse me. But I know what you mean about flat country, I must have mountains and hills, too.'

'Where do you have them?'

'In California. I am from the south, but I have heard people from the north of the state say there are places up there like Scotland.'

'Yes. Well, I hope I can be happy in other places than those just like my home. But I never will like plains. Let's sit down for a while. Are you happy to be going to the university?'

'Yes and no. It is a great privilege and I am dying to see it, but I have not really led a very disciplined life. Perhaps I will find it dull or too difficult.'

'Oh I trust not. Still, study is hard labor. Perhaps Bobbie was right when he said:

> What's a' your jargon o' your schools,
> Your Latin names for horns an' stools?
> If honest Nature made you fools,
> What sairs your grammars?
> Ye'd better taen up spades and shools,
> Or knappin-hammers.
>
> A set o' dull, conceited hashes
> Confuse their brains in college-classes;
> They gang in stirks and come out asses,
> Plain truth to speak;
> An' syne they think to climb Parnassus
> By dint o Greek!'

'He was just great, wasn't he? I love the sound of your language even though I often don't understand it.'

'I didn't mean to imply, of course, that *you* gang in a stirk and will come out an ass, but some do.'

René laughed.

'I'm sure of that, Miss McInness. I too am trying to climb Parnassus, but not by dint o' Greek.'

'Ah then, I hope you have ae spark o' Nature's fire, as Bobbie says next.'

'Yes. That is what it takes. I hope so too. That is what I want most.'

'Have you read much of Burns?'

'Not nearly as much as I should or would like,' admitted René.

'Let me lend you a copy. It is in my cabin. Come along and I will fetch it for you.'

They walked down a flight and then through a long corridor toward the bow of the ship. There was hardly anyone about. This was the time of evening when everyone gathered in the public rooms for drink, dancing or entertainment. Even the stewards were busy elsewhere.

'Sit down a moment while I find it,' she said and rummaged in a suitcase.

There was hardly any place to sit but on the bunk in that tiny room with one porthole to the sky. She straightened up awkwardly and sat down beside him.

'May I read you one or two of my favorites? At least I can speak the dialect.'

'Please do, Miss McInness.'

'Gail to you,' she said and looked into his eyes searchingly.

She read 'Of A' the Airts', and then 'A Red, Red Rose', Her eyes grew bright and her body became animated.

'Did he not have the gift and did he not understand us Scottish lasses?'

René smiled and she read 'Green Grow the Rashes'.

'An' then she made the lasses, O,' she repeated with a sigh. 'Oh, René, don't you know what the lasses are made for?'

She pulled him down on the bunk and covered his face with kisses, her breast heaving. They lay so for a few minutes.

'I see why Bobbie Burns loved the Scottish lasses, O,' said the young man softly.

She kissed him again.

'But, Gail, we mustn't. You are sweet but I'm not free. We must not break each other's hearts.'

She sighed.

'You are not one who can enjoy the moment. I'm afraid ye lack Nature's fire. And I want ye so.'

He kissed her gently. 'You would be wonderful to love. But I can't. We mustn't.'

'All right, you cautious American boy. Did I muss your hair? Let me kiss you once more and I will let you go.'

It was a long and passionate kiss. He untangled himself from her and closed the door gently as he left. At breakfast the next morning the married couple were just as moony, and René and Miss McInness were just as friendly and innocent as ever. But he contrived not to be alone with her again.

Chapter Four

'Mr. Levin? I'm John Phillips. Welcome to England. Did you have a good crossing?'

'Hello, Mr. Phillips. Yes, after the first day or two when the sea was rough.'

René had just emerged from customs, this confusing morning. Although he was back on dry land, he felt the ship rolling and pitching under his feet. The customs shed yawned empty and dim, but now he was outside in the rather pale sunshine, it was good to see green trees and hear a bird sing.

Mr. Phillips helped route the young traveler's trunk and then assisted him to a seat in one of the train compartments. Suddenly a whistle shrieked up ahead and the coaches moved off toward London.

'It won't take long,' assured the middle-aged Englishman. 'You will get used to living in our country. It is much smaller than your own.'

'This is so exciting for me. I can hardly believe that I am in England at last. I will probably pester you to death with questions.'

'Quite all right. It is always interesting to visit another part of the world.'

'Mr. Phillips, what are those red berries hanging from some of the trees out there?'

'Oh, those are rowan berries. You don't have them where you live do you? By the way, how did you leave Mr. Phineas? Well, I hope.'

'Yes, he seemed quite well and generally contented when I left. I think he would have liked to come with me, though. How I wish he could have!'

'Indeed, yes. But I am sure he is better off in California. We simply cannot boast of our climate. You know, too, that Cambridge is flat, low, and damp. I hope you are not prone to bronchitis.'

'No, not that I know of. I will miss seeing mountains but not too much, I'm sure. After all, I am here to study.'

'Well, but you must get out and around. It is not all that bad. You can visit the beauty spots during vacations.'

René was surprised when they got to London that they did not simply change trains. Instead, Mr. Phillips led him to a cab in which they careered through busy streets to a large old hotel. An open lift pulled them up several flights, expelling them into a thickly carpeted hallway.

'I hope you will find this comfortable,' said the older man as they entered a large old-fashioned bedroom.

'Of course, Mr. Phillips, but are we staying overnight?'

'Oh yes. You must see some of London before you bury yourself in the college.'

'But this is a great imposition upon you. I'm sure you have more to do than to guide me about.'

'Not really. I shall enjoy the holiday, too. Now let's clean up and have a good tuck-in.'

'You will have to tell me how to behave, Mr. Phillips – what fork to use for what, in case I do things too American-like.'

'Tush. We have many Americans with us. They don't often disgrace themselves. But feel free to ask anything, of course.'

The next day the accommodating Englishman led the young man through all the tourist places – the Tower of London, Westminster Abbey, the Houses of Parliament – and they spent two hours at the British Museum. René's head was in a whirl by the time they returned for dinner. He felt as though he had dined on a rich English dinner, but he felt immensely satisfied, too. He, a boy from California, was actually seeing, touching these overwhelming old historical relics. They were real, and impressive. Mr. Phillips asked him if he would like to see more, but René suggested instead that they go on to Cambridge the next day. He wanted to settle in.

'I say, fresher, are you put up next to me?'

A tall, gangling, friendly looking young man addressed this question to René as he emerged from his rooms for the first time. He had been reading a bundle of mail left on his table by the porter. Now he was trying to get used to wearing the short, blue academic gown over his American suit.

'How do you do. Yes, this is where I have been put. It seems very pleasant. Are your rooms about the same?'

'Come in and see. Excuse me, I'm Benjamin Stein. You're a Yank, aren't you? No offense, now.'

'Yes, I've just arrived.'

'Well, sit down. Have a smoke. No? We'll corrupt you before you return home. Are you going to join any of these societies?'

He indicated a pile of open envelopes on his desk like those René had just been reading.

'Probably not. But partly it's because I'm too green and don't know how to play cricket or row or debate. I'm sorry, I forgot to introduce myself. I'm René Levin.'

The Englishman casually took his hand.

'Glad to know you, Levin. Why don't you hang out with me until you are better acquainted?'

Is this the shy, reserved Englishman I've heard about? René asked himself.

'That's awfully good of you, Stein. I certainly could use some friendly guidance. I feel I'm making all kinds of faux pas without even knowing it. The porter looks pityingly at me already.'

'Oh, Grigsby's all right. He's just sizing you up. He's actually used to Americans. But he has to get us all educated. He looks the same way at me. I'm only a fresher, too. We've much to learn, I'm sure, But I do know a few other students and a don or two.'

'And you're English.'

'Can't deny it. But this place is full of chaps from all over. Some can't even speak American.'

He grinned at René and got up from his chair.

'Come on. I'll show you around. Who's going to be your supervisor, your tutor.'

'A Mr. Jarnagan.'

'Brrr. He's a bear. Not really, though. You'll get along with him. No nonsense, though. No nonsense with any of then actually. But it's not really too bad I hear. Just a hell of a lot of hard work – reading, you know.'

He strode over to the door upon hearing a knock and admitted a fair-haired, aristocratic-looking young man with a mischievous twinkle in his eye and a pipe in his mouth. As did the other two, he wore the short, blue academic gown on his back.

'Come in, Ev. Meet my neighbor, René Levin.'

'Howdjado, Levin, a fellow fresher I see.'

'This is Evelyn Palmer-Hunt, René,' said Benjamin.

'Very glad to meet you, Mr. Palmer-Hunt. Why does that name sound familiar?'

'I can't escape fame. Pater makes those motor cars.'

'Oh, of course.'

'Well, Ev, if you don't mind I was just going to show our friend about a bit,' explained Stein. 'He's just off the boat, he says.'

'By all means.' Evelyn agreed. 'I'll join the tour if you'll have me. We can show him the main attractions, eh Ben? Where to eat, for instance.'

They descended the stairway and proceeded on their walk. The grounds were swarming with incoming students, dons, porters, bedders and others. René made his new friends explain the various costumes, the doctors' and masters' robes, and a thousand and one other things about the history and architecture of the colleges. A young don joined their party and was able to answer many of the questions the English freshers could not.

Later they walked along the 'backs', beside the river and finally rented a boat and paddled up and down the Cam under the old humped bridges. René began to feel rather more at home and was happy to have already met such casually pleasant fellow students.

Chapter Five

Dear Mr. Phineas

This is indeed a wonderful place, though at first I found it to be gloomy and dreary. The land is dreadfully flat, and the weather has been cold and drizzly. But now I don't really mind. I am kept too busy to notice; there are so many books to read and people to talk to.

I am amazed, for one thing, at how many clubs there are here, everything from philately to squash rackets. I am afraid I have been a disappointment to my fellow students in not joining something. I am neither fraternal nor athletic, whereas most of them are very sporty. I did not realize that the students would take sports so seriously and work at them as strenuously as they do.

You know that I was doubtful about making friends here as I do not usually find it easy. However, except for the athletic crowd, I have had a modest success. Most of my good luck in this regard has come through a fellow who rooms next to me, Benjamin Stein. He is extremely kind and sympathetic. I just now realize in writing the name that he must be Jewish. I am not used to the fact that a man with such a British accent could be a Jew. He does not seem to be especially Jewish, however. I'm sure he's not orthodox. He attends chapel. Of course you know that we all must attend chapel early every morning, or in lieu of that we must rush down to the porter's lodge and sign our names to a list. I must admit I often do the latter, although I have attended services at King's chapel and listened to their heavenly choir.

But to get back to friends, Ben has several whom I like. The most interesting fellow but also the most exasperating, is Evelyn Palmer-Hunt, of the motor car family. He is extremely likeable but is a sensualist and somewhat spoilt. It is disturbing that he is so pleasant when actually he is rather wicked. He has a good mind but is lazy and capricious in his studies. He doubts that he will actually go through and take a degree, and sometimes I doubt whether he will, too. But he can memorize and quote old English poetry when it appeals to him, and he is really rather well-read.

A third member of the group is someone I know somewhat less well, but who is pleasant and friendly to me. They call him 'Doctor' Johnson. Apparently at one time he studied, or started to study, medicine. He is really, I think, the best scholar among us but is quieter and less colorful, perhaps, than the others.

I still have qualms about considering myself a scholar; however, my tutor says I am doing well enough, and he is kind enough to say that he likes the way I write. Apparently that does count for much, although, of course, one must have something to say – a foundation of knowledge – and I would be lost without that which you have given me.

Much of what I have written, you probably already know about, but I will carry on anyway since it is all new and interesting to me. Did you know, for instance, that there are two small courts here at Trinity called 'the spitoon' and 'the billiard table' because of the shape and disposition of their drainage gratings? The attention to such details is not surprising, here where it rains so much and so often. Of course the greenness of everything is a result of this, and is a marvel to a Southern Californian.

But let me tell you of something funny and, after all, 'athletic' that I accomplished. One day I said something to

Ben and Ev about the clocks that ring here at Trinity, especially at noon, there seem to be two, and they do not strike simultaneously. Ev told me that there is a tradition that a really speedy undergraduate can run around the whole of Trinity great court or quadrangle during the time these clocks are striking twelve. Where I made my mistake was in mentioning that I used to hold a record in running the hundred-yard dash. Nothing would do after this but to promise to try to beat the bells. I was sure that I could not do it. I have not run in years, but Englishmen being what they are, they must take bets on my chances and make a sporting thing of it. To cut this story shorter, the next day I did don track clothes and finished the round just barely before the last clock stroke. Someone said the time was forty-three seconds. Now, apparently, they will forgive me for not participating in other athletic contests. We do go out and row on the little river on pleasant days, but to a real athlete this is probably 'sissy'.

As to the poetry, I have not been writing much just lately. Perhaps I will get fully used to Cambridge eventually and then will feel like doing some more. Now I must mostly read others verses, and some of them are a little dull. I have not joined a literary society because most of their members seem to want to engage in endless, futile discussions and then to try to write like Eliot or Pound.

The other day I did come across the little poem, 'I, Dancing,' that you sent to the Harvard professor and that you said he liked. If I can get into the mood, later on I will try some more like that, or something more 'modern' perhaps, and submit it to one of the student magazines. Could something like 'Dancing' every appeal to undergraduate sophisticates, though? Perhaps with some kind of mutatis mutandis. Mostly, the student writers try to be deadly serious and at the same time try to seem lightly 'sophisticated', to be Freudianly metaphorical if one can use such a clumsy term. Beauty is not at all the interest now; it is psychology, which for some reason is always so dreary and hopeless. Did Henry James, or his brother, start all this? But he, of course, wasn't a follower of Freud. What a thought!

These student writers are world-weary without ever having known the world. They are lightly satirical without ever having suffered; and no one can really write satire who hasn't suffered. They are sorry for themselves without ever having lost anything worth regretting. I am much out of tune with these present-day attitudes, and of course those who hold them find me hopelessly naïve.

This fashionable, self-conscious agonizing over the supposed degeneracy of society, where did it really start; with Arnold, with Eliot? I think man will never get used to change. Change is always for the worst when you are aware of it. A young, vigorous, expanding society, though, makes changes rather than regretting them. But it's the kind of change that matters, of course. Nana, Gervaise, what downward spirals! Is man perfectible, or is he after all merely a little boy thumbing his nose at the universe, scribbling graffiti on the walls of the world, urinating on the flowers of creation? Exhibiting his contempt for all that he cannot understand, he struts and postures, a jigging urchin in the warming light of day. But when night comes he tries to hurry home, scurrying through the graveyard of past hopes, where he attempts to whistle up courage against the immensity of his littleness while cocking a furtive eye at the high, faint, impersonal light of a distant galaxy.

Will we ever grow up to our possibilities, or will we succumb to our actualities?

Love,
René

P.S. When I write to you I get carried away. It's your fault. You let me rave on. So I almost forgot to tell you that

Benjamin is a recorder player. We are looking forward to playing duets. He thinks we can actually put on some concerts for our fellow students. He's even commandeered a small hall and made me promise to appear. So I'm glad I brought my Dolmetsch with me. Please tell Mrs. B. I hope she stays well. Again love.

R.

Chapter Six

One evening René invited his new friends to share his rooms and perhaps engage in what he called a 'bull session', though this term seemed to puzzle them a bit. The skies turned dark and cloudy and a chilly wind whipped around the ancient stone building. René opened the door to the young men and they trampled in and deposited themselves on to the scattered furniture.

Evelyn put his feet up on the fender and leaned back in an armchair comfortably. The other two got up and milled about, sampling René's library or critically inspecting his few prints.

'Now then,' said Evelyn, 'Where did you say you hail from, which ultima thule?'

'My home is situated approximately five hundred miles south of Brobdingnag, that is to say in Spanish El Dorado.'

'Oh, then money is no problem. I thought I noticed your pockets sagging under the weight of Iberian doubloons.'

'Alas, no. Those are merely the shells of ancient wampum. You see, Drake got there before me.'

Evelyn guffawed.

'Ancient wampum. That's good. But I suppose it will buy few pints of porter.'

'Your supposition is correct,' continued René. 'When the publican threw it on his counter it rang hollow.'

'Hollow, hallo, holloa. Thy fate jerks bitter tears. Here, my good man, this will wet your whistle.'

He flipped a half crown into the American boy's open palm.

'Oh, thank you, sir,' simpered René, putting the coin carefully into his pocket. 'I did impeticos thy gratility.'

'That thee did, good clown. And see to it that after your drink, you make water in a sink-a-pace.'

Benjamin joined in.

'What are these two fools doing in Illyria?'

'They delight in masques and revels altogether,' Johnson replied.

Evelyn pulled a pipe out of one pocket, a pouch out of another, and elaborately prepared to smoke. The other two students sat down near the grate. 'Doctor' Johnson held a book in his hand.

'Bretheren, our subject this evening is the obsolescence of art. I take as my text the following: 'Science and pragmatism are gradually but steadily destroying art, since the latter depends upon myth, legend, superstition, and dreams, which can hardly be allowed in a purely rational society.'

'Sounds like some third-rate journalism to me,' commented Benjamin.

'No. This is word from on high. Gentlemen, art is on the way out. Let us pray.'

'Why does this Cassandra say that myth, legend, etcetera, can hardly be allowed in a rational society?' asked Evelyn, spouting a great jet of smoke. 'Will a steam engine run less well if the fireman believes he is shoveling coal into a demon's mouth, instead of supplying carbonaceous fuel to be oxidized in order to vaporize water in the boiler tubes?'

'It might,' said René, 'if he ever got into his head the fancy that the demon wanted a human sacrifice, for instance, and threw himself into the furnace. Such irrational impulses used to exist in old irrational societies, you know.'

'Shadrach, Mesach, n' Abednego' intoned Benjamin, beating time on top of a nearby table.

'But what *I* find faulty in the text', continued René, 'is the term "rational society". Since when has there ever been one?'

'Ever since Newton and Darwin, my son,' intoned young Benjamin. 'Don't you know that the universe is run by clockwork and the soul is merely a highly adapted cerebellum?'

'Cerebrum, you idiot,' said Johnson.

Evelyn waved him off.

'There's your scientist again. Exactitude, Perhaps it's actually in the pineal gland.'

'Or perhaps there ain't one,' replied the 'doctor', pretending to be nettled.

'Then we should examine critically the stated thesis that art depends upon superstition, legend, etcetera,' put in Benjamin, the youngest brother.

'I think that is true,' said René. 'Try to imagine that all art – statues, paintings, music and stories – based on or containing "myths" are suddenly to be obliterated. There wouldn't be much left.'

'Not nearly so much, but still quite a bit. Bach fugues, non-representational or decorative art, in fact much of modern art.'

Evelyn gestured with his pipe.

'In fact that's often the aim of modern art, to be non-allusive.'

'But then there's Eliot and Pound,' reminded the 'doctor'.

'Ergo, all generalizations are false, including this one,' pontificated the pipe-waver.

'There's a rumor that Eliot and Pound are poets,' said Benjamin, now safely out of Egypt.

'And there's another ugly rumor that they are Americans,' added 'Doctor' Johnson.

'To top it all,' said Evelyn, pointing his pipe at René, 'it has been bruited about that we have one of these American versifiers in our very midst. Is this one more result of George the Third's ineptitude?'

'Away with these Yankee Doodles. What chance has a poor Britisher got?' threatened the 'doctor'.

René pretended to shrink in fright.

'We will allow this rebel to retain his head if he can read us even just one decent sonnet that he has writ. Is that not merciful, Yankee Levin?' asked the smoking one.

'Most generous, kind sirs, if you will completely forget about Pound, Eliot, and all other good poets, and will delete the word "decent" from the requirement.'

'Harsh terms from a rebel, but being Britishers we will accede,' stated Joseph's brother.

René read his 'exercise', sonnet, the one he had written for Mr. Phineas:

Often in the dewy breath of night,
Or seldom in the heated still of noon,
Flies low that feckless lady moth, the moon.
As slim or full she tumbles toward the light.
But never lost in stars, not satellite,
His majesty the sun throws down the boon
Of fire and light from out his hot balloon,
Ne'er pale and rarely grudging of his might.
Yet when I think of her whom I do love
And long to scan her face or kiss her hair,
I shun the blaze of flaming royalty
And choose to wait the cooler orb above

From which the softer rays fall clear and fair
To gleam her face and glow our ecstasy.

'What say the jury?' asked Johnson. 'Although it is not an English sonnet, shall we let him keep that orb, his head?'

'Yea, let him join his two fellow countrymen. Give him sanctuary, eh Benjamin?'

'Yea, verily,' voted the beloved son of Isaac. 'However, seriously, I would like a copy of that. I detect some slightly suspicious word contrasts here and there.'

'Yes, Columbian Apollo, type us out copies, will you?'

Evelyn smiled and knocked the dottle out of his pipe.

'If this keeps up, you will have to get out a book. I can just see it, a slim volume titled, let's see, "Western Winds" or "South of Brobdingnag".'

'I blush with pleasure at your confidence, gentlemen. Now, to celebrate that unlikely occasion, here is a libation.'

René poured out four glasses of sherry.

'I propose that even more unlikely and distant occasion… our graduation,' volunteered Evelyn.

They drank slowly, but with relish.

'Only a Spaniard or an American can afford such delicious sherry. That hollow wampum must have deceived the wine merchant,' said the son of the right hand.

'Yes, but now, our libation is poured solely into our gullets,' pointed out the good 'doctor'. 'If we were proper Greeks we would have spilled a few drops to the gods.'

'You are too technical my friend Johnson,' complained Evelyn the bold. 'In this case we are the gods. Besides this sherry is too expensive to waste in these parlous times. Let us glow our ecstasy.'

'Besides which the porter would complain bitterly of the spots on the rug. But since we are gods, as our friend dared to state, let us propitiate ourselves further.'

René refilled their glasses.

'Jove, I am in a jovial mood,' stated Benjamin the blessed.

'That's quite all right, my boy Mercury. Tonight you may all share my prerogative. I have lain thunderbolts aside,' allowed the Olympian Evelyn. 'Apollo Levin, will you not smite again your bloomin' lyre?'

'Nay, immortals, I must preserve something for the copyright. Why do we not hear from Aesculapius?'

'What would you all, a recital of the bones of the skull?' queried the 'doctor' jumping up and running his fingers over Evelyn's cranium. 'Alas, poor Yorick, I do not know thee as well as I should... occipital, parietal, frontal, temporal...'

Evelyn pushed him off.

'Enough; there are other parts of the anatomy more interesting.'

'I wondered how long it would take the conversation to come around to them,' said the 'doctor'.

'How are the arrangements coming along for your party, Evelyn?' asked Benjamin, correctly following the line of thought.

'Ah, we need one more virgin... for the Yankee. What color of thatch do you prefer, Levin: red, yellow, black?'

'I have always wondered,' said René, 'why women are classified mainly by the color of their hair. Is there any scientific basis for this?'

'Ah, there is an investigation you should pursue,' advised Johnson. 'A poet should become cognizant of this esoteric matter.'

'Erotic, he means,' waved Evelyn.

He had filled and relighted his pipe.

'Seriously, though Levin, I have just thought of a beauty who would be just right for you; she is dark like you. It's possible she has even read a poem, Angelica, is her name.'

'Very well, Evelyn, but tell her not to expect too much. There's a girl at home...'

'Here, that won't do. When in Rome, you know... When the cat's away,' reminded Benjamin.

'Gentlemen, time. Please, it's time,' intoned publican Johnson.

'Good heavens, so it is. Why didn't you chase us out 'ere now, René?' worried Evelyn the prompt.

'I have been enamored of your company, gentlemen, but I suppose that we must part.'

'Indeed we must,' verified the 'doctor'.

Evelyn and the 'doctor' donned their overcoats and gloves. They all thanked their host warmly as he opened the door for their exit.

'And don't forget, young man, you have Angelica to look forward to,' waved Evelyn as he descended. 'Shantih, shantih, shantih.'

Chapter Seven

Mr. Evelyn Palmer-Hunt's digs were large and impressive as befitted the scion of a wealthy motor manufacturer. Even in these financially uncertain times he managed to live luxuriously and to entertain lavishly. The lights blazed in the drawing room and the people blazed under them.

As usual René felt rather uncomfortable at such a gathering. He enjoyed talking to a few friends but always disliked larger, noisier social brawls. It all seemed so senseless, even sinister. People wandered and whirled like lost souls in the second circle of Inferno, and the confusion and hot wind of their pointless promenading enveloped him.

'René,' called the host, emerging out of the circling throng. 'Come here. I want you to meet Angelica. And here is Mona Stuart and Ron Bagbee, you know, the Devonshire poet.'

They wavered. in front of his eyes as though distorted by desert heat. He shook their hands and smiled. Angelica, a tall, dark, young lady in a striking white gown tucked her hand under his arm and led him to a sofa. The others followed.

'I am so pleased to meet you, Mr. Levin,' stated the Devonshire poet. 'Evelyn has been raving to me about your work.'

'Evelyn raves too easily,' said René smiling. 'I can say so because he has departed.'

'Have a drink, Mr. Levin,' proffered Miss Stuart, a short, friendly-looking pixie of a girl. 'Heavens, we are all ahead of you. You must have just arrived.'

'Yes,' answered René. 'But I'm an awful sissy. I'll take only a little sherry.'

For some reason Angelica seemed pleased to hear this and she smiled at the American boy in an encouraging way.

'It's the gods' truth,' confirmed 'Doctor' Johnson, flying by. 'He won't touch another liquor, our Spanish American. He hasn't learned how.'

'That's good, René,' said Angelica. 'I only want sherry myself. But what did he mean, "Spanish American"? You don't have Spanish-looking skin.'

'I'm not really Spanish,' the young man explained. 'My home is in California, the part of America originally belonging to Spain.'

'Oh, how romantic. Robert Louis Stevenson and cinema stars.'

'Something like that, though I've known neither.'

They were comparatively alone for a moment. The others had whirled off and only strangers stood nearby. But peace could not last in Inferno, a jazz band had been tuning up at the other end of the room and suddenly struck up a loud popular tune. Everyone whirled out onto the floor while a servant sprinkled powdered wax on the parquet.

'Will you dance?' asked René gallantly. 'I should warn you that I hardly know how.'

'Yes, let's. We can hardly do more than toddle around in this smash, anyway.'

Her voice had a husky tone but she was mercifully free of the bored drawl fashionable in society at the time.

They toddled for a while and then stopped to pick up small glasses of sherry from a waiter, which they sipped perfunctorily.

'Look, René, you don't have to stick with me every moment. Run along and talk to some of your student friends while I retire for a little while.'

'All right, Angelica. I will find you again.'

René wandered through the holocaust, occasionally seeing and greeting fellow students who introduced him to innumerable women. Later he found himself sitting on a sofa near Miss Stuart.

'You know, it's stupid of me to think so, but you look very much like someone I know,' she babbled.

'Oh, I'm a double to several people in Britain, I'm told. Who was the poor fellow?'

'He is a black Highlander. Of course he was larger, heavier than you, but otherwise sported the same dark, dashing good looks. Are you Scottish by any chance?'

'No. My father is Jewish-American and my mother French-American. But I don't usually talk about it. Have I had too much wine?'

The pixie girl's face grew bored.

'Hardly. You are the only sober man here.'

Finally the guests began to thin out. The infernal wind moderated to a warm breeze. René started to hunt for the butler to retrieve his topcoat.

'Are you mad?' demanded a flushed Evelyn, holding on to his arm. 'The fun is just beginning. Soon the throng will have departed and we will ascend to our bowers of bliss. Come. I'll show you your particular paradise.'

They climbed a broad stairway, a few straggling guests passing them. Evelyn led to a door and threw it open.

Inside was a softly lit bedroom where Angelica lounged in a boudoir chair wearing a negligée.

'Now to it, old chap,' said Evelyn, slapping him on the back. 'Don't come out till break of day. My gorgeous, long-limbed blonde awaits me. Toodle-oo.'

He closed the door as he left, leering lightly at the girl. She rose and advanced towards René, embracing him.

'Really, you know, I'm awfully naive, but I didn't know Evelyn was serious when he said it would be this kind of party,' René confided.

She backed away.

'Don't you like me, René? Won't I do?'

She opened her gown provocatively.

'You're a beautiful woman, Angelica, too beautiful to be in this business.'

'Lor, René, you're not going to turn moral on me, are you? Come now, that's a good chap.'

She started to help him out of his clothes. He smiled and continued to undress.

'Listen Angelica, I'm not going to make love to you. I'm sleepy and I'm going to bed, even in that cupid's boat thing. I hope it's comfortable. And you're welcome to half of it. Hop in. But I don't want your body.'

She stamped her foot.

'What's wrong with my body? Mr. Palmer-Hunt had to pay five pounds just to give it to you. Now it's yours, all of it.'

René winced at the mention of money.

'No, thank you. You see there's a woman in California and after loving her I couldn't. Evelyn didn't tell you, I see. He means well. But, aren't you glad you won't have to work for the money? A good night's sleep and on your way.'

He stepped into the dressing closet and slipped into a pair of bright blue Russian pajamas that were lying across the back of a chair. When he emerged Angelica was in bed. She stared at him incredulously. He found the light switch, turned it, and slipped into the bed, turning his back on the baffled woman. After a while she settled her head on her pillow and addressed his back.

'She must be quite some young lady, this one in California.'

He grunted and yawned.

'Tell me, René,' she touched him lightly on the shoulder. 'Is she dark like me?'

She could hardly hear him as he fell asleep saying, 'Spun gold, spun gold.'

When the young man awoke in the pale daylight he was startled to find his head cradled by two voluptuous breasts and to find two white arms enveloping him. He gently disengaged himself and stepped out of the absurd, boat-like bed.

'Where are you going, lover?' Angelica asked, awaking and pulling her slight negligée around her.

'Home. I want to get away before the rest of them stir. You stay there. I'll dress in the closet and be away in no time.'

'Oh, very well. Are you angry with me for holding you like that?'

'No, Angelica, of course not. Go back to sleep now. And thank you.'

He smiled at her as he closed the closet door. When he came out she was apparently asleep. He kissed her lightly on the forehead and then tiptoed down the broad stairs, found the blank-faced butler, and emerged from the front door to walk home in the early morning fog.

Part Eight

Chapter One

René and some of his undergraduate friends decided to pool their resources during the summer vacation in order to make a tour of the continent. Discussion raged as to just where to go and how long to stay in each place. However, after toying with the idea of visiting several countries, they began to realize that their funds would be inadequate. One of the group said he knew of a town house in Florence where they could rent rooms cheaply, and they finally agreed to lodge there and to confine their holiday to that Italian city. The group persuaded a young don to act as guide and chaperone in Florence since Benjamin and Evelyn wanted to bring along their lady friends.

When the party departed during the second week in June it consisted of seven young men and the two women. René and his friends looked forward to this Italian visit with eager anticipation. In addition to Ben and Moira, and Evelyn and Miss Prentiss, Robert Le Blanc, (an American who had recently come to the university by way of Paris, where he had been studying painting), joined the group. He was a rather tall, thin fellow, a 'Nordic' type with blue eyes and blond hair. He and his sister were the adored children of a wealthy San Francisco importer. He had attached himself to one of the Parisian ateliers for a year or two and then, becoming dissatisfied, had enrolled at Trinity to read Renaissance art. He had become especially fond of René, and like Evelyn, predicted great success for his friend's poetry.

The air rang with quips and farewells as the party boarded the London train, although the weather was not at all gay. A drizzling rain descended from louring clouds which seemed to brush the flat Cambridge countryside. In London they dashed quickly from station to station and boarded the train to Dover. There they caught a channel ferry where most of them fell sick. However, at Calais the sun was shining and spirits revived on the train to Paris. The young people promised themselves a stop-over in Paris on their way back. They ogled the city hungrily while hurriedly proceeding across town to the Gare de Lyon and the train south.

René was so excited at finally being on the Continent that he could hardly draw himself away from the train windows. As they sped across the famous land he saw it not as it was but as it once had been. The fields, forests and towns came alive with the characters of literature. Every familiar place name produced a sympathetic vibration within him like that of the strings of a piano when the hold pedal is pressed and a note is sung. He saw the characters of Balzac, Flaubert, Hugo and Proust going in and out of farm houses and city dwellings as the express hurled itself south.

Some of the students made a pact to speak nothing but French while in France. Moira was especially adept at the language, having attended a girls' school where this custom was enforced. But the rest could not adhere to their agreement, and broke into their native tongue whenever they grew excited, which was often. Robert and René sat next to each other and talked about art, looking out of the windows. The tutor lectured the group on French history, literature, and art all the way to the border. Evelyn and Miss Prentiss toyed with a small chess set and tried to look bored.

Ben and René had brought along their recorders, which they had to declare at the douane. Despite the encouragement of their fellows, they lacked the nerve to play them on the train. They promised one another that they would search out other old-instrument players, if there were any, in Florence.

Finally, the train pulled into the Stazione Centrale with a shriek of its whistle. People started to leave the crowded cars even before they had stopped moving. The student group, their don in front, waited decorously for the other passengers to run down the steps and then emerged in a single file. They engaged two taxis to shuttle them to the old rented house on the Lungarno Acciaioli. It was now dark, but the motor car headlights were flashed on only briefly at intersections.

Dinner awaited them at the house. The don had written ahead to arrange this. Although most of the group wanted to explore the city after eating, some, including René and Robert, felt tired and decided to rest. These two shared a high-ceilinged room with a view of the Arno which slipped silently by. Sonorously quoting snatches of Dante, René lay back on his bed while Robert unpacked his luggage and set up his water-color equipment. He was too tired to paint that night, however, and the two soon fell asleep to the sound of the bells of a nearby campanile.

The pealing of bells awoke everyone early the next morning. They agreed that they would stay together as a group for a few days and follow their don as he conducted them through the famous churches and galleries. They then planned to go their separate ways, meeting for dinner at the house to compare experiences and rave about their latest discoveries.

The Duomo, the ancient Baptistery, and Giotto's tower occupied their first morning. As Professor Prentice began to lead them through the jewel boxes of Renaissance treasures the students were hushed with awe. Even the young ladies stopped talking and followed along quietly with widening eyes. Here before them were the beauties whose images they had seen in numerous books, photographs and paintings. Here where they could be touched were the Ghiberti doors, acting now as the students' gates to paradise. Robert and René devoured them with their eyes and then looked at each other furtively. They could not speak. Beauty had struck them dumb. The others, however, began to chatter excitedly, even in the presence of these holy objects.

A week passed swiftly. In bed René closed his eyes, and a dizzying procession of paintings, statues, and buildings whirled past his dazzled interior vision. It was too much. He thought it would take years to see all this beauty and to incorporate it into one's being. He knew that museums and cathedrals are like a sonnet sequence: they can only be absorbed one room, one poem, at a time. But René already knew certain works that he would return to again and again.

That human beings could create such a profusion of visual beauty was both inspiring and humbling. What could a young man of this time hope to create in words that would be worthy of such a heritage?

Chapter Two

René and Benjamin leaned on the balustrade across the street from their house and watched the muddy Arno swirl westward toward the distant sea.

'Since you've been wandering off so early every day, Mr. Levin, I've taken it upon myself to hunt up some musicians,' announced Ben.

'Good, Ben. I've been bemused ever since we came here. I admit I've not been worth a damn. I'm glad you have your wits about you, anyway.'

'Well really, Professor Prentice did all the work. He seems to know almost everyone here and is so accommodating.'

'Yes, he's very kind. But are they agreeable, the musicians? Do any of them speak English?'

'Happily, yes. Giordano Zanobi is the director. He has gotten together a Baroque group. They have an old harpsichord and some recorders and viols. He seems anxious to have us join them. Somehow he seems to have heard of you. I told him we'd be over this evening. You will come, won't you?'

'Of course, Ben. I'm afraid I'm awfully rusty, though. Have you practiced any lately?'

'A little. But you'll soon warm up. So do come back for dinner in time. I'll take you to the place where they meet.'

'Very well. I will.'

'Where do you go these days? Or is it a secret?'

'Oh, I just wander around. Sometimes I sit down for a while and write. I'm exploring some of the less historic areas of the town. Of course that's silly; the whole place is a history book. But I like to get away from the tourists.'

'All right. See you tonight, then.'

Ben obviously would have liked to accompany René on his explorations, but the latter wanted to wander alone. He strolled off toward a neighborhood of poor working people he had discovered a day or two previously. As he walked into a small piazza he encountered a gaggle of ragamuffins fighting and squabbling. A little girl with a face like a *della Robbia* cherub clung to a large, tall-swishing tabby cat while several little boys tried to grab it out of her arms. One of them struck her on the face while another grabbed at her ankles. A third pulled the cat's tail viciously.

René could not stand by and see the girl attacked. He knew it was foolish to intervene, but he pulled the boys back and stood in front of the child.

'*Basta*!' he yelled, waving his arms.

The boys looked startled but took to their heels to escape the foreigner. The little girl smiled up at him like a cherub and took his hand, holding the cat precariously under her other arm. René reached down and took the animal in his arms. He stroked its head and it purred, seeming to vibrate all over. The brown-haired, dark-eyed little *figlia* tugged at his left hand, after he transferred the cat to his shoulder, and drew him down a narrow street. He follow somewhat reluctantly. He knew his Italian might not be adequate to explain this situation to an adult.

'*Lei parla inglese*?' he asked her, but it was obvious that she spoke no English.

She conducted him through several alley-like streets until they stopped before a house that looked like all the others in that part of town, crowded together and rather dirty. The shutters screened most of the several stories of front windows and were propped open at the bottom with window boxes of bright red geraniums hanging under some of them. A woman who sat on the front stone steps looked up suspiciously as they approached.

The little girl broke into rapid speech, pointing at René and the cat and spitting out the names 'Giuseppe' and 'Giulio' contemptuously several times.

'*Mi scusi,*' attempted René doubtfully. '*C'e qualcuno che parla l'inglese*?'

'*Aspetoti un momento, per cortesia,*' replied the woman and ran up the steps into the house.

Thank heavens someone speaks English, René thought as the woman returned with a young man in tow.

He looked at René and scowled.

'Pardon me. My name is Levin. I found this little girl in the piazza being beaten by some little boys. I chased them away, and she insisted upon bringing me here.'

The young Italian relaxed and smiled lightly.

'You are an American, no? I am Giovanni Giusto, and this is my small sister. I excuse if she bother you.'

'No bother at all, Mr. Giusto.'

René held out his hand, which the other man grasped after a short hesitation.

'The boys were trying to take this cat away from her. They were hitting her.'

'Pardon, this is our mother. She want to thank you,' said Giovanni after a short, sharp conversation with the woman.

René bowed to her and said, '*Piacere di fare la sua conoscenzo, signora.*'

She smiled and spoke rapidly to her son. He turned again to René.

'Franca is always saving the cats. My mother says thank you for help her out of trouble. Are you *turista*?'

'Well, I am staying here most of the summer with some other college students.'

'Oh, Harvard?'

'No, I am at Cambridge, in England,'

'But you are American?'

'Yes, I come from California.'

The young man turned to his mother and gesticulated as he spoke rapidly.

To René he said, 'I have uncle in California – Modesto – you know him? Benedetto Francione.'

'No. I'm sorry. That is not close to where I live. California is almost as long as Italy you know.'

Giovanni looked skeptical at this information but transmitted it to his mother.

René felt that it was time for him to leave.

'Giovanni, Signora Giusto, Franca, I am so pleased to have made your acquaintance, I hope the boys will not hit Franca any more. I did not like that. Now I will go. *Arrivederla*. Franca, *arrivederci*.'

'No, no, *aspetti*,' wailed the little girl.

'Yes, I must. Now be a good girl,' admonished René, forgetting that she could not understand him.

Franca ran up the steps to where the cat was sitting, sunning itself and washing its stomach. She picked it up unceremoniously, ran down to the young American and handed it to him. She spoke rapidly to her brother.

'She is crazy. She want to give you the cat. She think that is thanks. Franca, *basta*!'

'*Grazie*, Franca. Yes, I will take the cat if you don't want him. I like cats and will keep him while I am here. *Grazie* ancora, Franca. *Arrivederci*.'

He walked down the narrow street with the cat on his shoulder. At the intersection he turned and waved, and they all waved back to him.

Signor Zanobi and his musicians were gracious and friendly towards René and Benjamin. They were obviously quite at ease with their instruments and with Baroque music. Of course they were especially strong in the Italian masters. René expressed his regret at being out of practice and reminded the Florentines that he would be sight-reading. The director accepted this as modesty.

'A friend of mine heard you play in England. He knows good recorder playing when he hears it. We have extra copies of alto parts for you and soprano for Mr. Stein. When you have warmed up we would be pleased to try this Paradisi with you.'

'How about it, Ben, are you game?'

'Yes, I'll do my best not to disgrace us,' joked Benjamin as he withdrew his recorder from its case and warmed it in his hands.

Their host arranged chairs and stands for them. They were all placed on a raised platform at one end of a large, empty room with a high ceiling. This chamber, with its stone walls and floor, caused the music to take on a startlingly reverberant, live quality as they began to play.

The Paradisi went well. René's Dolmetsch instrument sang and soared above the harpsichord and string continuo. The Italians smiled at him after the first movement. Ben kept his soprano soft and sweet so that it blended well with the other Instruments. At the end the Italians broke out excitedly and lavished praise on the two visitors through the translation of Signor Zanobi.

The evening was a great success. They tried some Gabrielli and then a Telemann sonata which René had played before. He looked out once into the unlighted part of the room and was startled to see that there were people standing in the dark, listening to them. By the end of the Telemann a fair-sized group had gathered. He learned later that they were members of a chorus that had been practicing in another part of the building.

'Mr. Levin, Mr. Stein, please, you must join us in a public performance before you leave Florence,' wheedled the director.

The visitors rather hesitantly agreed to comply with this request, and a schedule of rehearsals was set up.

René and Ben felt that they would never forget the pleasure of playing with their Italian friends. The keenest aspect of that pleasure was the participation in the recreation of such pure and sensuous beauty. The only greater pleasure imaginable to René would be the original creation, the composition, of such music.

When the concert was finished René realized for the first time that the full Trinity group was in the hall. They ran up to him and Ben and badgered them with mock-impolite comments on their performance. In truth, they were impressed, and Robert pumped René's arm excitedly.

'It isn't fair,' he said, 'that you should have so many talents. Probably you could draw and paint if you would just try – a regular Renaissance gentleman.

'Not really,' laughed René. 'You're the artist, not I. Besides, I'm not dashing with the women.'

'You could be,' said Moira as she and Ben joined in.

They took their leave of the Florentine musicians and walked leisurely back toward their lodging. The warm summer air and the black sky sprinkled with stars made them want to indulge in some swashbuckling Renaissance adventure. No such opportunity presented itself, however, and as they neared the house Dr. Prentice quoted:

> In the shade it sings and springs; in the shine such
>   foam-bows flash
> On the horses with curling fish-tails, that prance and
>   paddle and pash

Round the lady atop in her conch – fifty gazers do
not abash,
Though all that she wears is some weeks round her
waist in a sort of sash.

'That's what we should do!' shouted Evelyn. 'Anyone for a splash in the fountain?'

'You'd have to go as naked as the lady in the conch,' jibed one of the others.

'Dear me… I didn't really mean to suggest any such prank,' faltered the young don.

'Never mind. We'll hold on to this would-be dolphin,' said Benjamin. 'Besides, here we are at home. He can swim in the marble bath if he wants.'

Laura Prentiss put one hand on René's arm and the other on Ben's.

'Thank you for that beautiful music. It was a revelation,' she said.

'Yes, we all thank and are proud of our talented companions,' intoned the don as they climbed the steps and entered the front door.

Chapter Three

The night before the Cambridge students were to return to England, René lay in his bed reading. Robert had already gone to sleep so his friend put aside his book and turned out the light in order not to disturb him, Eventually he fell into a state that was half-waking and half-sleeping

Franca was glad to take back the cat. I think she will take good care of him. Is there something unusual about people who like cats? Most people don't. Bastet, swing your sistrum and gaze long into our eyes. At what a hazard are domestic beasts' lives anyway – entirely at the mercy of undependable man, and once some of them were gods. Why are we so cruel...? To each other, too...? especially! Rafe Caber and Gervaise and Jean Calas. But a cat toys with a lizard before biting it in two... Cruelty or instinct? He has hypnotized his victim. It almost doesn't mind.

Not more than trembling bones
Nor less than canceled breath,
Deep-welled, yet light-trapped
Stays the lambent tempest.
But though the claw is kept,
The muscle loosed,
The eye retract,
Will not this lightning leap
When sudden stirs a leaf?

Cruel Florence, Firenze, Florentia. Cunning and treachery, murder and exile, Michaelangelo, Savonarola and Dante… and beauty ineffable.

> *Nel mezzo del cammin de nostra vita*
> *Mi ritrovai pera una selva oscura*

Una selva oscura indeed… and what is that running through the Tuscan dusk? Those are hooves pounding the ground, suddenly hollow as they drum over an Etruscan tomb, secret and dark and old. A man and his wife embrace in effigy. What is this smile, this happy death? Can they tell us? But we must follow away. The hooves grow faint. Wait, for we must see, must know. Today the sun shone in Leo. The orange-red earth of Tuscany glowed and stirred to the ox-drawn plow. Its blade turned up the head of a bronze god. He stared amazed at our latter light. This ancient land smells of pagan delights: demigods in chase and forest orgies. Listen the hooves have ceased. The flute begins. It ravishes my soul. Nowhere in this vale of Vallombrosa, dark with Etruscan shades, can now be seen the leaf-strewn brooks. But I hear the sighs, the pantings, the gurgling delights. I encircle a hamadryad. Her hair feels like spring leaves; her skin smells of wet bark; her lips taste of ripe fruit. Ah, joy, joy! But suddenly a gust of wind blows the bushes to the ground and a jag of lightning flames the sky. A black hole gapes in the hill behind me. It is the gate of hell. Ave Maria; ora pro nobis. I will walk out of this wood of danger and delight. The journey to the underworld has been made. Hell has been harrowed, and a new dispensation offered man. We now have a choice, a possibility.

The young man fell asleep to the sound of church bells, and the old Arno continued its journey, sliding quietly under the Ponte Santa Trinita on its way to Pisa and the sea.

Chapter Four

Gusts of wind swooped at the windows and fluted across the chimney pots. René stirred the fire in his grate and sat down near it, trying to warm his California blood. It would be a good time to stay in and read, although he did feel a bit restless on this blustery November night.

A banging on the door put an end to thoughts of quiet study. Ben and Evelyn and several others crowded around the entrance. They were all dressed to go out.

'Gunpowder, treason, and plot,' cried 'Doctor' Johnson. 'Better than a Boston tea party. Come out and help set the world on fire.'

'That's right, it is the fifth. I was forgetting.'

René hurriedly donned his overcoat and gown, turned out the lights, and joined them on the landing.

Other groups of students clotted in the halls and on the stairs, then spilled out into the court and through the narrow streets where the wind buffeted them along. Cries and commands flew between the gathering plotters.

'Fetch the scaffolding from that building. Carry those planks, lads, one of you at each end. Hurry now. To the squares. Did you bring the kindling, Scoggs?'

'Oh, it'll be a good one tonight,' promised Ben. 'With this wind we'll fire the whole town.'

René was swept along, wondering. This was not the twentieth century. They were embroiled in a Jacobean intrigue. The old, crude, wild England engulfed him.

I must have taken part in this once before, he thought. Where are the rearing horses, the lanthorns, the scheming Papists? I cam smell the powder in the cellar now. Guy, where is your long match?'

They debouched into the village square. Here electric lights slightly marred the seventeenth-century vision. These were after all merely university undergraduates. But they had regressed to a mob of plotters on this night of traditional mischief-making.

'The progs are busy this eve,' chortled Evelyn. 'There'll be many a fine to pay and reprimand to endure tomorrow.'

'Well, we really shouldn't damage or steal,' admitted René.

'But that's half the fun, Yank,' panted a fat young fresher as he flung a heavy board up onto the growing pile and then examined his soft, white fingers for splinters.

Someone started striking matches, which the wind promptly puffed out. But finally with the help of an old newspaper and some small sticks a start was made. Soon flames leapt up, nattering and cracking in the gusts like a whipped flag. When the bonfire finally filled out, the students moved back from the heat while the townspeople shook their heads and grumbled.

'Now three cheers for old Fawkes. Hip, hip...'

Everyone joined in, and the fire began to burn itself out.

I think I see Huss or Jeanne writhing in that incandescence, thought René. He stood as if stupefied while the red tongues devoured the wood and licked at each other.

'Speak,' he conjured the forking flames.

Yes, it is we. All who have been burned and all who still burn and will burn. Behold him who feigned madness in Ithaca but was caught out and sent to Troy. Returning I lost all my men, but Athene bright eyes brought me finally home. It is not true that I voyaged again. The Italian lies. There are many here, not all in hell. Let me speak. I am Antineus, a Christian. Nero burned me as a torch in his garden. The Roman guests laughed, but where are they now? Mine is life everlasting! And I, Huss, Master of Arts, do I not burn with a fearful light? God is my witness. The church will remember me. Kyrie Eleison! And I want you English to remember me as an excellent general. Dieu et mon pays. It was not you, but the Inquisition, that consigned Jeanneton D'arc to the flames. Jesus! Jesus! Ashes to ashes, blown away through time in a swirl of wind. Thus will we all.

'Come on, René, don't stand there all night in a brown study. There's nothing left now, but it was a corking bonfire, wasn't it? Now you know how to celebrate old gunpowder Fawkes.'

Ben took his bemused American friend by the arm and steered him toward their college. The wind had died down a little, and the air was cold and damp.

'Yes, it was a bonfire. It has burned a long time. How else can we kill our heretics without bloodletting?' demanded René of his puzzled companion as they hurried through the narrow streets while the high stars threw down their cold fire upon them.

'But the men, the women, where are they now? What do we do to each other? What makes us? *De heretico comburendo*.'

'I don't know,' Ben said, shaking his head. 'Maybe there *is* a devil burning in Hell who prods us all. Make a poem about this, why not?'

'I will, I will. I blaze with it. Thanks, Ben. Good night.'

Chapter Five

That winter René retreated into himself although not because of melancholy or excess of study. For no reason that he could fathom, and at this most unlikely time of year – when the trees were bare, the sky leaden, and the flat countryside was whipped by cold winds and occasionally powdered with snow – he felt an access of song. He spent many hours writing and rewriting poetry far into the night. Benjamin gave up expecting him to play duets with him. He became scarce even to his other friends. Evelyn, Robert, and 'Doctor' Johnson finally understood that he was to be left to himself. He saw them only at dinner, at chapel, and at occasional lectures.

It was an ecstasy, but not always felicitous. Sometimes René came to himself late at night, tired and trembling and a little blurred. But the lines of words flew across the paper, and they were good.

I don't know where this comes from, he thought, but thank you, Muse.

Finally, one morning in February he came out of his retreat. He knocked on Benjamin's door and found Ev there also.

'Salute, returned soldier,' mocked Evelyn. 'How did you leave the holy land?'

'Littered with broken lances, I mean pencils,' wanly joked René. 'And how are you two scholars? Is the world still one with you?'

'Yes, and its name is exams,' stated Ben. 'I suppose a hermit like you is not concerned with that little trifle?'

'Say not so, I must be. But, Ev, you are still here. You have so far stayed the course.'

'There's not much else one can do this time of year. It is the season made for study. The fire in the blood becomes a mere spark in the embers.'

'Good. Now keep it banked another year until Tripos. Then behold, B.A.'

'*Aut insanit homo aut versus facit,*' quoted the motor magnate's son.

'Yes, that's just what I've been doing,' admitted René, 'making verses or raving, and you've been reading Horace.'

'Well, rave on,' put in Benjamin. 'It is good to hear you make noises like a human being again. Now perhaps you'll join me in some duets again.'

'Yes, I would like to.'

'And how is Tess, the robotess?'

'As well oiled in the joints and as efficient as ever. No blown fuses yet.'

'Now who in the hell is that?' demanded Evelyn. 'You've never told me about her?'

'Oh, that's my scout,' explained Benjamin. 'You wealthy out-lodgers wouldn't know about them.'

'But why is she a robotess?'

'She just is. You ought to see her work.'

Ben stood up and pretended to make his bed in startlingly swift, jerky, mechanical fashion.

Ev howled and René smiled hesitantly.

'Not that she isn't a wonderful scout and a good-hearted soul to boot, Ev,' added Ben. 'But she does work as though she were doing her jerks. I can't imagine where she learned to move like that.'

'Well, Rossums built it into her, no doubt,' said René a little distractedly. 'But one reason I came to see you this morning, gentlemen, is that I have had a somewhat unsettling experience… stranger even than watching a robot make one's bed.'

'Oh? I thought you looked a trifle shaken, *mon ami*,' said Evelyn. 'Did you see a ghost? Tell us your Gothic tale.'

'Well, since I am among friends. But promise you won't trundle me off to an asylum.'

'We promise,' they both intoned solemnly.

'Do you look at yourself in an especially introspective way while you are shaving in the morning?'

'Yes, I usually use that occasion to deplore my lack of manly beauty and to chide myself for other obvious deficiencies. That fellow staring back at me from the mirror takes an awful ragging,' admitted Benjamin.

'Right-o. I suppose we all behave in similar fashion during that solemn ritual,' said Evelyn, 'but what happened to you and your alter ego?'

'I hesitate… but, well, this morning as I was looking at myself in the mirror, and talking to myself in my head, I bent down to rinse my razor, and when I straightened up again… really, it sounds too incredible now… but it *was* disconcerting. When I looked up again there was no one there.'

'I say,' breathed Ben.

'You mean you were there but *it* wasn't?' asked Ev, staring.

'Yes.'

'I'd say it was time you *were* coming out of retirement.'

'Oh I know… nerves and all that. Still, I seem to be all right now, don't I?'

'Perfectly. This flesh is quite solid.'

'Well, thank you. I just wanted to be sure…'

'That you had not thawed and resolved into a dew? No. you are here, and so are we. Ben, why don't you leg it next door and test that mirror on the wall?'

'You afraid to, Ev?' twitted Benjamin.

'Well, a little,' admitted Evelyn.

When Ben returned, looking sheepish, they both stared at him expectantly. He grinned a twisted grin at René.

'Didn't you know? Did you fly into a rage? It's smashed into a thousand pieces!'

René sat down heavily.

'I did not do it, friends. I did not.'

'Well, well,' calmed Evelyn, 'it's some optical phenomenon. The glass must have been under some kind of tension, so much so that it finally shattered. I insist upon helping our friend to procure a newer, less ghostly looking-glass.'

'Thanks, Ev. You could be right, I suppose, about the mirror. I don't know. But I'll get another from the porter, one in which I can see myself. You must admit, though, that it was an upsetting experience… and now to find it smashed… how strange!'

'Admitted; but let's hold on to the real, solid world yet awhile. It is not for us to probe the vast spaces between atomic particles as they do at Cavendish. Remember how Samil Johnson kicked the stone to refute Bishop Berkeley? Come on now, let us put some visible food into our too too solid bodies.'

They joked René out of his distracted mood and walked him over to hall for luncheon. However, when he wasn't looking at them for a moment, Benjamin shook his head at Evelyn and frowned. The latter shrugged his shoulders and rolled his eyes. They would watch after their American friend more closely for a while.

Chapter Six

'Merie sungen the munechis binnen Ely Tha Cnut ching rew ther by,' sang Evelyn as he strolled with René toward Trinity Hall.

Spring leaves were popping out of the old tree branches, and the Cam ran full and muddy between its newly green banks.

'And how fares our peregrine poet this lovely spring day?'

'He fares quite well, Canute, and has in fact been inspired to produce a new spate of verse. This English spring, coming after the English winter, is indeed a heady wine. Seriously, though, Ev, I gave old Hamilton a box of my stuff, and he waxed enthusiastic. He actually thinks it's good enough to publish.'

'I told you so. I knew it. If Professor Hamilton says so, you're made. Congratulations, Apollo!'

'Well, of course we have to see if the publishers agree with the professor.'

'My boy, any publisher who didn't agree with Hamilton on modern poetry would go out and shoot himself. Don't be an ass. Let's celebrate at my digs tonight.'

'Thank you, Ev, but let's wait until it's more definite, and then, please, not a crowd – just we few.'

'All right, old top, I won't even invite Angelica.'

'Poor Angelica. Isn't there any way to get her out of that business?'

'Not really, you idealist. She's of age. You could keep her for yourself if you were wealthy enough.'

'That would still be business. It's beastly.'

'Yes, I suppose it is, really. I'll try at least not to encourage the girl, Saint René. But it's a hard, cold world. There are so many of us wicked creatures in it.'

'Not realizing when we are being wicked does most harm.'

'Yes, Alyosha. Let me touch the hem of your cassock.'

'Oh, you're incorrigible. But anyway, I'll autograph a copy of the first edition for you if you'll reform.'

'By all means, so I can say I knew him when.'

They turned into the great court through the venerable great gate. The sacred lawns shone newly green, and a faint mist arose as the declining sun warmed the dewy grass. They plunged into the teeming hall just as the clock struck, and fell to their quick repast. They ate in the din of several hundred undergraduates being served and eating rapidly so as to be out of hall in the required twenty-five minutes.

It was difficult to converse in the bedlam, but Evelyn talked and waved his arms, What René could hear of his utterance seemed to be concerned with the imminent Mays and the possibility of his failing and being sent down in disgrace. René shook his head, but Evelyn nodded his lugubriously as they finished eating and genuflected toward the dons at high table.

'In that case, Ev, you need to study; and frankly so do I. Then I'm to see Hamilton again this evening.'

'I'm beginning to wonder if reading alone really helps me much. Can you remember much of that muck about old Wilmot and "The Satire Against Man"?'

'Well, hopefully enough to get through an essay, anyway. Come on now, Ev, you have a good memory if you'll just buckle down and put it to work.'

'Aye, there's the rub. There are so many pleasant diversions now that spring is here. but I'll follow your Erasmic example this night, anyway. I'll burn the midnight paraffin perusing Wilmot, Pomfret, and Prior, damn them.'

'Good, and don't be led astray by John W. when he says:

I'd be a dog, a monkey, or a bear,
or anything, but that vain animal,
Who is so proud of being rational...

'Oh ye gods, here you are quoting what I haven't even read. All right. Your humble servant departs to his study and his lamp.'

'Cheerio, Ev, you'll like some of those old eighteenth-century boys when you really get into them. You'll like their satire.'

'Maybe, but I, too, would rather be a monkey or a bear now that May is here, tra la. Ta-ta.'

René left his friend at the gate and turned back to walk across court, up the stairway, and into his rooms.

It *is* hard to keep your nose in a long eighteenth-century poem when the new leaves are popping out, he thought. But soon summer and freedom. Come on you vain animals – doctors, examiners, dons – so proud of being rational.

'I have taken the liberty of winnowing your harvest, Mr. Levin,' stated Professor Hamilton later that evening. 'Here are the poems I think Chatto can't refuse. But, of course you are the author. You may have favorites among those I have cast aside.'

'I'm sure I would hesitate to quarrel with your taste, Dr. Hamilton.'

'Don't be sure.'

The peppery don squirmed in his chair as though he anticipated some opposition. His eyes scanned the young man's face expectantly. Then he smiled.

'At any rate, look over my selection in the next day or two. Differ with me where you must, but quickly. We must get the final typing done by the end of the week. Fame and publishers will not wait.'

'Well, fame may. But I will go through these by tomorrow evening if possible. I owe you much, sir. I should never have thought of submitting them myself, I think, especially not to an English publisher.'

'Really, it is we who owe you. I am happy that you are among us. You know our poetic tradition: Milton, Wordsworth, Tennyson and the rest. But we have been in need of a good modern voice. It was kind of your Mr. Phineas to direct you our way.'

'I can certainly agree to that, anyway.'

'Well, come, let's have coffee.'

The small but lively professor jumped up like a grasshopper and called a servant who soon brought in a steaming, aromatic pot of coffee, together with another of milk and two empty cups, on a tray.

'Black or white, Mr. Levin?'

'White, thank you,' René replied, and the servant poured out coffee and milk simultaneously into his china cup.

'You have said that you discovered poetry through Whitman at an early age. Yet you do not write like Whitman,' probed the professor.

'No. Finding Whitman early was an accident. His book happened to be where I could read it. First impressions are strongest and lasting, I suppose. He showed me what could be done with language and with close observation. I admire him, but I am not at all like him. So I try to be like myself.'

'Well, but what about Eliot and his "Tradition and the Individual Talent"? Do you agree that good poetry must be in a tradition, that it is tradition and not merely personal effusion!'

'I think that is probably true, but I don't think it's consciously in mind when one is writing. Modern poetry probably is often too personal and private. But in the end one writes what one must, and it is only afterward that he discovers where it fits, or whether it fits, into the overall tradition. And, of course, I would find it very difficult to believe that anything I write can or will have any appreciable effect on the whole body of poetry in English.'

'Do you think Eliot's poetry has such an effect?'

'Yes, but he, like Whitman, is one of the great innovators.'

'Well, we shall see, of course. I mean we shall see some day if you might also be a permanent influence. Don't be incredulous. It's possible.'

René shrugged his shoulders and drank the last of his coffee. Dr. Hamilton put down his empty cup, and it was obviously time for the young student to leave.

'The important thing about your poetry is that it is unequivocally and unashamedly beautiful. That is daring, but I think you can bring it off. We had thought that beauty had fled this wasteland. Let's talk some more about this another time. Now do make your selections for the book soon. No more thanks, now. Goodbye.'

René slipped back into his rooms and pulled down a copy of Milton. He would glance through the results of Hamilton's winnowing tomorrow.

Chapter Seven

This summer René would stay in England. He had hoped to visit home but the financial depression was severe, so severe that many American students in England and Europe had to return home permanently, their education incomplete. René did not complain, but instead he wrote letters to Mother and to Mr. Phineas, anxiously inquiring whether or not they could afford for him to stay the final year. They reassured him that their incomes had been cut, but that since money was worth more, he could stay and graduate.

He felt useless and somewhat guilty after the end of the term. He knew it was time, perhaps the last chance he would get, to visit the English countryside and to discover, as Mr. Phineas had said, whether the magic was in the country or in the literature. He would travel cheaply, walking when possible. Benjamin would be his companion. Moira wanted to go with them, but this was to be a bachelor excursion.

'I don't care how silly you think it is of me,' announced René to his friend. 'I want to spend midsummer night in the forest of Arden.'

'Not silly at all, old chap. I think it's a corking idea, reassured Benjamin. 'We can take the train over to Henley-in-Arden and tramp around in the woods all night – if it doesn't rain.'

'Oh it can't rain, not that night.'

'You've been here too long to make such an asinine remark. But let's hope.'

They seemed to be in luck. As the railway guard opened the door to their train the sun shone warmly in a clear, blue sky.

'Are you expecting them all to be there tonight, René: Titania, Oberon, and Robin Goodfellow?'

'Yes, at least that fairy crew, because they are immortals.'

'Yes, I wonder what they have been up to all these years.'

'I expect the king and queen have quarreled many times, and Lord knows how many churns of butter and mugs of ale Puck has spoiled by now.'

'I hope he's not been around today,' said Benjamin, because I'm getting hungry and thirsty, and there's a good inn at Henley where we can sup.'

'All right, but let's not linger there, or we'll miss the magic.'

'Tut, old chap, you've forgotten how long the light lasts in these latitudes on this night of all nights.'

'It's very good of you to come with me, Ben, and to humor me in this madness.'

'Not at all. I'm fully as mad. It will be a lark.'

Puck had not spoiled the ale at the inn. After a good meal the two young men wandered off into the woods. Following a tramp through several groves of old trees, they came to the edge of a small meadow and sat down on a scattering of haulm with their backs to a gnarled old giant of an oak. René picked up a few acorns and examined them closely.

'I thought surely I would find an elf or two,' he said. 'They must be reveling in another part of the forest.'

'Probably. By the way, did you bring your recorder?' asked Benjamin. 'I have mine.'

'Oh, good. Yes, I stuck mine in my jacket pocket. Good thing you reminded me. I may be sitting on it. Do you think we could do the Fairy queen rondo without music?'

'Yes. Let's try.'

Mendelssohn's lilting tune sounded through the evening air and rose to the tops of the old trees. The nearly-full moon began to move up over the forest, its light filtering through the leaves.

'If this won't summon them, I don't know what will. Now, Ben, let's try the jig. That should set them dancing.'

The lively, fairy-like notes soared up and away from the two young men's pipes.

Suddenly Benjamin put down his instrument and plucked at René s sleeve.

'Over there in that patch of flowers, look,' he whispered, 'and listen.'

A host of tiny people seemed to be moving in a dance or procession. A taller and most imperious lady spoke in a silvery, faint voice:

Come, now a roundel and a fairy song
Sing me now asleep.

As well as the young men could tell at that distance and in that light, she seemed then to curl up in the bell of a cowslip. They heard the rest of the band singing:

Philomele with melody
Sing in our sweet lullaby.
Lulla, lulla, lullaby; lulla, lulla, lullaby…

Their eyelids grew heavy as the band swung around their tree. Their hands relaxed and their recorders dropped from their grasps. Now only the sound of a twittering nightingale floated through the silvered forest.

BUTTERFLY Who be these mortals?

HUMBLEBEE Strangers to Arden, but not from Athens by their garb.

CATKIN Let us wake them and try their wits. How, good Robin, will you do it for us?

ROBIN I will tickle their nostrils, pull their hair and snarl it in locks. I will affright them with goblin dreams. They will start up in trembles.

CATKIN Gently. They also may be good fellows. Did you not hear their piping?

RENEUS (*waking and running his fingers over his head*)
Oh what a nest of spiders crooks my hair.
Fie on it. Benean, you start. Are you awake?

BENEAN Grinning grimalkin scratched my eyes and bit the end of my nose just now, it seemed.

ROBIN Quickly mortals, to your feet. The little ones surround you, in every flower, leaf, cranny, niche.
Look to your wits,
Or they'll give you fits.

RENEUS What would they of us, two harmless wanderers in the forest? And who be you?

ROBIN Robin, called Goodfellow;
That am I.

Do you so name me
If hence you would hie.

BENEAN Good master Goodfellow, we bear you good will. We came here in hopes of seeing the faery.

ROBIN So you have done, and they have upon you cast a spell. But if you can answer three questions with wit and truth,
You to your homes
May swiftly fly
And bless the ones
Who let you by,
For you have gazed
Upon the queen,
Asleep, amazed,
And seldom seen.

RENEUS We mean no harm to royal majesty.
We'd love to join her fairy fantasy.
But if you wish us gone, we'll try
To answer fair and featly; so say I.

BUTTERFLY This mortal speaks well. To you, then, I pose the first riddle. Your friend may answer if so he's able. What mouse can eat the moon?

BENEAN Ah, it must then indeed be made of cheese. But I do not know of any mouse could jump so high.

RENEUS The reremouse it must be,
Who spreading leathern sail

Bites off a slice of moon
When flitting through its pale.

HUMBLEBEE You have outwitted one wit, to wit: it, Flutter, feckless butterfly. Now try my sting. What flowery way leads to loss of flowers?

BENEAN I can only suppose a schoolgirl, having picked a bouquet, may toss it to the wind when next she spies a field of more beauteous blossoms.

RENEUS Still, that is not true loss,
But when a maiden lightly trips
The primrose path of love,
Her leman may take more than lips.

CATKIN You have humbled the humming humblebee. Now may he humbler be. Buzz away, bumbler. Yet have I a third crackwit to tickle your pate. I scratch you with: How may live corn move from place to place?

BENEAN Perchance a farmer might grow grain in a pot and carry it with him to market.

RENEUS Methinks it soon would die.
But does not the lordly unicorn
Bear his? No lie.

ROBIN You have scat the cat and tweaked his wiry whiskers. Pussy willow, will you now purr perhaps?
This mortal's wits

Are sharper than
Sir Catkin's fits
Or Butters plan.
E'en Humble's sting
Be not his ban.

We beg your pardon for any slight inconvenience, gentlemen. Your scratches, snarls, and bites were only dreams. When you awake, we will be gone. Remember us not unkindly when next you stroll this way. Come, fairies, let us depart.

René stretched and yawned as the sky began to lighten. Benjamin woke with a start and gingerly felt his nose and eyelids. They looked at each other curiously.

'I certainly didn't expect to sleep here all night, did you, René? I feel as though something, perhaps some drug, made me unusually drowsy and dreamy.'

'Yes, something did, the fairies of course. You know they can on midsummer night. Look, there are our recorders. We must have fallen asleep!'

'All I remember is seeing little people over there and hearing them sing. Do you suppose it was our imagination?'

'Ben, everything is. We are such stuff as dreams are made on.'

'And I dreamed a cat scratched my eyes and bit my nose. I can still feel it. And look at your hair. It's all in tangles.'

'Well, elves were bound to be about. Shall we walk back to the inn for breakfast?'

At the inn the proprietor was apologetic. Somehow or other all the milk had turned sour overnight.

Chapter Eight

Aries Ensorcelled appeared in the shops and in the hands of students sunning themselves on the grassy banks or strolling through the narrow Cambridge streets. Professor Hamilton gathered a group of undergraduates at his quarters one evening and made René attend to talk and try to explain his poems.

'It's a strange feeling, seeing these words in print,' said the author to Benjamin one sunny afternoon.

'Of course, you'd never call it a good feeling, a thrill, a splendid accomplishment.'

'Oh, it feels good, all right, but rather unreal. Some of these poems seem written by a stranger. It's almost as though I was a medium and someone else did the composing.'

'That seems to happen with you artists. Didn't Handel say something similar about some of his songs?'

'Well, Handel, but what a genius! Ben, you're carried away, but thanks. And now I must send off a copy to my real teacher in California.'

'Your Mr. Phineas? Heavens, yes. Will he be unhappy that you published in England? No, I remember he's English.'

'Yes. Let's walk over to the post office. I have a copy wrapped and addressed.'

On their way back from the post office, the sun disappeared, and by the time they reached their college rain was falling in large, heavy drops. René left his friend at his room and returning to his own found copies of London papers waiting for him. Hamilton must have sent them over because they contained reviews of his book.

The reviewers were, on the whole, kind. Two felt that the poems, while well written, were too far out of the mainstream of current fashion. 'In this world of war and strikes and grinding poverty and psychic pain, what have we to do with such withdrawn and delicate musings, even if beautifully expressed?' asked one.

But others were charmed and seemed surprised that 'the language could still weave such spells,' as one of them put it. 'They're in an old tradition, and there's more here than first meets the eye. I feel a Japanese way of looking at things. This young man will bear watching,' wrote one perceptive reader.

I hope the book beats the reviews to Mr. P. thought René. He used to take *The Times* but it's awfully slow getting there. I wonder what he'll really think of all this? A small chill wavered through his body for no apparent reason when he thought of Mr. Phineas, so far away now: I must have gotten colder than I thought in that shower. I'll stoke up a little fire in the grate and browse through that stiff new book by that brash young Cambridge undergraduate.

The solemn, pompous, but somehow moving, ceremonies were over. René Levin, A.B. and even Evelyn Palmer-Hunt, A.B. though admittedly not a first with honors like the former. The scholars scattered like leaves in October but not before René had troubled to greet each friend and exchange farewells because the time had finally arrived – he was going home.

Professor Hamilton gave him the name of a teacher at the California University in Berkeley and made him more or less promise to look him up. 'Delighted with your book's success, aren't you?' probed the bright-eyed little man. 'The published tells me it's selling unusually well for an unknown young poet, and of course, he's written you about bringing out an American edition. You must go on, Levin, and develop your gift. Do send me copies of anything new you write – and the very best of success and happiness to you.'

René shook his hand and felt a pang of regret. I'm going to miss these people and this atmosphere intensely, he thought. Our lives seem to be a series of unitings and partings with only sometimes the happiness of re-unitings. Will I ever see this kind man and these pale yellow stones and green lawns again?

Back in his quarters René resumed packing his few belongings at the urging of Grigsby, the porter, who smiled at the young man paternally now. Grig and the college have finally molded me into a gentleman – almost, laughed René inwardly. He shuffled through a sheaf of letters the porter had left on the table by the door until he came to one from California addressed in a familiar but now shaky script. His face fell and became troubled as he scanned the short letter. Mr. Phineas was obviously ill. Hence, the uncertain handwriting. Although he tried to make light of it, Mr. Phineas conveyed to his young friend that he was 'somewhat under the weather' and had taken leave 'only temporarily, of course' from the library. He expressed pleasurable anticipation at reading his former pupil's first book of poems and hoped that he would soon have a copy in his hands.

René sat down hard and shook his head. He must get better. I must see him again, and he must see the book. It was for him. He felt that these wishes would come to pass since he in his youthful faith willed them.

Suddenly life seemed to speed up and to pass, as in a

too-fast movie. The blurred activities of leave taking, saying goodbye to the now loved friends, speeding to London, boarding the enormous ocean liner, getting seasick but then feeling better, debarking in New York, going through customs, hailing a taxi, catching a train. René gradually slowed to a crawl in his reclining seat as the snake slid west. His eyelids drooped. He seemed to sleep.

Oh, Mr. Phineas, don't go yet. Let me talk to you some more. Let's talk about Cambridge. Let's learn more about words. En archei en hoc logos. *But I'm afraid. I'm afraid you have left already. Have you shuffled off this mortal coil so soon? Oh, goodbye. God indeed be with you. Death, oh Death, be kind.*

René woke with a start. He felt sure now that Phineas was gone.

Part Nine

Chapter One

As the streamlined train dashed out of the Los Angeles station on the last lap of the long journey, René looked out of the window with a sense of misgiving mingled with love. He did not see the ugly junk yards and industrial trash heaps alongside the city tracks. Nor did he notice the little-town shacks or even the laden orange trees farther south. Not until the train curved toward the ocean and raced along the empty beaches did he feel that he was coming home. The fog lurked offshore like a fleet of sailboats. He saw the endless ocean into which he had gone a boy and come out a man one starlit night.

What would she be like now: married, a plump, practical housewife, perhaps with a baby at her breast? Impossible! Not that silky-haired Nereid with the glistening white, wet body and sea-green eyes. But it was all too possible – in fact, probable. Furthermore, why should it matter to me, a man grown, 'sophisticated', a published poet? They say you can't really ever go home again. But we want to, intensely. And wonderful Muv married to a stranger. Who could be worthy of her? And old Fed slaving away in an office, but his office, in San Diego, the would-be millionaire. And Mr. Phineas gone, the finest human being possible to imagine, some of the best part of myself gone to oblivion with him. Thank heaven he got to see the book, anyway. Did it really please him? His letter said so.

The porter came to get his luggage. The train slowed down and stopped at the little town, now a little larger and newer looking. The young man caught sight of his mother. He thought she looked older. She was alone and that was all and that was more than enough.

'Ansel couldn't leave his work, René. You will like him and he will like my famous author son.'

As if to corroborate her pride a sweating young man ran up to them and shouted, 'Mr. Levin, I am with *The News-Post*. May I ask you for an interview for a feature article on you and your work?'

'Oh, I suppose so, but not now. I'll come down to your office in a day or two.'

'Tomorrow, please, Mr. Levin; deadlines, you know. Just ask for Harry. Thank you, now.'

Ora pulled the rather dazed young, man, her grown son, to an automobile and climbed in behind the steering wheel.

'What's good is that things don't really seem to have changed much,' he said, 'even if you have learned to run a motor and have a new husband.'

'You've changed, though. Young people always do, of course. Can you feel at home among us who haven't, while you have gone on so far?'

'Oh, Mother, what I want is for everyone and everything to be the same. I resent every new building in the town, all the latest "improvements".'

'Well, at least you haven't acquired an English accent – only a very slight one, anyway. But how will you feel about our new house and about Ansel?'

'I don't really know, of course, Mother, but I'm sure I'll like anything and anyone you do.'

'Thank you, René. I see you really haven't changed, and I'm glad.'

The new house was, as a matter of fact, a disappointment. No eucalyptus trees or bougainvillea vines graced this undistinguished, suburban-style residence, and no floor-to-ceiling bookshelves lined the living room walls. The little piano was still there, however, and René admitted to himself that the place was more comfortable and easier to keep neat than the other one. Nevertheless, his heart remained in the house in which he had 'been married' and had lived the earlier, more vivid part of his life. He chided himself for being a sentimentalist and remembered the many inevitable changes that must take place among the living. Mr. Phineas, of course, was beyond change now. In fact, he had always seemed to be eternal.

'Well, René, this is a pleasure, said a pleasant-faced, tall, graying man who strode into the living room late in the afternoon.

'Mr. Riley, Ansel, I have been looking forward to meeting you for a long time, of course. I hope you weren't expecting too much.'

'Yes, I was, but don't be so self-deprecating. It is an honor to have you as a son.'

'It probably isn't, but it is good of you to think so.'

'René, right off the bat I'll have to tell you that I can't really appreciate your book. Forgive me for that. But I tremendously admire you for the accomplishment and expect you to write much more.'

'Oh, don't think any more about that book. I'm tired of it already. It's people that matter.'

'Yes, but books are written by people, and there aren't many who can write successfully. We feel you are a very special person. Make yourself completely at home, of course, and let me know if there is anything I can do to help.'

'Thanks. I'll probably spend a few days just loafing and getting reacquainted with everyone.'

'Let's see, you don't drive, do you?'

'No, and I realize that is becoming a necessity. But I won't need a motor to get around here, anyway.'

'Good. If you do want to go farther, Ora will probably have time to take you. Excuse me now. I'll go and wash up.'

René walked into the kitchen and hugged his mother a moment.

'He seems to be a good man. Of course he would be if you married him.'

'I'm glad you like him.'

'Oh, Mother, baked beans for supper! It's been a long time.'

'Yes, and I expect you to eat them all.'

'By the way, how about Fed?'

'He'll be up Saturday. He usually comes up over the weekends. He really is working hard at his business. Now, don't make fun of him.'

'Wouldn't think of it. I have more respect for things like that than I used to. I do hope he won't turn into a Kiwani like Mr. Hornbeck, though.'

'You know better than that. If he joins a club it'll only be a means to an end: more business.'

'I suppose he's doing the right thing. He fits in this world. I'm not sure if I do.'

'Utter nonsense. You're of a rarer sort and hence even more needed.'

'That is good to know. Remind me often.'

Supper was a rather gay affair. René warmed to Ansel, not because they shared intellectual ground, but because he seemed a happy, unselfconscious, and above all, kindly man. And he obviously loved Ora.

'There are so many things and people I want to catch up on that it will take a while,' said René at the end of the meal. 'I'm not going to sit around all evening boring you with questions, though. My legs need exercise, so I'm going to wander around town this evening for a while. Hope you don't mind.'

Mrs. Riley did mind, but she didn't say so, and the young man strode off in the direction of the old library. He couldn't find it, though, it had been torn down. The trees and building had completely disappeared.

That is as should be. He's gone. It's gone. Both unique. I suppose there's a slick new building somewhere else full of shiny new volumes with very little in them and shiny new lady clerks with very little in them. Of course I'm being childish. But it is perhaps good not to live too long, especially now when everything moves so fast and nothing is sacred. He would show me clear that it's probably always been that way. The long view. But we live a short life, and these things matter. En archei en hoc logos. Will it be at the end, though? We may end up using sign language, numbers strung together like ideograms. 7382946, but 51903031. Kiss me, 829375, 4013 me. What subtlety in 2739 instead of 2937. The word will never die, he said. Art is as necessary as bread. The Sphynx still gazes with a wild surmise at the desert where generations of puny men have grown and died unknown, But stronger and longer-lived than the Sphynx is the idea in the word. The clay tablets of Ashurbanipal and the rolls of the Torah. I christen thee Marilyn, I now pronounce you man and wife. And I pronounce this man dead.

René's steps had led him to the white house on the corner of Mission Street. He awoke with a start and ducked behind an oleander just as he caught himself about to walk up the steps and knock on the screen door. This, at least, had not changed much. The roof was now of cedar shakes, but the house was still the same shape; it was still white and it was still there.

He hoped the Morrises still lived there, although he knew they might not. He hoped that Reverend Morris still preached at the Presbyterian church every Sunday and did very little else, yes, and that *she* still lived there and was still his flower-faced little girt with the light-yellow hair and the sea-green eyes and... what utter folly, René Levin... but, oh!

Marilyn opened the screen door, waved to someone inside, and turned down the walk. Her hair still shone pale gold. She was more beautiful and piquant than ever. She was alone... unmarried? What foolishness to expect that, he told himself, as he strode after her up the street.

When they reached the next street light – high up, glaring, and surrounded by fluttering moths – he slowed and said, 'Marilyn.'

She stopped, put her hand to her mouth, turned around, and stared,

'No one can say my name like that. Is it you?'

'It is,' he said, coming into the full light. 'Are you... may I... can you?'

'He threw out his arms. She rushed into them with a little cry.

'Oh René, my René. I was afraid never again... never... again...'

This is it. This is what it is all about. Nothing else matters. Stars reel and earth shakes. The heavens declare the glory of God, and this woman sheweth his handiwork. How could you have wrought so well, Mr. Morris, in a Presbyterian bed? Mirabile dictu, out of a dull, tired man, got 'tween steep and awake this Rose of Sharon, this fairest among women. Thou art all fair, my love, and I am the one who will proclaim it.

'Where are you going, Marilyn?'

'Nowhere. Nowhere important. Nowhere without you, Where are you going?'

'I was going to you, I see that now. All the way from Cambridge.'

'No. There are many people… your mother…'

'Yes, and they are important, but I didn't really get here until… now. But I must not say all this. Who is your sweetheart? Are you engaged, married?'

'Yes, and have six children, you utterly dumb, blind idiot.'

'But it would be impossible. The whole bachelor population must gather in your living room every night like the suitors of Penelope. Your beauty must fetch them like a flock of birds to the lighthouse.'

'And you think that I could bear to let one touch me when there is someone who can talk like that and look like this to me?'

'Oh, Marilyn, I am not worthy of this at all. You are so gay and pretty. You must live.'

'I have started to do so again, René Levin.'

She took his hand in hers and they walked down the street. They turned the corner and walked west to the pier and then down to the sand, along the wet, firm border just outside the waves, and south toward the dunes. He had come home.

Chapter Two

Early Saturday afternoon Fed drove into the driveway in a large, new sedan. He unloaded some packages of presents for Ora and then came into the living room, looking for René.

'Well, Ren, welcome home. It sounds like you did knock those Limeys dead after all.'

René stood up and grasped the hand of his older brother. Fred had grown more solid looking and was dressed in a dark gray business suit.

'Hello, Fed. I hear you've been knocking some Yankees dead, too.'

'Well, not really, but we're getting along. Wish I could appreciate your book the way the critics do, but you know me. I never could understand poetry.'

'Forget it. I've moved on from there by now, anyway. How does it feel to be president of a company?'

'Right now in this depression it's scary. But there are lots of opportunities around if you can dig up a little money.'

'Is that how you did it, Fed?'

'Yes. I took what I had saved up from the paper. Since money is worth so much now I was able to buy this manufacturing outfit in San Diego that was going under. Now if I can just keep it going until business gets better, we'll have something.'

'Come on and eat something, you two, before it gets any later,' urged their mother emerging from the kitchen.

Fed was full of schemes and predictions throughout dinner. He listened politely to René's stories of England and university life, but it was obvious that his mind was on the business and its problems. He explained that he was in the process of establishing dealerships and franchises for his products – a line of household appliances – throughout the country.

'I never appreciated the importance of advertising before this,' he announced. 'Our things are better than some of the well-known brands, but people don't know that and are suspicious of such a little-known name.'

After the meal the two brothers sat in the living room while Mrs. Riley bustled in the kitchen. A new radio set blared its mechanical voice at them until René asked Fed to turn it off.

'It's good that you got to talk to Dad on your way over,' said Fred.

'Yes, it was a very short visit and I felt very strange, but I'm glad I got to see him and that we could be friends.'

'Do you know I saw him, too?'

'No, Fed, when was that? He said he wanted to talk to you.'

'It wasn't too long ago. About a year ago he called me up in San Diego and said he would be coming out here and wanted to see me. I told him he could stay with me but he took a hotel room. He didn't want to come up here and face Mother, but he looked over my business and insisted on putting some money in it. That just about saved my life.'

'Fed, do you know what ever became of the woman he…?'

'No. He won't talk about it. Too painful, I suppose.'

'Does he live alone, then?'

'Oh, didn't you know? He's married, but I don't know a thing about his new wife, either.'

'Well, it's good he helped you out, Fed.'

'Yes, and that reminds me. He wanted to know how he could help you. And I'd like to know how, too.'

'That's good of you – and Father – but I don't know myself just what I will do next. I promised several people I would write another book, but the sort of thing I write won't support me.'

'No. I suppose not. Would you be interested in any kind of job I could give you – such as advertising?'

'It's awfully good of you to think of me, Fed, but I doubt that I could do anything useful that way. I'll tell you what. I'll live off my friends and family for another year, and write. Then if I haven't thought of any other way to make a living, I'll ask you for some routine kind of office job that anyone who can read or write can do.'

'All right, but a Cambridge graduate should have something better than that.'

'Not necessarily, Fed. Oftentimes the best job for a writer is some small, routine thing that leaves his mind free for writing.'

'Well, if that's what you want, we'll give it to you. But don't forget Dad, too. He might have something better.'

'I'd rather stay here, Fed. Thanks for your help.'

Mr. Riley walked into the room, and they conversed in small town generalities until time for the evening meal. He turned on the metallic radio music for them to dine to.

René's mother came into his bedroom to talk to him a little before bedtime, an old custom of hers.

'Mother, I've been meaning to ask you about Mrs. Briscecov. Did you mention in one of your letters that she had moved away?'

'Yes, she came to see me about a month after Mr. Phineas died and said she was going to live with a relative of hers, another musician, in the East somewhere. I have the address. She was quite broken up over his death.'

'So was I, Mother. Weren't we extraordinarily lucky to have him here? I never could seem to thank him or repay him adequately for all he did.'

'I think he felt adequately repaid when he saw your book. In fact he probably was satisfied long before that.'

'He was a really good man. I hope I can grow to be like him. I brought Mrs. Briscecov a new Dolmetsch recorder. I must send it to her. I am sorry not to get to see her again and tell her about recorder playing in England and Italy.'

'Yes, she would have liked that.'

'I didn't tell you I played in a concert over there, did I?'

'No, but I'm glad you've kept up your music, René.'

'Alas, there is probably no one here now I can play with.'

'In that case you must play alone. I can accompany you anyway.'

'That's right, Muv. That will be wonderful.'

'Now, did Fed talk to you about a job?'

'Yes, he said I could go to work for him, advertising or something similar; but I told him I would sponge off you and Ansel for a year while I write another book. Is that all right?'

'Yes, René, that is what I want to tell you. Don't feel pressed to go out and get a job just to pay your board and room. Ansel wants you to know you are welcome to live with us and write.'

'You and he are spoiling me, but I will let you, at least until I have written one more book.'

'That is good. Good night now, son.'

'Good night, Mother.'

Chapter Three

The fog had rolled in thickly this night in early November. The few automobiles on the streets of the town crawled cautiously, their lights forming hollow, white cotton balls inside which they floated uncertainly and from which they could not escape.

René studied in his room while Mr. and Mrs. Riley occupied the living room, both reading the evening paper. A faint knock at the front door brought Ansel to his feet. When he opened it a young Japanese boy emerged from the mist and haltingly asked for René.

'You come, please, Mr. Levin? Kyoko ask. She is not well.'

'Oh, Kyoko. It has been so long. I supposed she had forgotten me. Is she...? She must be quite ill. Oh, how dreadful!'

The young man ran to the closet for hat and coat.

'I'll go, of course. Mother, Ansel, see you later.'

He followed the Japanese boy through the damp, clinging cloud. His face and clothing soon became wet. However, his guide seemed to have no difficulties finding a way through the deserted streets. Blobs of light, some colored, loomed up as they walked through the business district. Then they were on the road to the outskirts. How could the young Nisei see? He did, however, and they finally reached the small cottage. It was so clean and clear in the Japanese style that René felt he should remove his shoes, but the other man didn't. Two older, worried-looking people greeted and bowed: Mr. and Mrs. Kitagawa. They led him to a bedroom where a small lamp revealed a low cot on which lay a young woman, breathing with difficulty. It was Kyoko.

René threw off his coat and knelt by the cot.

'Kyoko,' he cried, 'why didn't you send for me? Oh, I know, I have been away so long. But I have been home more than a week. Oh. Kyoko.'

He made motions to touch her without actually doing so. He outlined her face and hair with his fingers. She looked at him and tried to smile. He dared to stroked her black hair. Then he jumped up.

'We must get the best doctors. Send to San Diego, to the big city at once!'

The other young man pointed to a man sitting in a corner of the room. He was an impassive Japanese.

'He is the doctor.'

'Oh, Doctor, I am sorry. But would you mind? For consultation, you see.'

The doctor shook his head slightly and whispered in his ear.

'It would do no good. Believe me, we have done what can be done. We should have seen her much sooner. We are susceptible to this disease. I am so very sorry for her, for them, for you.'

René wrung his hands. He wanted to dash out to a telephone, but he did not want to leave Kyoko.

'Excuse me, what is your name?' he asked, and bowed to the young man who had brought him.

'I am Okichi.'

'Please, Okichi,' he said softly but insistently, 'would you carry a note back to my house? I hate to ask you on such a night, but it is important.'

Okichi bowed and said, '*Hai*, yes, I will do that.'

René found a scrap of paper and a fountain pen in his pocket. He went into the other room and scribbled a note to his mother asking her to work miracles by telephone. Okichi left without saying more.

René returned to the cot and knelt again.

'Oh, Kyoko, rest. I will work for you. Lay everything on me. I have been so bad to you. I am so very sorry.'

The girl moved her arm slightly and put her fingers lightly on his lips. He took them and put them gently inside his mouth. He heard someone in the room suck in his breath, but the girl smiled faintly.

René sat back on his heels and held Kyoko's hand and thought.

She is the flower and this cot is the tokonoma. We are here to worship and to watch this flower die. There is no point in asking why life is so wasteful, why clods like me keep on living and beautiful, perfectly good angels like this die young. Oh, if I had had the courage and sense to stay and marry this lovely girl, would she be happy and well now? Perhaps not, and after all, what a futile question. We always think we can remold life nearer to the heart's desire. Here I am childishly speculating while Kyoko lies dying. But what else can I do? I can cleanse my mind of all these trivial tag-ends and concentrate on the flower in the tokonoma. They are right. We Westerners are scatterbrained and superficial.

A man craned his head through the doorway and beckoned to the Japanese doctor. It was Dr. Horace. They went into another room and talked a little while. Then Dr. Horace beckoned to René.

'I am sorry, young man, about this girl. Dr. Sakamoto was called in by her family, but it was too late. She has the fast-moving kind of consumption that plagues these people especially. There is nothing we can do now to save her. I am truly sorry.'

'Thank you for coming and thank you, too, Dr. Sakemoto. It is hard to accept what you say.'

'Yes, it is always hard to accept this. It never gets to be any easier. Good night. Again I am sorry.'

Dr. Horace bowed slightly to everyone in the room and left the house.

They renewed their vigil. René held the girl's hand constantly. He put it to his wet cheek often.

Why did she ask for me after all his time? That is what stabs my heart like a hot steel knife. If I am going to affect people like this just by being near them for a while, I should be put away in a cave in the desert. Oh, what terrible things we can do without ever realizing it. Now I see why wisdom is so necessary. Why was I not first made wise before I was allowed to love? but, please. The last blossoms are falling into the river. The thrush flutters and prepares to fly into the dawn.

Kyoko died so quietly that no one but the doctor noticed what had happened. He took her hand from René's and folded her arms over her breast. A faint light diffused the fog as the dawn began another day. René kissed her forehead and walked out into the misty air. Another portion of his soul had gone with her. He learned again that we grow lighter and smaller each time we lose someone we love. He stumbled blindly homeward as the heartless birds sang their joyous matins.

At the funeral he remembered a haiku.

Sorrowful butterflies
fan the peaceful face
that now lies seeing heaven.

Chapter Four

Mrs. Levin woke her younger son late in the afternoon to ask him if he could eat something.

'I suppose I must, Mother, but I don't want to.'

'Yes, you must,' she said, and made him put on a robe and sit down at the kitchen table.

He listlessly spooned some soup into his mouth and nibbled at a slice of buttered toast.

'I am a little surprised at you, René. I didn't suppose this would hit you as hard as it has. Can't you recall some of the wisdom and philosophy you must have acquired the past few years?'

'Mother, I haven't acquired much until just now. I thought I had learned to see and perhaps to describe well what I have seen. But that is nothing. The most important things cannot be seen. They must be known and then acted upon. Kyoko would have felt the same way about me if she had not been beautiful, but would I have paid any attention to her then? I'm afraid I have formed a cult of the beautiful, and look what it has led to! Now I must change and try to acquire wisdom.'

'Well, you are acquiring it. This is one of the ways. It is a hard way, but the only way most of us ever gain it.'

'I do earnestly hope that the rest of the wisdom I may be able to acquire will not be gained at the expense of anyone else but me – certainly not at the expense of an angel like Kyoko, Mother.'

‘Yes, that is a good hope, although you will come to see that you are not so much at fault in this as you think.’

‘I hope so. But I see the great dangers that wait for anyone who single-mindedly worships art, for instance. Did you know that Henry James once went to the funeral of a neighboring youngster, even though he knew he wasn’t welcome? He was disliked by these neighbors, but he sat in the pew directly behind the mourning family so he could watch their actions and manifestations of grief. In gathering grist for his mill he became inhuman. If art has to be bought at this high a price, it is not worth it. I, too, have been too much an observer and recorder, and so I have failed to behave rightly toward other people. I thought that my behavior was harmless because it arose from love, but I see now that does not make it right. Love is even more powerful than I realized, but it can be a power for wrong. How strange!’

His mother buttered him another piece of toast.

‘Yes,’ she said, ‘any of the powerful emotions can cause wrong or right, and sometimes both at the same time. We sometimes forget their great power or we have to learn it.’

‘I suppose that means that even hate, for instance, can sometimes do good; for example, the hatred of evil. But what really matters, I begin to see, is that we think of the consequences of what we are about to do. This requires wisdom to foresee what the consequences are likely to be. Some emotional people say that this is to act in a calculating manner and is therefore bad, but they are wrong.’

‘Yes, that is what being an adult means. That and accepting the consequences if you do something wrong in spite of forethought.’

‘Thank you, Mother, for the toast and the insight. I think I can face up to life again. And I will try very hard not to hurt anyone ever again.’

'Of course you will; but this will not stop you from being an artist. It will make you a better one.'

'Mother, I have just had a thought; I am going to write a novel, not another book of poems. I am going to try to show what we have just said, to show it in a story. I will dedicate it to Kyoko's memory.'

'That will be good, son. Now let's go into the living room and keep Ansel company.'

'All right. I think, though, if you don't mind, I will get dressed and hunt up the new library. I want to borrow some books to help get me started on the novel.'

'Yes, it will be good for you to go out for a little while.'

For the next few days René pored over books and scribbled pages of notes. The main ideas for a novel began to take shape. However, every now and then he threw up the whole project and sat in dejection, thinking of Kyoko. One day he visited the little house of the Kitigawas to ask them if he could have one of the girl's kimonos to keep. His strong desire for this overcame his qualms that they might feel resentful toward him for neglecting their daughter for so long. But they did not seem to hate him. They were not the kind of people to blame someone for the inscrutable turns of fate. They gave him the kimono, wrapped in bright red tissue paper. He tried to express his sympathy and sorrow to them but they remained impassive. He bowed and they bowed as he walked out of the little house for the last time.

One evening he called to ask for Marilyn. They walked and talked and finally sat on a bench in the park near the new library.

'René, I am sorry, about the Japanese girl. She was very pretty,' Marilyn said.

'Yes. It is extremely sad and I have much to make up for there. Marilyn, you are always telling me that I don't understand about us and that I have a lot to learn. Well, I have learned that you are right. I shouldn't have loved because of beauty. If you don't love for other reasons than beauty, you don't really love.'

'Then I'm afraid you don't really love me. Remember, you said you wouldn't if I weren't beautiful.'

'I'm afraid of that, too, Marilyn. Oh, what a dog I am, I am going to have to learn to see if I can really love. I am going to have to go away again to do this.'

'Oh, no, René.'

'Yes, For a while. But not far away, and not for years as in England. I am going to San Francisco to write a novel. In it I hope to work some of these things out. And again, Marin-lyn, you must be free. Your beauty and liveliness must not go to waste.'

'And again I say pooh-pooh to you and your theories. I will be here waiting when you get back.'

'Oh, Marilyn, that is a twist of the knife.'

'I can't help it, René. I am glad you are going to find out about love. I just hope it will not be with someone else, though. That would kill *me*.'

'Oh, don't, don't. No. That is the main reason I am doing this, to learn how to love without hurting. I am not going to look at any women. At least you can be sure of that. I will be a monk. Really, Marilyn.'

'That is your intention now, anyway, But regardless of what happens, I will be waiting.'

'Poor patient Griselda,' he said and folded her tight in his arms.

'One thing, though, René,' she cried. 'Let me come see you if I get too lonely.'

'No. I will come see you, every few months. And yet you *can* come to see me. That will be good, whenever I need inspiration.'

'Or when I need it.'

They walked home arm in arm.

'Why are you going to San Francisco, René? It is so far away,' she asked as they reached her house.

'I forgot to tell you, A chap I met at Cambridge comes from San Francisco. He is home now, too, and wrote me a letter saying he has money and that I can have a room in his studio. He's a painter. I feel that I have to get away somewhere like that where I can really concentrate and try to forget unhappy things.'

'I see, Well, goodbye again, sweetheart; we say goodbye so often, don't we?'

'I'm so very sorry I'm such a will-o'-the-wisp, Marylin. Maybe I can straighten myself out some day. Don't cry. You can come see me soon. Really. You can stay with Robert's parents. They live next door. And he'll like you. He'll want to paint you.'

She tried to smile as she slipped through the front door.

Part Ten

Chapter One

Robert Le Blanc was delighted to learn that René would accept the offer to occupy a room in his house while attempting to write his first novel. He met his friend at the railroad station and whisked him to his hilltop studio in a cab.

'Now that I'm here, I'm a little embarrassed, Bob. You are so generous. I won't be able to pay my way, you know.'

'Great Scott, no. Who ever heard of a prosperous young poet? I told you it would be our pleasure to have you here indefinitely. I don't pay my way, you know.'

'But, Bob, of course your parents would help you. But they've never even seen me. How do they know I'm worth it?' worried René.

'Because I've told them. That's all it takes. Frankly, they have spoiled Karen and me rotten, but they like to, and they really can afford to, even now in a depression. Call it luck, but take advantage of it. Another aspect of all this is that my father loves to patronize the arts and artists. He's really very artistic; he has to be in his business. But he's never had a chance to help a literary type like you, before. So let him have his fun.'

'Well, I'm here on your hands now. But it seems to me that all my life I've been taking instead of giving, and here I am, at it still.'

'If you must look at things that way, you can consider that giving us a good novel will make it all square.'

'Of course I hope to do that. But it takes much faith on your father's part to count on a novel from a beginner.'

'We'll gamble on you. After all, he's read your poems and likes them. Now, aren't you hungry? Let's wash up and go to a French restaurant I know. Really quite economical, too.'

René laughed at Robert's last dig and the young men sallied out on foot to a small restaurant with big checkered table cloths and baskets of good French bread on the table.

'Isn't it barbarous? A French meal but no wine. We'll have to postpone that until we get back home,' grumbled Robert.

'Oh, then, you have a cellar?'

'Of course; my father couldn't live without the amenities. Surely before long we'll abandon the noble experiment and return to civilized customs on this side of the world. But now, tell me about yourself. Was it good to get home?'

'Yes and no, Bob. I've had an extremely sad experience. A girl I loved once just died. She asked for me just before she died. I have turned over a new leaf. The novel will, I hope, be an expiation. I have learned that love of beauty is not nearly enough, even for an artist.'

'I am sorry about the girl. That must have been shattering. But your last remark is extremely interesting. What more do we need besides love of beauty and the ability to create it?'

'Wisdom,' said René. 'And we're always forgetting that. But let's talk about less solemn things tonight. What is your sister like?'

'Karen? Oh, people say she's very much like me, poor thing. But she seems to be happy. She's married, and she has twins, a boy and a girl of eight. You *must* meet them.'

'I would like to. I haven't known any children in years.'

'Karen and her husband live not too far from here. We'll go see them soon.'

'Good. I hope they'll like me.'

'It's foregone. By the way do you have any female attachments at present?'

'I'm in a complicated situation. There is a beautiful girl at home, but she is so foolish. We are not engaged but she will not have anything to do with anyone but me. All the time I was at Cambridge she waited. Now she is waiting again. I can't get her to forget me.'

'Perhaps she loves you, René.'

'I'm afraid so. You see, that's part of the trouble I am in and must set right. I have loved her and the other girl spontaneously without realizing that this could cause great unhappiness. I'm not a little small-town businessman who can just marry and settle down. Who knows when or if I ever can? So I should not have loved.'

'It's pretty hard not to.'

'Well, of course one can't help doing so, really. I didn't promise anything like marriage, but still I didn't manage it right. I will have to work this all out in my own mind. The problem is how to love without hurting.'

'I'm not sure that can be done,' said Robert, shaking his head.

'There must be a way.'

'Well now, you must be tired, so let's get back to the studio. I want you to meet my parents tomorrow, Then we'll not interrupt you.'

'Thank you, Bob. You are a perfect friend and host. My cup is running over already.'

René found a desk in his room, equipped with pads of paper, pencils, and a typewriter. He unpacked his suitcase and spread out his preliminary notes on the desk top.

Dear Kyoko, he thought, this is for you.

He wrote until after eleven. It seemed good, but he felt the need of a critic, someone like Mr. Phineas. Suddenly this old man seemed to be present.

This room is full of ghosts tonight, René mused. I'm glad they're here.

He went to bed and slept well.

'If you can stand the fare, you are welcome to eat with me, said Robert, poking his head inside René's door at lunch time.

They ate in the artist's studio: cheese, beaten biscuits and Italian sausage. René wandered about, inspecting the work in various stages of completion.

'I like that,' he exclaimed, pointing to a watercolor portrait of a blonde, blue-eyed woman.

That's Karen. Glad you like it. I do too. By the way, sometime when your inspiration has left you, if it ever does, I'd like you to sit again.'

'All right. I think I'll probably write most of the time in the afternoon and evening. Do you mind working in the morning?'

'Not at all. Prefer it, in fact.'

'Bob, you are so generous it will sound dreadful to ask any more favors, but I will.'

'Fire away.'

'The girl I told you about, Marilyn, I rashly told her she could come up here sometime. Could we put her up somewhere?'

'Of course. My parents next door have several extra rooms.'

'One of the reasons I said she could come was that I think you would like to paint her.'

'Good. She must be beautiful.'

'Yes. She is.'

René spent most of the afternoon at his desk. At five o'clock he got up to stretch his legs, climbing and descending the streets in the windy, damp air. When he returned, Robert was waiting.

'Let's eat with my people tonight. Nothing formal. Go wash up if you like.'

René washed his face and hands and combed his unruly hair. After being introduced to Mr. and Mrs. Le Blanc, he sat down with them in a small dining room and ate. There was wine on the table.

'I have told Robert how grateful I am for letting me stay here,' said René. 'Now I want you to know.'

'It is our pleasure, Mr. Levin,' replied Robert's father in a rather clipped accent. 'We like your poetry and Bob likes you. He says you have started writing already. Hope you don't feel pushed about it.'

He smiled at the young man.

'No, not at all; I have a lot to say and you have fixed me such a pleasant room. I just hope I can do justice to your kindness.'

'You will,' said Mrs. Le Blanc, tall and Scandinavian-looking, as all the Le Blancs were. 'But don't work *too* hard. Karen would like to meet you when you have time.'

'Yes, I want to meet her and the children.'

'Let's go over there tomorrow night after supper,' put in Robert. 'All right, René?'

'Of course. That will be great.'

Katherine, Karen to her intimates, was instantly recognizable to René from the portrait by her brother. Her husband was a dark, rather somber man, but accessible and courteous. The twins were irresistible. René was amazed to learn that the girl's name was Lyndall. She was more lively than her brother, a rather dreamy, quiet child named Lynn.

After dinner the twins appropriated René. Karen tried to drag them away from him now and then, but they soon returned. Lyndall sat on his lap and teased while Lynn sat at his feet and called him 'Runny'.

'Runny,' he said, 'what did you do when you were my size? Did you like to fight?'

'No. I hated fighting. Do you like to fight? Are you good at it? I don't see any black eyes or bashed noses.'

'No. I don't like to. But what do you do when a fellow hits you?'

'I'll tell you a story about that sometime,' promised René, 'I was just awful lucky.'

'Tell us now,' ordered Lyndall, wiggling.

She rarely took her eyes from his face. Was it his curly eyelashes?

'What do *you* know about fighting, violet eyes? Who would ever fight you?'

'He does,' she said, making a face at Lynn. 'We fight lots.'

'I'm disillusioned,' laughed René. 'I assumed you were an angel.' Suddenly he frowned. No, that was Kyoko, he thought.

'You're mad at me,' wailed the little girl.

'I am not. Do you want to hear the story?'

'I'm waiting, Runny,' reminded the little boy, hugging his legs.

'Well, once upon a time there was a young man about your size, and he had to go to school. At this school the boys played on one side of the playground and the girls played on the other side. One day the young man got tired of wrestling and punching and he saw some nice girls playing hopscotch, so he went over and played with them.'

'I bet the other boys didn't like that,' interrupted Lynn.

'Sh. Who cares about them?' said Lyndall.

'Well, anyway, the next day when the young man came to school, a bunch of boys grabbed him and got ready to beat him up.'

'See,' said Lynn,

'So a giant came and picked him up and carried him away, I bet,' offered Lyndall.

'However did you know?' exclaimed René. 'That's almost what *did* happen.'

He looked into her dancing violet eyes.

'I'm physic,' she declared.

When the laughter subsided, Karen told her daughter the word she really wanted.

'Anyway, you know what I mean,' she pouted.

'Yes, I know, and you must be,' reassured René.

'Now tell us what really happened,' prompted Lynn.

'A big boy by the name of Takeo came to the young man's rescue. He wouldn't let the other boys hurt him. The other boys called Takeo a giant. He was a good giant.'

'And I know who the young man was, too.' announced Lyndall.

'Who?' asked René, looking astonished.

The little girl poked her finger into René s chest.

'And I love you,' she said, hugging him.

Chapter Two

René sat for Robert three or four mornings a week now. The artist often apologized for taking up so much of his guest's time. He said he couldn't understand, why he had such difficulty getting down what he wanted to represent when he tried to paint his friend.

The young author usually wrote in the afternoon or caught a bus to the public library where he pored over reference books to confirm details in his story. The cold, foggy, windy weather did not bother him as long as he was absorbed in his work. Later he would miss the southern sunshine.

Robert took him out to various small, good restaurants where they sampled sea food, or Italian dishes, or Hungarian goulash. Once or twice a week they ate with the Le Blancs and once or twice a week they dined with Karen and her family. René looked forward most of all to playing with the twins. They made him feel the goodness of life again. They made him realize, too, how much he might be missing. If he settled down and got a job he too might have a wife and lovely children. But he knew that this was not for him yet.

The precocious twins admitted René to all their secret world. The family had two young cats, named Mozzle and Pootle by the children. Around these pets the boy and girl had erected an imaginary country: Cat land. All the riches of their inventive and changeable fancy were applied to this private Cockaigne.

'Runny, here is our latest newspaper. Don't you want to read about how General Pootle put down a rebellion and punished the calico cats?'

'Yes I do, Lynn, and what's that picture you're working on, Lyndall?'

She looked up at him with a blue smear of crayon on her chin.

'This is the Mozzle cat factory.'

She had drawn a complicated machine that appeared to be turning out cats like sausages from a grinder.

Lately René would go off to the breakfast nook and play with the twins after supper while the rest of the family visited in the living room, No one seemed to find this impolite or disconcerting.

'How did you happen to name your cats?' asked René one time. 'I had a cat named Kinky once.'

'Well, Mozzle is the noise the black one makes when he washes and bites himself,' explained Lyndall reasonably.

'And Pootle is the noise the gray one makes when he purrs and meows at the same time,' added Lynn.

'I see. Those are noise names. Ours was a look name. Our cat had a crooked tail.'

'Did you learn to talk with her?' asked Lyndall.

'Not very well. Have you learned your cats' language?'

'All cats talk the same language,' averred the little girl. 'We can say some things.' She made a noise that sounded like 'perrier'.

'That means, "Don't be silly",' she explained.

'Oh,' said René, solemnly, 'I'll try to remember that – "perrier".'

Lynn and Lyndall had accumulated a pile of papers relating to Cat land. These consisted of drawings of battles between warring factions, domestic activities, and social functions. In addition, a number of issues of the newspaper, 'The Caterwaul' had been compiled, each painstakingly hand-lettered and profusely illustrated, Only a few special people were allowed to browse through this stack of treasures. René would take some back to the studio each time to serve as bedtime reading. Often later he would ask for an explanation of obscure incomprehensible points when he brought them back.

'Lynn, what are all these cats doing in this building? Each one has his tail stuck into some kind of socket. And then wires run out from the building on pylons.'

'Of course, Runny, that's the power plant. When cats purr they make electricity. The electricity runs out their tails into wires that go out to all the houses to light all the lights in the town.'

'I see. Are these special power-producing cats, then?'

'No, every cat in Cat land has to take his turn in a power house.'

'Can they keep on purring long enough to make it worthwhile?'

'Sure. All they have to do is think happy thoughts.'

René picked up Lynn and tossed him in the air. 'You and violet-eyes are my happy thoughts. Don't let me down, now. Keep on purring.'

'We will, we will,' promised Lyndall.

What a shame they ever have to grow up – children and kittens. I suppose that shows I'm not mature. If they didn't grow up, they couldn't reproduce. Why is it so important for life to go on and on? There must be something extremely important up ahead there in time that makes us keep working so hard and long to try to reach it. Not we as individuals; we are just stepping-stones for life. We hand it on and drop out like runners in a relay race. What can that goal, that end, possibly be? Have we been thrown out in some gigantic explosion and are now falling back toward the center, toward a final reunion with God? That doesn't satisfy me. I doubt that we can ever know why. That's why I'll stay with the whats. I told Mr. Phineas I was no philosopher. Art thou there, truepenny?

The novel slowly took form. For a poet novel writing seemed a difficult art. So many words to say, really, so little. But he learned the art of piling on, of building, the ant-like activity of carrying a straw here and of adding a grain there. Thus the pyramids were built, block upon block upon block – and then the facing, the smoothing off, the finishing and polishing – rewriting and rewriting the rewrites. He decided to send a copy of what he had accomplished so far to Professor Hamilton. However, he had many doubts. Hamilton was severe and uncompromising; he might topple the work of months by a few harsh words. Nevertheless, it must be done. He arranged for a copy to be typewritten – at the Le Blancs expense of course. They laughed at his concern over the cost. They even understood when he wouldn't let them read it. So, with a rather apologetic letter of explanation, the package was mailed to England. In the meantime René added and changed. The pyramid was far from complete.

Chapter Three

Dearest Marilyn,

You must come up and meet the Le Blancs. And I need you. You know you said you would. I am enclosing a letter to your mother and father from Mr. Le Blanc. You will stay with them. It's perfectly respectable. Robert and I don't even live in the same house. If your parents are still doubtful, get them to ask Mother. Remember, I am now a monk. However, I have fallen in love with a girl up here. She's eight years old and you will love her too. The Le Blancs are wealthy, so here is your railroad ticket. Show your mother that it is a round trip ticket. All you have to do is send back a postcard telling what train and what date. We'll meet you at the station, Please, Marilyn, come soon,

Love,
René

A week later a postal card arrived saying, 'Thursday, 6.30 p.m.' No signature. That Marilyn!

When they met the train, at first they were afraid she hadn't come, but then René saw her in a dark blue dress and a white hat, lost in the midst of a crowd of people and a pile of luggage. They rushed into each other's arms. Robert held back discreetly. Finally they came back to earth and René introduced her to Bob.

'Hello, Marilyn. I see all that raving René has been doing about you is true.'

'He does rave a lot, doesn't he? Glad to meet you Mr. Le Blanc.'

'Robert or Bob to you. Here's a cab. Let's get out of this crush. Have you eaten?'

'Yes, on the train.'

'All right, we'll head for home.'

Marilyn seemed happy but more than a little flustered by all the unusual activity and these new people. At the house the Le Blancs were gracious and informal and soon put her at ease. They showed her to her room and told her to rest awhile if she wished. She came downstairs shortly, and sat with them in the living room.

'I know it sounds trite, but it's true,' said Mrs. Le Blanc. 'We want you to feel that this is your home, and we will not stand on any ceremonies. We live informally. The whole house is yours, Miss Morris.'

'Thank you. I am not used to being away from home. You will forgive a small-town girl if she doesn't always know how to act in a big city?'

'No, because you couldn't do anything needing forgiveness. We are so happy to have you. Did your mother worry about you coming?'

'Yes, a little. You know mothers. I have never been so far alone. Thank you for that letter, Mr. Le Blanc.'

'Not at all,' he replied. 'Glad it worked.'

Robert had been looking at the girl intently ever since she arrived. She seemed to be a little embarrassed by his scrutiny.

'Don't mind Bob,' advised René. 'He's an artist, you know. He's measuring the proportions of your face or something. He even looks at me that way... well, almost that way. Next thing he'll want to twist your head around in various positions and in various lights. He's likely to make you famous, you know. He has canvases in some of the best galleries.'

'Oh, René, really…'

'He's right, Marilyn,' put in Robert. 'As soon as you get rested and have seen some of the town, you must, simply must, sit for me.'

'It will be an honor, Robert.'

'Hooray,' he exulted. 'I can hardly wait.'

'Now you boys run along,' ordered Mrs. Le Blanc. Marilyn is tired, I'm sure. We'll see you sometime after breakfast.'

'Where do they eat?' asked Marilyn.

'We throw something together in Bob's studio,' explained René.

'Myra's right, though. We'll run along and see you tomorrow. Right, Bob?'

'Absolutely. Good night, Marilyn.'

She smiled at the artist as the two young men walked out.

'She's ravishing, simply ravishing, René, you old dog. How can you stay away from that cup of honey?' raved Robert as they entered the studio next door.

'It didn't take her long to hook you, too, I see,' laughed René.

'Cruel man, how can you talk about her so? Hook, indeed.'

'Oh, it's unconscious, I admit. But you see what I mean about beauty and why I used to call her Circe.'

'I see the beauty, but she's no witch.'

'Oh no? Well she's bewitched you already, I think.'

Robert sighed.

'Yes, I'm afraid she has, you lucky dog.'

The following two days were spent in showing Marilyn the city, Bob and René took her everywhere, even on several of the ferry boats across the bay. She shivered a little in the cold, foggy wind, but it all seemed like fairyland nevertheless. And Bob seemed to lose his heart completely, but Marilyn had eyes only for René. Mrs. Le Blanc made her son stay away from them in the evenings so the girl and the young writer could have some time alone together. One evening they went to a restaurant at the top of a tall building where they had a panoramic view of the city and the water while they ate. The next evening Marilyn said she wanted to be with René in a quiet place, so they visited in his studio. The Le Blancs didn't feel it necessary to chaperone them every moment, and the girl wanted to see where René lived and wrote.

'Isn't this pleasant, Marin-lyn? Aren't they wonderful people to let me stay here?'

'Yes, René, it seems like a dream. No wonder you like them so.'

'Well, you've made a big conquest of Bob, too, you know. He really is an up-and-coming artist, an important one already.'

'I'll stick with my important writer, thank you.'

She drew close to him and looked into his face.

'You do look a little older and more serious. How is the book coming along?'

'It has been hard. I had to work some things out before I could decide what to make my characters do. The story isn't turning out as I had first planned, either. Novels are queer that way. They have a life of their own and you have to follow along with it.'

'May I see some of it?'

'Yes, you may, but it won't make much sense right now. It's all in bits and pieces.'

'René, have you learned more about love?'

'I don't know. Bob says you can't love without hurting. Sooner or later you will. "Each man kills the thing he loves," as Wilde said. If not kills, at least hurts.'

'And yet you can't go through life not loving.'

'Exactly. I suppose the ideal solution would be to acquire as much wisdom as possible before you fall in love with someone so you will do the least amount of hurting afterward. Have you noticed that older people are better at this? Look at Ansel and Mother and then look at Mother and my father... much younger. And then look at us loving each other when we were children. I think children hurt each other the most of all... no forethought, just spontaneous affection.'

'But it was good, just the same. I suppose I'll always be a child.'

'So one of us has to grow up. I'm trying to.'

'It would be nice if in growing up, you wouldn't grow away.'

'Ouch. Marilyn, you know that if I would allow myself to be my old spontaneous self I would love you to repletion. Do you think I have forgotten that night on the beach?'

'Do you think I have?'

'Suppose we were to let go like that again, here on this bed, right now. What ecstasy! And then suppose you became pregnant. Suppose you had on the beach... then what, little Aphrodite?'

'You would *have* to marry me. Then you would always resent me.'

'And you me. See what I mean by wisdom? It's better to wait until we can be sure of all this and how to handle it. It's hard, sweetheart, and I sometimes feel like throwing all sense to the wind and running off with you to a Gretna Green, but you know how that would end... no money, your indignant family, my unhappy family. It would soon turn sour in our mouths. See, I really love you too much to do anything like that. Our love must be happy afterwards. Just wait until you meet Karen and her children. That's the kind of love we must have!'

'All right. I can wait as long as I know you love me and really want me. What worries me the most is that you are such an artist and such a highly educated man. You will probably become famous. Then you could have all manner of wonderful women; smart, intellectual, well-read, witty. I'm not like that and never will be. Then what regrets you'll have.'

'What you say shows your generosity and what might be called surface sense, but it's not *real* sense. Read back in history and you'll see that artists don't get along well with blue-stocking women, not really, I certainly don't anyway. I hate gatherings of "smart", "intellectual" people, especially women. I know I shouldn't say this right now because it will just make it harder for us, but I do love you. You are the one for me, just as you are. I really don't think I'll ever change my mind about us. I don't think you ought to gamble on my uncertain future, Marilyn, but if you really want to… that's the way I feel about you.'

She smothered him with kisses and cried on his shoulder. She hugged him in a bear's grip and snuggled her golden head on his chest.

'Here now, my proud beauty. If you keep that up, I'll lose my good intentions.'

'Oh, how I wish we could make love again. But you are right. I will be a good girl for a little longer anyway.'

She sprang up and stood before the mirror of his dressing table. She brushed her hair with one of his military brushes and smoothed her dress. Then she turned around and smiled.

'You are the most beautiful creature this side of paradise,' he exclaimed. 'No wonder Bob wants to paint you. And be careful with that young man, he may not be as strong as we are.'

'All right, René, Now escort me home.'

Chapter Four

The older Le Blancs and their guests visited Karen and her family after supper on a weekend evening. The twins appropriated Marilyn as earlier they had appropriated René.

'Tell us a story, Marilyn,' ordered Lyndall, 'with cats in it.'

'I've heard about your cat stories,' she replied. 'I don't know cat language the way you do. So you tell me one.'

'All right. Once upon a time President Mozzle…'

'Who?'

'President Mozzle. I guess you haven't met him. Here, I'll introduce you.'

She flew out to the kitchen and returned with a young, black, short-haired cat in her arms. She held up one of its paws so Marilyn could 'shake hands'. With a little coaching the older girl got the idea.

'This is President Mozzle of Cat land.'

'Pleased to meet you, I'm sure.'

The cat squirmed down and ran back to the kitchen.

'He has some important unfinished business,' Lynne explained, gazing adoringly into Marilyn's eyes.

'Anyway, President Mozzle heard that the calico cats were acting up again,' continued Lyndall. 'So he called in his army and made them sharpen their claws. Then he sent a big old orange cat over to where the calicos stayed. He said, "Listen, you undecided colors, are you going to behave and help us run Cat land, or are we going to have to bite your ears and pull out some fur"?'

'And you know what the calico cats said?' broke in Lynn. 'They said, "meowrftt sssss". That's an awful insult.'

'It certainly sounds like one. I would be awfully mad if anyone said that to me,' commented Marilyn.

'Oh, do you know what it means?' asked Lyndall.

'I'm afraid to ask, it sounds so bad. Maybe you can whisper it in my ear.'

Lyndall cupped her hands over one of Marilyn's ears and whispered excitedly. Marilyn pretended to look shocked.

'Heavens!' she exclaimed.

'Yes. So when the orange cat told President Mozzle, he declared war.'

'I should think so,' said Marilyn.

'So they fought and bit and scratched, and the battlefield got to looking like one big cat, all covered with fur,' declared Lyndall.

'But then, here came the Titter Tatters,' put in Lynn.

'The what?'

'We'll have to tell you about them,' he continued. 'I'll draw you a picture of one.'

He drew a creature made up simply of lines, one for each arm and leg and one for the trunk. At the end of each arm and leg line appeared an arrow head.

'Are they really as sharp as they look?'

'Yes. So they can hurt fierce,' said Lyndall, jumping up and down.

'What did they do to the cats?' prompted Marilyn.

'They flew at both sides and stuck them with their sharp hands and feet.'

'And all the cats ran home and hid,' yelled Lynn.

'But what did they do about the Titter Tatters?'

'Cats are pretty smart,' avowed the little girl. 'They decided to make a lot of cats out of real soft wood, you know – dummy cats. Then one dark night they put all the dummy cats out in the field where they had been fighting before.'

'So next morning the Titter Tatters flew at the wooden cats and got stuck in them. They're still there, too,' finished Lynn.

'Serves the nasty creatures right, I'd say. But did the calico cats ever apologize to the others?'

'Yes, they went to see President Mozzle and said, "Purriplp, purriplp, let's be friends".'

Marilyn hugged the little girl and boy and said, 'And let us be friends, too.'

'Oh, we are. You're so nice and so much fun... and so pretty.'

She joined the rest of the group in the living room after the children had been put to bed.

'I hope they didn't wear you out with cat stories, Marilyn. They will if you let them. But that shows they like you, anyway,' said Karen.

'Of course not. They are fun. I wish I had two like them of my own.'

'I'm jealous,' pretended René. 'They used to play with me.'

'You have them all the time. Don't be greedy,' Marilyn flashed back.

'All right. I knew they would like you, though.'

'How is the portrait coming, Robert?' asked Karen.

'Very well, I think. With such a subject how can I fail?'

'But he won't let me look at it,' complained Marilyn.

'He never will, Marilyn, when he's working on one.'

'I'm doing this one awfully fast. It won't be finished when you have to go home, Marilyn,' explained Robert. 'But I want you to see it then, anyway.'

He seemed unusually excited whenever he talked about the painting. His family knew this meant that it really was going well.

'Let's go home now, boys and girls,' said Mrs. Le Blanc.

'It's been such a pleasure meeting you, Mr. and Mrs. Leighton, and your delightful children,' averred Marilyn. 'You are so fortunate to have them.'

'Thank you, Marilyn. I'm sure you will be just as lucky some day,' teased Karen.

They drove home through a mist. The fog horns moaned intermittently out in the bay as they descended from the car and went their various ways to bed.

Chapter Five

Marilyn could stay only three weeks at the longest. Her mother would rather have had her home sooner. So Robert sped the painting of her portrait, making her sit for him every morning for two or three hours. Then they and René would go out to eat together. Most afternoons René and Marilyn went sightseeing or exploring. He felt that a little rest from the novel would be good, and he wanted to be with her more and more. Although he could not talk to her about art or ideas, he loved being with her, looking at her, and the gay, careless sound of her voice, and her childlike simplicity and natural womanliness. As long as she was with him she was happy, and this made him additionally happy.

One day they took the ferry to Berkeley and walked up to the campus of the university. Although very different from the colleges of Cambridge, it had the atmosphere of intelligent bustle, of professorial concern and youthful enthusiasm, that make most universities attractive. The campus, too, was old enough not to seem as raw and businesslike as most of the ones in the south.

On an impulse René decided to inquire after Professor Watts, the friend of Hamilton of Cambridge. He remembered that he had half-promised Dr. Hamilton to make the acquaintance of the California teacher. Marilyn tended to pull back, overawed by the solemn quiet and dignity of the humanities department and the faculty offices. But René pulled her after him and found the professor's office. He was in and able to receive them. Piles of papers littered his large desk, and books old and new crowded the shelves and tables.

Dr. Watts beamed when René introduced himself and his friend.

'It's about time you were showing up here, young man. I have been dying to meet the author of *Aries Ensorcelled.* Are you not proud of him, Miss Morris?'

'Yes, I am.'

'Indeed, yes. Some of those poems are required reading in my classes now. How was Hamilton last time you saw him, Mr. Levin?'

'He was as fiery and peppery as ever, Dr. Watts. He especially asked me to look you up. I have been slow about it.'

'Well here you are, anyway, and as a matter of fact, just in time.'

'Oh?'

'Yes. Do you live near here now?'

'In San Francisco for a while. I am working on a novel.'

'What a versatile young man. First you write a book of verse that sets the critics on their ears, even the august Eliot takes notice, and now you switch genres and tackle a novel. Plays next?'

'I doubt that, Dr. Watts; and perhaps the novel won't work.'

'I doubt *that*, Mr. Levin. But about my question... we have a series of Friday evening talks throughout the spring semester. I would be most grateful if you would be the speaker at one soon. I strongly urge this. Everyone around here is interested in your work, but no one has met you. We didn't even know you were in the neighborhood. Now please do agree.'

'I am inclined to say no, Dr. Watts. I am not a speaker. What could I say about the poems?'

'You writers often ask that question; you needn't talk about your poems. Any literary subject that appeals to you will do. These are informal things for the humanities students and professors, not much more than a large class. I'm not going to let you refuse. A young writer like you needs friends and an audience. Make him do it, Miss Morris.'

'Yes, I hope he will.'

'When, Professor?'

'Two weeks from yesterday at eight o'clock. Let's pick a subject now so it can be announced – any subject. You don't even have to stick to it.'

'Please do René. I'll be here and can hear it,' urged Marilyn.

'Well, all right, if you're sure it's really informal. Would you think I am crazy if I called my talk "Love and Wisdom"?'

'Of course not. Sounds intriguing. We would be happy, of course, if you could say *something* about your work. The students are always especially interested in hearing an author discuss his work.'

'My novel is partly concerned with the subject. I might even read part of one chapter.'

'Now you are really talking. I am so glad you came by, You need speak only an hour. Then afterward, if you are willing you might answer questions in an informal discussion.'

'I'll think about that.'

'Good. Now why don't both of you come straight to my office since you know where it is? Get here about seven thirty and I'll show you where the small hall is. Remember, it really is informal and relaxed. Don't prepare a formal talk, just some notes at the most. If you want to read a chapter or some poems, that's fine'

'All right, Dr. Watts; you seem to have talked me into something. We won't keep you any longer now.'

'I would like to talk to you about your work, but perhaps you'll tell me what I want to know in your address. I am happy to have you as an emissary from Dr. Hamilton, too. It has been a pleasure to meet you, Miss Morris. Thanks so much for helping to persuade our reluctant poet to talk.'

He graciously bowed them out of his office, and they walked around the campus another half hour before going down the hill to the ferry.

Robert and Mr. Le Blanc insisted upon accompanying Marilyn and René to Berkeley, the evening of the talk. The hall was larger and more full than René had expected, but he braced himself and plunged into his chosen topic.

'Let's look at love and wisdom,' he began, 'two such large and amorphous qualities that philosophers quail at even naming them. But we are not philosophers and can therefore be bold and, if necessary, foolish. It is good to try to grapple with subjects such as these from, time to time, As a scholar one must be more narrow and specific, but as an artist or an appreciator of art one can range high and far. If one falls, the descent will not be intellectually catastrophic, and in the meantime one may taste the fruits of Olympus.

'By my title I mean to imply that there is, or that there should be, a connection between the two qualities. I have learned, and many of you have also, probably, that loving unwisely can produce great harm. I'm not talking about the physical results of promiscuity now, although they are certainly often cruel enough. But I'm talking about many kinds of love used unwisely: disinterested love, parental love, religious love.

'At first it would seem that love, like goodness, could not, by its very nature, ever cause harm. Why has the universe not been arranged so that love, which is by its very nature spontaneous, produces only good in the lover and the beloved? We don't know why, of course, but so it is.

'Since this is true, we must learn how to love in such a way that in doing so we do not harm ourselves or others. The thought of governance of what seems so spontaneous is repugnant to many. But it is vital. We must learn the wisdom of governance, of forethought, at the same time as learning to love.

'It has been suggested by many that in the realm of sexual love, at least, it is impossible not to hurt, that the nature of the passion is such that one, and usually both, of the parties is so exposed and vulnerable as to make wounding inevitable. I do not believe that we should succumb to this philosophy. The inculcation of greater wisdom at an earlier age can prevent the kind of emotional exploitation that is too common in this relation.

'The results of a lack of wisdom in parental love are too well known to you to require repetition. Misuse of love among other members of a family is also a popular subject. A sister may lavish affection upon a young brother, thereby breaking the heart of another brother, and so forth. Religious wars and inquisitions are, of course, conducted in the name of love. Remember the grand inquisitor in *The Brothers Karamazov*?

'You may say that these are not manifestations of real love, but they may be. They may simply be applications of love without wisdom.

'Love may be seen as a kind of undirected power, one of the most potent sources of energy, spiritual and physical. Wisdom may be seen as the switchboard and wires which carry and control this otherwise unmanageable force. The force must be there, of course, but its presence alone isn't enough. It must be carefully directed and controlled, or, like fire, it may destroy even its originator. It behooves us all to acquire as early as possible the directing wisdom. It should be learned at our mother's knees.

'Very well, I am an impossible idealist, and these are amorphous generalities. Let's consider a possibly real situation. The following is an excerpt from a story now in progress which is very much concerned with the topic under discussion.

Laura put down the paper and arose wearily from her chair. She had heard the gate slam angrily as Martin turned in from the lane. Why did all his movements seem to be exaggerated and expressive of impatience or irascibility? Other men could come home from work calmly and at peace.

Martin strode into the kitchen and embraced the tired woman in an iron grip, even before putting down his lunch box or taking off his heavy, rough jacket. He scowled at her and at the stove.

'God I'm tired. That damned winch broke down again. What's cooking there, Laurie? Something to revive an overworked body?'

'Irish stew, Min. Not fancy but hearty.'

He took a ladle and started to dip into the boiling pot. She grabbed his hand and arrested the movement.

'Not yet. You'd scald your mouth. It isn't quite ready yet, anyway.'

She smiled at him tenderly but he frowned and turned away brusquely. Even in such little matters he couldn't be gracious or kindly. He stomped into the washroom as Colin opened the front door and made for the kitchen.

'You look tired, Laurie. Can't you go lie down for an hour? I'll watch the pot.'

'No, Colin; it's about ready to take off. Pretty soon, anyway. And Min is already trying to dip into it.'

'Min can wait for once or fend for himself.'

'In the house he's not much good, Colin, like a bear in a toy shop. I'd hate to see this place after he'd lived in it a week alone.'

'If it weren't for the work it would make for you later, that would be a good lesson for him.'

'But I'm here.'

'That's just the trouble. You're here, and he takes advantage of every minute of the fact.'

'Well, that's the way he is, but I love him.'

'That's what he really takes advantage of, Laurie. You've spoiled him rotten with your love.'

'Who's spoiled rotten?' thundered Martin emerging from the washroom dripping water on the clean kitchen floor. 'Hey, Colin?'

'We are, Min. Laurie spoils us. She spoils everyone. We ought to spoil her for a change.'

Martin stared at Laura.

'What's he talking about? Am I spoiled? Do you spoil us rotten?' he asked belligerently.

'No, Min. Settle down. Colin was just joking friendly. Here, sit by the fire and look at the paper.'

Martin sat down in the rocker with an aggrieved air and stared at the newspaper. Now and then he lowered it and glared at Colin. The older man shook his head at Laura when Martin wasn't looking and then left quietly by the front door.

'Now that snoopy is gone,' said Martin, 'I want to tell you about something.'

'That isn't nice, to call our friend that, Min.'

'Never mind him. Now listen. I'm going to stay at work late tomorrow. I'll drive the truck home after dark and I want you to have the cellar door unlocked and the outside lights turned out. Hear?'

Laura looked at him sharply. 'What are you up to, Min?'

'I'm just transferring some stuff temporarily. It's all right, but I don't want anyone else to know about it. You do what I say and you'll be glad, real glad.'

'All right, Min. Now eat your supper and then let's go to a show. You used to take me, remember?'

'Damn it, Laurie, I'm awful tired. Can't you go?'

'Never mind. We'll go when you're not tired. Eat now.'

Martin drove the truck, with the lights out, far back into the driveway the next night and spent more than an hour carrying some heavy objects down the cellar stairs. The doorbell rang, but Laura managed to get rid of Mrs. Osborne without letting her into the house. Martin remained quiet until she left.

Laura knew better than to question Martin when he came back after returning the truck to the warehouse. However, she looked at him anxiously. He seemed nervous and excited which was unusual for the aggressive, but not jumpy man.

The next two days passed uneventfully enough, but as they were eating supper the third day a heavy fist rapped on the front door. Martin leapt to the back door guiltily, a uniformed police officer staring at him from outside, Laura, her heart turning over, opened the front door to another officer.

'We have a search warrant, ma'am. You must let me into your cellar.'

She did so and turned the light on for him. Martin sat on a kitchen chair and glared at the first policeman, who had entered the rear door.

The officer came up from the cellar and announced, 'It's there, all right. I'm arresting you Martin Lascelles for possession of stolen goods. You'll have to come along to the station.'

Laura clung to her man, but the officer handcuffed him and led him out to the police car parked in the driveway.

'Laurie, I'm not really guilty. I can explain. Help me out, Laurie. Tell the judge I didn't steal. Get a good lawyer, Laura, We can get out of this.'

She collapsed onto a sofa as the car drove away. So this is what can happen when you love a man too much, she thought. It can make him weak instead of strong. He was spoiled. If I hadn't spoiled him, might he have grown up and faced things like a man instead of staying like a willful, self-centered, foolish little boy all these years?

Laura knew the answer to that now, too late.

'I can imagine – perhaps I can actually see – you smiling or shaking your heads. There are many things that shape a man's character, and hence his actions, you will say. Of course that is true. Nevertheless, unwisely applied love is one of the major forces for wrong, To repeat, it is not love that is harmful but the unwise, unforethinking application of this powerful force. We know that truth also has this shattering power. We are seekers after truth, but we cannot always face it when we have found it. We need the wisdom to accept truth without letting it destroy us. Those who love need the wisdom to direct that power In such a way as not to destroy its object. This object may be one's self, of course.

'Wisdom is the greatest of all virtues – greater by far than mere goodness, which without wisdom can do incalculable harm. Almost as much harm is done by the stupid good as by the malicious. Wisdom encompasses virtue. Who could imagine a wise but evil man?

'Let us proceed to investigate anew the means by which we may acquire this wisdom and refute the sad dictum of Oscar Wilde. And having acquired it, let us proceed to share it and apply it unceasingly.

'Thank you.'

Dr. Watts announced that René chose not to answer questions in a public exchange but would be pleased to meet and talk to anyone in the lounge afterwards.

'I feel honored that this young author who has won such wide respect and acclaim for his first book of verse, *Aries Ensorcelled,* has consented to address us here this evening. I believe this is his first public appearance, and I do hope it is not his last.'

Polite applause was followed by a movement of the audience toward the doors. A few minutes later a number of the students and professors gathered in the lounge to shake the author's hand and exchange the usual pleasantries. Marilyn and the Le Blancs sat in chairs at one end of the room and beamed at the perspiring young man.

Finally the people drifted out and Dr. Watts led René and the Le Blancs back to his office.

'I won't keep you long,' he said, 'but I do want you to hear this. I would like to offer you a job, Mr. Levin. Oh, I know you are busy on a novel now. But when you get through with it, I urge you to consider serving as an author in residence here. Thus, you can both write and teach. We need the influence of young, successful literary men like you. this will give you the opportunity to love with wisdom. That is what good teaching really is. And, of course, it will provide you with a livelihood.'

'I am thunderstruck, Dr. Watts. My head is awhirl. But this does sound quite tempting. May I return soon to learn more about the duties?'

'Of course. It is late now, run along home; but do come back and we will thresh out the details. Thank you again for a most interesting, and rather surprising, talk. It has been good to meet you, too, Messers Le Blanc.'

Marilyn looked at René in an especially happy and expectant way as they rode in Mr. Le Blanc's car down to the ferry. He quite understood her. This could be the chance for a life together at last. He hoped his old foreboding would fade and that the future could be real and happy after all.

Chapter Six

The day before Marilyn was to return home, Robert beckoned René into his studio. In the center of the room rested a large easel, and on it sat the portrait. René had purposely avoided it before, thinking that the artist would want to surprise him with it when it was almost finished.

Robert had even trained a spotlight on the canvas this morning, and the impact was dramatic.

'Great heaven, Robert; this absolutely takes one's breath away. This is different from anything I have ever seen of yours. How perceptive of you to do her as a Renaissance lady!'

He walked back and forth in front of the canvas with mounting excitement, Robert sat on a stool at one side and looked actually flushed with excitement himself.

'Bob, this is simply a masterpiece. You have almost created a modern Gioconda. You have even used a da Vinci background... and *sfumato*! But that smile; that is hers absolutely; and enigmatic.

'She is that way sometimes. Why, this will create a sensation. You have been truly inspired!'

'I was, I was, by love!'

'Poor man. I didn't realize you were that smitten I feel guilty that she cleaves so strongly to me. No. I don't really feel guilty; I love her too. But I do feel dreadfully bad about how you must feel. What a shame there aren't two of her.'

'Amen.'

'Well, it would be terribly sad if it weren't for this masterpiece. The whole world will know how you feel about her now.'

'I don't give a damn about the whole world.'

'Not now, but you will. Can't you get any pleasure at all out of this accomplishment?'

'Yes, oh yes, especially if she likes it.'

'Surely she will. But Bob, face it. She's unsophisticated about art. It's just that this is so good it will impress her by sheer force.'

'Do you really think it is that good?'

'Yes, indeed.'

Robert put his chin in his hand.

'I must admit, shamelessly, I do too. But I'm too close to it really to tell,' he said.

'You *know* it this time. And you got her blue-green eyes just right, too. Shall we ask her to come over now and see it?'

'I'm rather afraid to, but let's.'

They flew to the house next door. Marilyn was busy packing, but they pulled her away, causing her to drop a bit of filmy underwear on the bedroom floor. Bob picked it up and acted as though he would like to keep it, but handed it to her with slightly trembling fingers. They dragged her downstairs and across to the studio. She stood in front of the easel a minute or more without speaking.

'It's... beautiful... much more than me. What did you do to me?'

'This is the way I see you,' said Robert tenderly.

She looked at him in amazement.

'I didn't know you felt like that. Did you, René?'

'Not to this extent, no. But now you see what you can do to people.'

She looked almost frightened, but she went up to Bob and kissed him on the cheek.

'I'm sorry you feel that way about me, Robert, but it did make a beautiful picture.'

He sat down on the stool limply.

'Thank you,' he said. 'Thank you.'

'Well come on now, this is no tragic situation,' insisted René. 'Let's celebrate. Let's go out to dinner tonight and drink champagne – on Bob's money, of course.'

'It's good of Bob to invite us,' teased Marilyn, 'but now I must finish packing.'

'Don't look so woebegone, Robert,' advised René. 'You have wrought a masterpiece. Cheer up, man, and invite us out.'

'I do, I do. That is a good idea in spite of the sad occasion.'

'Sad? That you have painted your best portrait yet?'

'Yes, Robert, you really should be proud,' said Marilyn seriously. 'I don't know what makes great art, but this seems great to me, although I feel immodest to think that it is a picture of me. Even so I think it's beautiful.'

'That's what matters to me,' said Bob, somewhat reviving. 'Now we'll help you back home to pack.'

'Go ahead, you two,' ordered René, 'I want to look at this some more by myself.'

They left as he studied the portrait from several angles and distances, smiling and shaking his head. Many people are going to see my Marilyn now, he thought. I wonder who will finally end up with her hanging, on his wall.

Although the champagne that evening had to be ginger-ale, the young friends managed to become intoxicated on talk and love. Marilyn felt that she would never again be the small-town girl she had been. Bob Le Blanc felt that he would never fully recover from unrequited love, but somehow his young spirits would not let him mope. And René felt that he was probably the most fortunate mortal this side of Eden. They walked home arm in arm and embraced each other indiscriminately in a sudden access of youthful *joie de vivre*. For a while they seemed to lose their individual identities and to merge into a kind of unified and heightened consciousness. Robert was to recall this happy transformation many times during the remainder of his life.

Chapter Seven

Robert and René both felt low after Marilyn's departure. They plunged into work so hard that they hardly spoke to each other for several days. It wasn't that they were less friendly; it was just that they reminded each other of the gay, yellow-haired girl who had been with them so recently. Bob would have been jealous or envious, but he couldn't be of René, so he was merely melancholy.

This morning, however, the painter burst into the writer's room and dropped a heavy package on the latter's desk.

'Now she's sending you presents,' he joked feebly.

They both could see that the package came from England. It must be the typescript of the unfinished novel.

'Great Scott,' exclaimed René. 'I didn't expect Hamilton to send it back. I hope he's not angry.'

'Well, here's a letter from him too, you pessimist. Have you the courage to read it?'

'Frankly no, Bob. But I can't show myself to be a coward in front of you. I'll just scan it to learn the worst.'

'Want me to leave?'

'No, stay and give me courage.'

René tore the envelope feverishly and extracted a rather short letter. He read it in silence and then relaxed visibly.

'He says it'll do, as long as I make the changes he has suggested on the copy.'

'Only that it'll do?'

'Spare my modesty, Bob. Actually he gets rather carried away toward the end.'

'Hooray. It's a success, then. Not that I ever doubted it.'

'Well, I did. He says he showed it to Chatto, the ones who published the poems, and they are insisting on bringing this out in England first, too.'

'That will make it all the more distinguished and impressive to Americans.'

'Will it? He says I'll get a letter from them soon discussing terms. Heavens, I didn't expect to make any money out of it.'

'There goes my last hope down the drain. Now she'll marry you for your money.'

'Over yours? You're mad. It probably won't even sell. By the way, how about the portrait?'

'I finally did get it finished and am submitting it to a special exhibit in New York. Marilyn said I could.'

'Oh she did, did she? Now *I'm* jealous. But seriously Bob, how can it help but steal the show?'

'You never know with these modern artists and juries. But I think it will too, of course.'

'When will you know?'

'Any day now.'

'I predict we'll both be in the press and the public eye soon. Especially you.'

'Well, we artists must expect that sort of thing when we're good. How about going to lunch now to celebrate.'

'Yes, let's. Then this afternoon I'm going to lie in a park somewhere and see what old Hamilton did to my masterpiece.'

René took a street car to Golden Gate Park, near the ocean. Lately, he had felt the need to get close to the old mother, the sea, as he used to at home. Since the weather was now warmer the shore should not be too uncomfortable. He sat down at the base of a tree and untied the string around the box containing his typescript. He was sitting on the slope of a knoll that descended toward the sea. He was close enough to the beach to see clearly the footprint's made in the wet sand by the surf fishermen and a few young people in bathing suits.

Dr. Hamilton's flowing, blue-penciled comments and corrections sprinkled the typewritten pages. René found a rock to put on top of the loose sheets he took from the cardboard box, one by one. It is always a little embarrassing to read one's work after the ardor of composition has cooled. However, on the whole it sounded better than he had remembered or expected. There were some purple patches that would have to be toned down, at least to a rich blue, and there were weak stretches that would have to be toned up. He agreed with most of Hamilton's comments and slashes. There is always a good deal that needs to be cut. He winced at an occasional jab of sarcasm. The old boy hadn't mellowed any, yet at least. 'Tommyrot!' he wrote across one section of philosophizing. 'Probably so,' agreed the young man. 'Wooden dialogue,' the professor claimed at another place. 'Shorten and tighten.' In a few places René disagreed flatly. He doesn't know the Japanese, he thought, but I'll try it on two or three others. I think it's right, though. 'Be sure to send me the completed and revised typescript,' commanded the good doctor. 'Don't send it to Chatto first.'

'All right, agreed the young author, 'and what do you say, Mr. Phineas?'

'Swear.'

'I do swear… that this will be true to the word. This is my word world. Rest and be not perturbed good spirit.'

The warmth of the westering sun, the soothing shush of the waves, and the distant cries of gulls and children combined to make René drowsy and he surrendered to the temptation to doze a little.

What are you smiling about, girl with the blue-green eyes? You don't know. It is the woman in you. You go far back and can't help it. Eve, if you hadn't eaten that fruit we wouldn't be here, but you did eat it and you saw you were naked and Adam saw he was naked and he knew you and here we are and you are still Eve, seven hundred generations removed. That is what you are smiling about and don't know it. And I am Adam, made in God's image after his likeness, and I had dominion over the fish of the sea and over the birds and cattle and over all the earth, And I gave names to the cattle, the birds, and the beasts, all of which had been made for me. I am still a name giver in the chain. I have created a world out of nothing, which will now exist perhaps forever. But I will not live forever. Eve, why did you not eat of the fruit of the tree of life? Not to be, to be, and then not to be. That is almost as bad as never having been. Almost, but not quite. By knowing you I will pass myself on. But I will not then be here to enjoy myself. What a mystery! The knowledge of good and evil. Everything, even love, can be good or evil. That is the consequence, Eve, Marin-lyn, Gail, Angelica… Kyoko. Evil to an angel. Kyoko, I want you to meet Lyndall. The innocent must know each other. Why do you smile that way? That is the knowing smile. You too? All Eve? Every one? And I Adam. They both ate of the fruit and then hid their nakedness. You say you are not contained between your hat and boots, Walt, that you believe in those winged purposes and that the nearest gnat is an explanation? Maybe so. It might be so if we could really understand. You tried to expand enough to encompass America and you want us to do so also. But that dream is beginning to crumble at the edges. And as for death, how can it be delicious? You insist that it is, that death is not the enemy, that Kyoko and Mr. Phineas are somehow, somewhere, still with us and we with them, that death is a necessary part of life. It is hard for us here to see this. We are still crossing the ferry. But time and youth are cruel and I cannot stay for the answer. I hear the dance of the blessed spirits and I must go on. 'A thousand warbling echoes have started to life within me, never to die.' I, too, am a god-man and gave them life.

And the waves plenish my ear, endlessly, endlessly, endlessly rocking.

A shout nearby awoke him rudely. People were running to the water's edge and pointing. Out beyond the surf a speck, a bobbing head, was drifting quickly away from the shore. A faint cry blew inland. Two of the bathing-suited youths tried to plunge in after, but it would have been hopeless and bystanders restrained them. Finally an automobile with screaming siren skidded to a halt, and a rocket trailing a rope was fired, but it was too late. The speck had disappeared under the water. Later a boat crisscrossed the water futilely.

'The rip tide is bad today,' a shaken surf fisherman said. 'I told them not to go in swimming. It's against the rules here anyway.'

'Who was it; do you know?' asked René piteously.

'It was a girl with yellow hair and green eyes, young and pretty. Someone said her name was Eve.'

René gathered up the pages of his novel and put them back in the box. Nothing could have seemed less important now than these sheets of paper covered with lines of black symbols.

Chapter Eight

The story was finished. Suddenly all the pieces fell into place. The pyramid was capped. René's last revisions, incorporating many of Dr. Hamilton's suggestions, had now been frozen into that final typewritten copy, which was on its way to England. *The Serpent's Tongue* would soon be published on both sides of the Atlantic. Dedicated to the memory of Kyoko Kitagawa, he hoped it would be worthy of her, and pleasing to his generous patron, Mr. Le Blanc.

The latter insisted that the young author remain with the family at least until the book would appear in the San Francisco shops early in September. René agreed. He needed time alone and rest from his labors of imagination.

One day he took the ferry to Berkeley. He found Dr. Watts still there even though the summer vacation had drained away most of the professors from their academic home.

'I will accept your kind offer, Professor, if you still feel, after the book comes out, that I can fill the post successfully,' René told him as he sat back in a crooked chair in the office.

'Good, Mr. Levin, good. We will schedule you for two seminars. You know the rest. You can write or talk or do whatever you like. The stipend is not great, but you will have time to think and read. Hopefully you will find some of your students and fellow professors stimulating. I'm sure they'll find you so. If you need any help in organizing the classes, you know where to come. But have you decided where you will live?'

'No, but I'll look around in San Francisco. I've grown fond of it. I even enjoy the ferry ride. Besides…'

'I think I sense what is coming.'

'Perhaps you do, Dr. Watts. The young lady…'

'I was right. Miss Morris. Is she to become Mrs. Levin?'

'You are prescient… if she will have me…'

'She will. I've seen how she looks at you. congratulations. She is charming… and lucky.'

'Wait until the reviews before saying that last.'

'I'm not worried. Now as soon as you have a permanent address again let me know it so we can mail you the autumn class schedule and other necessary information as it becomes available.'

'You can mail things to me care of the Le Blancs. I will write their address out for you now.'

'Thank you, René Levin. I am looking forward to reading your novel.'

'Thank you for the job, Dr. Watts. It will enable me to marry.'

'Certainly no more felicitous cause was ever served by a university salary. And of course you must continue to write.'

As René left the Ferry Building he felt restless and decided to walk about the town. He skirted the better-known areas, the tourist attractions, Chinatown and the civic center. At length he found himself in a Japanese neighborhood. As he walked slowly along he passed what was evidently a Buddhist temple. On an impulse he turned into the vestibule, exchanged his shoes for a pair of *zori*, and entered the central room. He squatted on a black cushion, facing the *butsudan* at the front of the room, There was no statue, It was apparently a Zen temple.

He remained there in silence for some time. Finally a priest entered and approached him.

'You are not concentrating,' he stated.

'No,' René admitted, 'I do not really know how.'

'Of course not. It must be learned. You must follow the way. You do not know how to breathe, for one thing. Then having learned to breathe, you would learn how to listen to yourself with detachment.'

'Then?'

'You are too impatient. But then you would clear your mind and concentrate on a koan: I hold a flute in my hand. I do not blow into it, but it is not silent. How is this?'

'I do not know.'

'I would not accept that answer. You would be sent back to think on this. It might take many days.'

They sat in silence, but there was no uneasiness or constraint, Finally René felt almost sleepy. The priest rapped him on the shoulder with a long wooden paddle.

'What do you want to know?' he asked.

'I want to know what is death.'

'It is life.'

'And what is life?'

'It is death.'

'And what was?'

'Will be.'

'And what is?'

'Is not.'

'Then…!'

'Never.'

'Oh…?'

'Ever.'

'I see.'

'No not yet. You could see by following the way. Now you can only sense an intimation. By meditation and concentration you could learn to forget yourself, thereby knowing yourself. You could see inward in order to see outward. Finally in a flash you would understand. That is *satori*. But you could not then describe this understanding.'

'Ah, then there are things beyond words.'

'Yes. But words can be means to the end. We are using words. They are preliminary, but they are not the essence. Come with me.'

The priest led the writer to a door. Opening it he showed him through a courtyard planted in the sparse Japanese style. From the far side they could see the sun, through a veil of fog, dipping into the western ocean. They watched it in silence as it slid behind the gray-blue horizon.

'Where is the sun?' asked the teacher.

'It is gone,' answered the pupil.

The priest seized the pupil's arm and twisted it behind his back. The young man exclaimed, and a red light danced in front of his eyes where the sun had been.

'Ah, the sun is not gone. It is here all the time. Ah... ah...' marveled the writer as the priest released his arm.

'Quite. Death, life, past, present, future, body, spirit – all are here, all are one. You could learn. You could understand.'

When René arrived back at his room he was greeted by an elated Robert, who waved a newspaper under his nose.

'Read it, René; it's the review of the exhibit. It's *The New York Times*.'

The young writer grinned and scanned the half column of newsprint.

> In the welter of paintings now showing and in the trend of art as it now progresses, a phenomenon has appeared at the Parke-Bernet gallery. Here, in the midst of an above-average invitational exhibition of young American artists, hangs an anachronism. It is

also a masterpiece. It is a portrait of a young woman done in a Leonardesque manner. Nothing could be more *outre* in this day and age, you say. Nothing could be more self-consciously reactionary. But art is not constrained by any such intellectual or fashionable limitations. This portrait proves that. This is a case in which the power of the work is so great and immediate and inescapable that it impresses itself upon the viewer and sweeps away all reservations. One's theories and set of attitudes are overwhelmed. This is what is really meant by *tour de force*.

The painter, a young San Franciscan, Robert Le Blanc, has been submitting superior work to the galleries for more than a year and is far from unknown to connoisseurs. He has always and obviously been influenced by the Italian renaissance – quite unashamedly – but he has never done anything as bold and as impressive and as uncompromisingly unmodern as this.

Temporarily restrain your prejudices and submit yourself to the impact of this rare, contemporary work of a genius. It is somehow satisfying to see the trend and the fashion so thoroughly set aside.

'Well, indeed, Bob. Now are you satisfied?'

'I am pleased, of course. I thought it was good. But I will never do another like it.'

'Oh come now. This is the beginning of a more brilliant phase in your career.'

'No. It was the model.'

'Nonsense. What would De Mornay, for instance, have done with the same model?'

'He wouldn't feel toward her the way I do.'

'Even so, one has to have the creative spirit. And you do. You're smitten now and can't believe it, but you'll be inspired by other models. Besides, you can do her again.'

'No… no, I couldn't. But thanks for the kind words.'

'They are true words. I know that this is a beginning, not just a flash.'

'Well, I won't argue with you. We shall see. And what have you been doing? Must you really leave when the book comes out?'

'Bob, I went over to Berkeley today. I took the job.'

Robert smiled.

'That's really good to hear. Now you must stay on here. You can pay a little rent if you insist.'

'No, Bob, you see, now with a job, an income… well I'm going to take a wife.'

For an instant Robert looked shocked. But he was a gentleman, and René was his best friend. He pumped his friend's arm and seemed overjoyed and stricken at the same time.

'That's splendid, wonderful, René, and that means you'll both be up here where we can see you all the time.'

'Do you think it will really be all right? Will it bother you too much seeing her with me?'

'No, no, half a loaf is better than none. Of course I don't mean to be crude. You know how I mean it.'

'Of course. I truly hope you'll enjoy being with her… with us. Now may I dare ask your help in finding us a place to live? Remember what a small salary I'll have.'

'There must be many professors living in Berkeley.'

'No, I mean here. I want to live on this side of the bay.'

'Better and better. Yes, we will ask Karen. She'll know of a good place… artistic, inexpensive, like a studio. The twins will be glad to hear this. They love you both.'

'Well, now I haven't really asked her yet, Bob.'

'A mere formality, you dope. When will you?'

'I'll run down there as soon as the book comes out. Then I'll have to hurry right back so I can start to teach. Do you really think I can? Can you imagine it?'

'Yes, I can.'

'Well, thank you. I can't. Do you suppose we could see your sister tonight?'

'Yes, let's do. She'll be excited by the news.'

'Yes, that was a rave review.'

'That's not what I mean, and you know it.'

'It's what *I* mean, though. Let's go show it to her.'

Part Eleven

Chapter One

Marilyn hadn't answered René's letter asking her to marry him. Now he was on his way down to ask her personally. The grain fields and the humpbacked hills south of the big city looked brown and dry after the rainless summer. Bougainvillea still bloomed over the old adobe mission, however, and ice plant pushed up fat, green fingers where the train neared the coast. The air was clear and the ocean Mediterranean blue as they flew south along the beaches.

As he walked down the coach steps at the station, René caught a glimpse of spun gold hair over sea-green eyes. It was Marilyn. She held out her arms while he dropped his suitcase and enfolded her.

'Yes,' she said, 'yes, yes, yes.'

'When?' he asked.

'Tonight if I had my way. But you know Mother and Father. It will have to be in church and with guests.'

He groaned.

'Well, it's only fair,' he admitted. 'You're their only daughter, their only child, and they don't really like me. The least we can do is let your father marry us.'

'Thank you, René, my soon husband.'

'Is Mother here?'

'I told your mother I would meet you and drive you home. I can drive now. Wasn't that understanding of her? I see what you mean about older people.'

'Yes, Marin-lyn. We are growing up too. And your face hangs in a famous art museum back east.'

'And your new book is selling at Sawyer's. I saw a lady buy one when I went in to look.'

They sat in a new, dark-green sedan while Marilyn shifted gears importantly and swung up the main street and then north along the ocean drive.

'But, Marin, I have to be back in Berkeley in two weeks. I'm a working man now. And Karen has an apartment picked out she hopes you'll like. Can we be married that soon without upsetting your parents?'

'Yes, I have talked them into it. It is out of your hands. We are now engaged and will be married two weeks from yesterday. I hope you don't mind.'

He kissed her on the cheek, and the car wobbled crazily in the deserted street.

'We should invite Leila and Lizzie. It will be the second time as far as they are concerned, won't it?'

'We will. I've been working on a list.'

'And yet you didn't answer my letter.'

'I wanted you to come back here – to tell you this way.'

They pulled into the Riley driveway and ran into the living room.

A copy of the novel reposed importantly on the library table. Ora came out of the kitchen and hugged her younger son. Then she hugged Marilyn.

'Come eat now,' she said. 'You will both be hungry.'

'Oh thank you, Mrs. Riley,' Marilyn said. 'But I promised Mother I'd come right home. I'll come back later if that's all right.'

'Marilyn has turned out to be an understanding young lady,' said Ora after the girl had left.

'Yes, Mother, we were just saying that we are growing up.'

They sat down to a small table in an alcove, and Mrs. Riley served a modest meal. The windows were open and the ocean breeze blew the net curtains across one end of the table. René ate hungrily for a while and then looked closely at his mother's face.

'That is an overwhelming story you have written, son. It sounds more like a man of forty than one of twenty. I still hope you aren't growing up too fast.'

'Thank you, Muv. That means something coming from you. Do you think there is any wisdom in the book?'

'Yes, much. And now you will have a chance to put it into practice, to see if it really is yours.'

'You mean Marilyn?'

'I mean Marilyn and marriage and work. You have led an almost charmed life. Let's hope it will continue to be so.'

'Yes, I've often thought about that. I don't know why I continue to be so lucky.'

'I think I know, but I won't say.'

'Well, I know one of the main reasons, anyway.' He looked intently at her.

She turned away in a fluster and carried some empty dishes into the kitchen.

Later the doorbell rang. It was the young man from the newspaper. He and René sat in the living room while he interviewed the young writer. It was impossible to convey any real literary or artistic meaning to the small-town reporter, so René simply answered his factual questions and helped him spell a few difficult words. He said nothing about his forthcoming marriage. That would have to come from the Morrises, through the society page he supposed.

Still later, Marilyn chugged up in the sedan and drove him to her parents' house on Mission Street. Mrs. Morris fluttered over him anxiously and asked innumerable questions about the university and about the apartment in San Francisco. The Reverend Mr. Morris came in eventually, shook his hand, and smiled enigmatically. René supposed he was expected to say something about taking care of their daughter forever afterward. Perhaps he was even supposed to ask Mr. Morris for her hand. Instead he talked about his new teaching job and avoided mentioning the novel.

I do feel sorry for them, he thought. They are really acting very decently. I know how many misgivings they must have about me.

'I love your daughter very much indeed,' he blurted out. 'I am so grateful to you for having her. I am glad that you are going to marry us, Mr. Morris. Please know that we will come see you often, and you must come up to see us.'

Mrs. Morris cried a little at this, but Marilyn looked gratified and Mr. Morris smiled faintly.

René was afraid that the minister would insist upon examining him on his religious faith, or the lack of it. Incongruously he saw in his mind the Zen priest and the red sunset. However, Mr. Morris refrained. Perhaps he suspected the worst and did not want to confirm it.

The young man excused himself early and begged his fiancée not to bother to drive him home.

'I'll walk, goldylocks. I'm used to it. Let's go out to the mission tomorrow and wander around in the valley. It's been years since I've really explored. Or are you too busy?'

'I am, but we will anyway. I'll come get you at nine.'

'Good night, Mrs. Lightning.'

'Good night, sweet prince. See, I can quote Shakespeare, too. René, how many children shall we have?'

'What a question, Eve. Let's wait and see if you first conceive twins.'

'But, husband, my name is not Eve.'

'It is, among others, fairest among women. You are life, teeming with life, and we will bring it forth.'

'Good, husband, soon!'

He walked home inebriated. He didn't notice until he crossed his mother's front porch that the air had become peculiarly still. Heavy rollers pounded the shore and made the house tremble slightly.

Madly the sea pushes upon the land… he thought.

Mrs. Riley spent a large part of the September Saturday afternoon shopping, paying bills, conducting small business affairs. She parked the car and proceeded to her errands on foot.

Coming out of the department store she noticed a crowd, mostly of children following something or someone. Probably just another advertising stunt, she thought, but she waited to see. Soon she could make out a white-clad figure moving as at the head of a procession. It was an old man with long white hair and a flowing white beard. He was clad in a toga-like garment, slightly dusty at the bottom where it lifted to reveal his sandaled feet as he walked. He carried a shepherd's crook, and pinned to it a sign read: 'Repent. The Day of Judgment is at Hand.'

Children followed him along the main street as though he were the piper of Hamelin, the little ones in awed silence, the older ones in attitudes ranging from curiosity to ridicule. From the latter came occasional cat-calls and mocking epithets. But the old man ignored them all and proceeded slowly on his way.

Mrs. Riley had met varieties of religious 'nuts': hermits, begging friars, mock Buddhist monks; but there was something moving and disturbing about this man. He seemed somehow less of a charlatan, and except for the sign on his crook, more like a real character out of the Bible, Isaiah perhaps.

When she returned home she deposited her packages on the dining room table and started to change into a housedress. An excited knock on the door brought her into the living room.

Amanda, the little girl from next door, rushed in without ceremony and cried, 'Mrs. Riley, oh Mrs. Riley, the world's coming to an end. Did you see him? God's in town!'

Chapter Two

It was good to have them all at home that evening. René down from San Francisco; Mr. Frederick Levin of Levin Enterprises up from San Diego in his big black automobile; Ansel, imperturbable and pleasant as ever; and Marilyn, the gay and beautiful, now officially engaged to René.

The sky outside was filled with darkening fish-scale clouds. The air seemed especially close and humid. There was no wind at all. The ocean waves curled back upon themselves and seemed not to want to run up on the shore.

'Earthquake weather,' said Ansel and shook his head. But Fed smiled indulgently and quoted statistics.

Mrs. Riley opened the living room windows, sat down on the sofa, and asked René about the new book.

'I just can't talk about it now. I've lived with it for too long, I suppose. Right now I feel as though I've put all of myself into it. I don't see how I can ever write any more. But I suppose that's natural at this stage, At any rate it is good to have finished. If I wanted to be poetically dramatic I might quote Prospero. My characters

were all spirits and
Are melted into air, into thin air;
And, like the baseless fabric of this vision,
These cloud-capped towers, the gorgeous palaces,
The solemn temples, the great globe itself,
Yea, all which it inherit, shall dissolve,
And, like this unsubstantial pageant faded

Leave not a rack behind. We are such stuff
As dreams are made on, and our little life
Is rounded with a sleep.

'The story seems to me now to be an "unsubstantial pageant faded".'

'Oh, you'll be making up new stories when you've seventy, won't he, Ansel?' put in Fed.

'I'm sure of it, and getting more and more famous.'

'Yes,' said Marilyn quietly but with conviction.

'Yes,' said Ora Riley with pride.

'Now that we've got that settled,' offered Fed with a big grin at René 'shall we go for a ride to cool off a bit?'

They were rising from their seats when a sound like the rumbling of a hundred express trains erupted under their feet. The earth moved, slowly at first, then faster and more violently in a gigantic devil's dance. The plaster began to fall from the ceiling and walls. Marilyn and Ora ran quickly into René s arms where he held them tightly, swaying. The lights went out, The other two men staggered toward the doorway. But the porch pilasters tipped and fell, blocking the way out. With a last great wrench the framework of the house twisted and collapsed.

It was now completely dark The new moon could not penetrate the thickening clouds. The old ocean retreated into itself uncovering the land beneath the water, revealing the hulks of sunken ships and the depths of watery canyons – but there was no one there to see them and no light to see them by. Then the waters came back. They swept up the beach in a boiling, liquid wall, over the tracks, roads and embankments, to engulf the wreckage of houses and the fallen walls of buildings. The waves then brought them all, with their pitiful contents, back into the ancient, surging sea.

A word then, (for I will conquer it,)
the word final, superior to all,
Death, death, death, death, death.

Sources of the quotations:

pp. 16, 67, 159, 289, 305, 309
OUT OF THE CRADLE ENDLESSLY ROCKING
Walt Whitman
pp. 32, 33
GULLIVER'S TRAVELS
Jonathan Swift
p. 57
THE WIND IN THE WILLOWS
Kenneth Grahame
p. 105
TRADITIONAL JAPANESE NURSERY SONGS
p. 160
THE SUN RISING
John Donne
p. 162
EPISTLE TO JOHN LAPRAIT, AN OLD SCOTTISH BARD
Robert Burns
pp. 198, 199
UP AT A VILLA-DOWN IN THE CITY
Robert Browning
p. 201
THE INFERNO
Dante Alighieri
p. 209
THE SONG OF CANUTE
Early English Ballad
p. 211
A SATIRE AGAINST MANKIND
John Wilmot, Earl of Rochester
p. 216
A MIDSUMMER NIGHT'S DREAM
William Shakespeare
pp. 307, 308
THE TEMPEST
William Shakespeare